THAT BRIGHT LAND

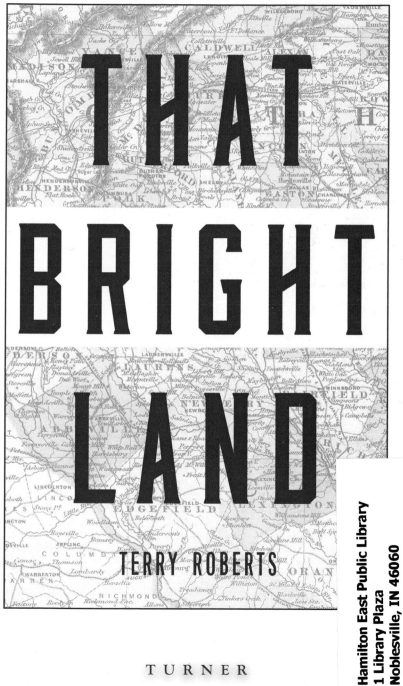

THAT BRIGHT LAND

TERRY ROBERTS

TURNER

Turner Publishing Company
Nashville, Tennessee
New York, New York

www.turnerpublishing.com

That Bright Land, A Novel

Cover design: Maddie Cothren
Book design: Glen Edelstein
Author photo: Michael Mauney

Library of Congress Cataloging-in-Publication Data

Names: Roberts, Terry, 1956- author.
Title: That bright land : a novel / Terry Roberts.
Description: Nashville, TN : Turner Publishing Company, [2016]
Identifiers: LCCN 2015037766| ISBN 9781630269760 (hardcover : acid-free paper) | ISBN 9781630269753 (softcover : acid-free paper) | ISBN 9781630269777 (ebook)
Classification: LCC PS3618.O3164 B75 2016 | DDC 813/.6--dc23
LC record available at http://lccn.loc.gov/2015037766

[9781630269753]

Printed in the United States of America
10 9 8 7 6 5 4 3 2 1

For John Ehle
Who First Cut the Path

I'm just a poor wayfaring stranger

Traveling through this world of woe.

Yet there's no sickness, toil nor danger

In that bright land to which I go.

I'm going there to see my father,

I'm going there no more to roam.

I'm just going over Jordan,

I'm just going over home.

"WAYFARING STRANGER"
(Nineteenth-Century American Traditional Song)

THAT BRIGHT LAND

PART ONE

CHAPTER ONE

In the summer of 1866 I went down South to find and kill a man. It's not what I would have chosen, and when I first arrived in the territory, I didn't want to admit that's what I was about. Nevertheless, I was well suited to the task—by my past and by the shadows it cast in my soul.

*　　*　　*

IN THOSE WILD DAYS after the war, the North Carolina Central Railroad tracks came to an abrupt halt at the foot of the Appalachian Mountains. From the last station on the line, I had to take a series of coaches and then a farmer's wagon to arrive at Alexander's Station, a drovers' outpost on the Buncombe Turnpike. When I climbed down from the wagon beside the turnpike that July day in 1866, I was amazed—stunned almost—by the dust and smell, as strong as anything I'd experienced since the last great gathering at Appomattox Court House the year before. There were acres of penned animals on the east bank of the French Broad River. Lots full of hogs, yes, and cattle, which I would have expected, but also horses, mules, geese, and turkeys. By God, turkeys on the hoof—or whatever the hell turkeys ramble down the road on. The smell was not that of a day-after battlefield—not blood and entrails smoking in the sun—but something healthy, something alive. Manure, yes, but also the dust-dry smell of hay and corn tossed into the pens by the bale and bushel. And the clouds of dust came not from barely shod human feet marching in ranks but from hoof and claw scratching in the dirt. It was a dusty, dirty piece of the world but full of life for all that.

I paid a bystander in torn overalls and busted boots to drag my trunk down the dirt street to an open square in front of Alexander's tavern. I could hear a woman singing inside, and there were drovers sprawled asleep on the long porch despite the heat of midday. A coach sat in the yard, hitched to a team of six fly-bitten, uniformly bay horses, waiting in the heavy air. As near as I could tell they were each branded with a large block "P" on rump and withers.

When I called up my name to the driver, a thin man with a tobacco-stained, gray beard, he motioned with his whip for me to climb inside the coach. "The tavern boys'll load your trunk," he said and then paused to spit a brown stream between his horses' backs. "Mr. Patton's expecting you down at Warm Springs."

James Patton was the owner of the Warm Springs Hotel and one of a handful of North Carolina contacts I had been given in Washington City. The brand on the horses' hides was very probably his sign, as he was reputed to own the stage lines as well as the hotel and a good deal of property in and around the Springs. Like the man who had sent me, Patton was a former Confederate, a traitor who'd made his way through the war. Indeed, who'd made his fortune, if what I'd heard was true.

While waiting for Patton's stage to pull out north toward the Springs, I went into the tavern for something strong, something to bite into the knot of the day. The place was mostly empty, though a few of the drovers were bent over tables in the main room, spooning a raw, onion-smelling stew out of wooden bowls into slobbering mouths. At the bar, a broad, Indian-looking woman was scrubbing away at the splintered wood. She glanced up and grinned. "Somethin' to eat?" she asked in a voice so husky that I looked again to be sure she was a woman. "Or drink?"

"Have you got anything like brandy?"

She threw her head back, her laugh as raspy as her voice. "Not like it. Hell no. The thing itself." She reached under the bar and sat a glass jar in front of me. She unscrewed the lid and held it up for me to smell, and I will tell you straight away, it smelled like something made in the hills south of heaven. Woodsmoke and honey and something else, something . . . ?

"I'll be damned," I said.

She nodded. "Applejack from near Barnard. Old man Freeman made it. Mostly Limbertwigs with a Buncombe or two thrown in the mill."

I reached my good right hand out to the jar, keeping my left out of sight, and I am glad to report that my right hand didn't tremor. That far, at least, I had come from the last days of the war.

I started to raise the jar to my lips, but her broad, brown hand on mine stopped me. "You want me to pour you out a tot?" she asked. "Or you want to purchase the jar?"

"How much?"

"Two dollars script or one dollar silver for the whole. I know it sounds like thievery, but it's worth every penny. Ask that gent-man down the way."

I glanced to my right, where a tall, portly, distinguished man stood with his own jar of the apple brandy, meticulously pouring out a measure into a cloudy glass. He nodded graciously. "The matron is correct," he said. He had a clipped, New England accent, the last sort of voice you'd have expected in Alexander's or anywhere south of Richmond. "At two dollars, this delightful potion represents an investment of your capital that you will not soon regret."

Hell, I thought, a banker. Or worse, a goddamned attorney. "Looks like you're not regretting it any," I said out loud.

"No, sir, I am not. And if, like me, you're getting ready to embark on that machine in the yard, you will want fortification."

When I stepped out onto the porch a moment later, my brandy jar in hand, I came face-to-face with three bearded men wearing the remains of uniforms, a confusing mix of faded blue and butternut gray. One of the three was carrying a rifle loosely at his side and started to raise the barrel in my direction until a second man reached out to stop him. The second man muttered, "that ain't him" in a hoarse voice, and they stepped aside to let me pass. They were looking for someone, and the first man continued to glare at me with naked hostility as I walked past.

*   *   *

THE GENTLEMAN FROM the bar was named Joseph B. Lyman. He too was on his way to Warm Springs, as a bonded and certified representative of the Western North Carolina Cooperative Manufacturing and Agricultural Association. Which sounds, of course, like so much horseshit, until he explained that it is a fancy name for a group of New York investors, who had sent him down south to study the possibility of buying up a large parcel of land in the French Broad River valley and redistributing it to hardworking families from the ghettos of New York. Families that yearned to escape the "industrial cesspool of the city and relocate into the bosom of nature where they could commune with nature's God."

Lyman claimed to be the agricultural editor of the *New York Tribune* and the author of a book titled—so help me God—*The Philosophy of Housekeeping*. He showed me a copy while we sat across from each other on the stage, and it turned out that by *Housekeeping* he meant everything from keeping bees to breeding cattle. As we nursed our jars of brandy while riding up the Buncombe Turnpike, it became apparent that I was to be impressed that a man like himself had come all the way from New York for mere land speculation. He implied he was being paid a handsome fee for his opinion but was too tactful to mention the sum.

When he finally got around to asking me why I was there, I gave him the official version, which was that I was there to investigate the dozens of disability claims submitted during the past year by veterans of the Union army from the isolated mountain counties of North Carolina.

"But I don't understand," Lyman said. "Are we not in the bowels of the Old Confederacy? And you're telling me these men served in the Army of the Republic?"

"North Carolina was a traitor state," I agreed. "Still is of course. Only Tennessee has rejoined the Union. Even so, Western North Carolina was divided. They didn't split off from the rest of the state like West Virginia, but there were apparently pockets of real patriots, and hundreds of men from the far western counties crossed into Tennessee to join up."

"And so these brave men have applied for pensions?"

"Oh, they already receive a pension. Most of them eight dollars a month in federal script. But since the laws changed this year, a number have applied for disability as well. Everything from missing arms and legs to paralysis and war madness."

"And your job is to . . . ?"

"My job is to ascertain whether they are indeed who they say they are and to do at least a preliminary evaluation of their medical condition."

Lyman leaned back in his seat, apparently impressed. "So you, sir, are a physician, a master of the healing arts?"

"No, Mr. Lyman. I'm not." I brought my left hand out of my coat pocket and touched his knee with the single, scarred finger. To his credit, he blanched but didn't turn his face away. "But after most of my hand was shot away by a blast of grapeshot at Fredericksburg, I became a surgeon's assistant, and I've held down hundreds of boys while a master of the healing arts sawed off their arms or legs. And held their hands and wiped their faces while afterwards they puked out their guts and died."

"I honor you for it," he said in a whisper, shrinking back into his side of the coach. "And I admire your continued dedication to our fighting men. The true patriots who—"

"I've come to do a job," I said. "As best I can. And there are those who think that my time in the medical corps qualifies me. That and the fact that I was born here."

I don't know what made me say that last part. Certainly, it wasn't something I was proud of, nor did I feel compelled to justify myself to Lyman. He was buttoned up as though by lock and key, and it looked as if his heart had shriveled up in his chest.

"Again you astonish me, Mr. Ballard. You are a native of . . ." And he waved his hand vaguely to indicate the howling wilderness outside.

"My mother took us north to Pennsylvania when I was eight years old," I said. "To Lancaster, where I grew up. I don't recall much of my childhood before that. As I said, I'm here to do a job and to get back to Washington City by the end of the summer." I pointed out the window with what was left of my hand. "The hell with this godforsaken place."

CHAPTER TWO

I had sworn never again to take up detective work, not after what I'd seen and done, but this time the work had sought me out. Ironically, it had sought me out several weeks before in the form of Zebulon Baird Vance. Ironic because he was my blood uncle, though I had not seen him for years.

*   *   *

ZEB VANCE AND his brother had been Confederate volunteers in 1861. By 1865, the brother had become a Reb general, and Zeb himself elected governor of North Carolina. Other than old Jeff Davis, he was the most famous Rebel politician there was, and he was my mother's brother—my blood uncle. In the spring of 1866, when I met him in Washington City, he had traveled back north to accept his official pardon from President Johnson. And when he summoned me from my desk at the War Department, I was ordered by my superiors to go.

In those days Washington City was like some sort of sprawling frontier town on market day. There were former soldiers and speculators everywhere: lounging, walking, whoring, spitting, looking for work of any kind, legal or otherwise. At the Nations Boarding House, I was sent upstairs to the second-floor parlor by a jerk of the proprietor's thumb, where I was met by a stout man who immediately asked me to call him Zeb. He strode across the room and grasped my good right hand hard in both of his. His own hands were broad, like the end of a plank, and so was the rest of him. He was shorter than me, but it didn't matter. He was twice as broad. Not fat, not by an ounce, but broad and strong and topped by an especially large, square head. He was all over hard and masculine. Wispy brown hair combed dry and a bushy mustache. He was nothing that I had expected, and he seemed so glad to see me that he almost knocked me down.

I was not glad to see him.

I let it be known that I didn't acknowledge my Southern family. Why? Because they had rejected my mother when she broke ranks to marry my father. Furthermore, I had left North Carolina at such a young age that I had almost no memories of the place. By God, I was from Pennsylvania and had fought for the Army of the Potomac.

We went back and forth, me calling him "Governor" or "Vance," and him calling me "a young pup with no respect for his elders." The language was growing heated, the name-calling more personal, when in midinsult he started to laugh. I was about to walk out when he stopped me. "You see!" he cried. "See how much alike we are?"

I must have seen, because I started to laugh.

It was then that Vance—for I refused to call him Uncle or Zeb—yelled to his wife Harriet for a bottle and glasses to be sent up.

*   *   *

THIRTY MINUTES LATER, after we'd had our toast to family, he spread a map on the wobbly tavern table in the corner of the room and began to point out various landmarks north of some riverside village called Asheville. I still wasn't entirely sure what he was about.

"So, you're telling me that Union veterans are dying out. I understand that. But why are Union veterans there in the first place?"

"Because, Jacob, even though the mountains sent thousands of men like me and my brother into the Confederate army, they also sent hundreds over into Tennessee to join up with the Feds. The Second and Third North Carolina Mounted Infantry were Federal troops based in Tennessee, made up mostly of men from Western North Carolina, and just as many Madison County men ended the war wearing blue as they did gray."

"Good for them," I said, feeling the need to remind the old man where my own allegiances lay. "But now you say they've suddenly started dying out. From wounds, from disease?"

"Hell no. Or at least not from war wounds. From gun and knife and . . . one of them was hung in his own tobacco barn. Somebody is killing them off."

"You sure none of this is self-slaughter?"

"You mean suicide?" he asked incredulously.

I nodded. "Suffering from what we call the *soldier's heart*. The veteran can't sleep no matter how much he drinks. And if he does, the nightmares consume him. Things he thought and did in the war rise up, and he can't escape the memories no matter. Only way out is a rope or a pistol."

"Hell no," he said, a flush rising into his cheeks again. "These men aren't killing themselves. Hell, some of them have been murdered in their beds or shot through the windows of their own homes."

"It's some of your damn Rebels don't want the war to be over," I said. "Some of them don't know when they've been whipped."

Vance only laughed, which apparently he did a lot. "Maybe, but what I want you to do is go down there and find out who in God's name is doing this. They have to be stopped, before they raise up the whole countryside."

"What do you mean, raise up the countryside?"

"Meaning that once Lee surrendered, every thinking man in the South gave up the fight and began to imagine being an American again. But, Jacob, there are a lot of nonthinking men and women down home who would just as soon keep fighting. And the mountains are the best place to light a fuse under the whole mess."

"Why there? I thought it was isolated as hell. Not close to anything that matters."

"Mountain people are touchy as hell," he said. "And they like to fight. Hell, look at you and me. If the mountains go back to war, armed bands of night riders raiding from valley to valley, then it would take a division of regular army just to restore order."

"And you don't want a division roaming the hills?"

"No, it would be Sherman's march all over again."

"So, what's at the heart of it? The killing, I mean."

"For once, this doesn't seem to be about the Negro. Former slaves in those parts, what few there are, seem to be going about their business undisturbed. This is something else."

"You think what's brewing down there is from the war?"

"It has to be. Some sort of vengeance left over from the dark years, and Lord knows there were some horrible things done back then, some by North Carolina troops in uniform." He shook his massive head sadly. "There's something that happened in particular that I need to tell you about."

"What's that? And why tell me?"

"I've heard from several men in Washington, Jacob, that you did good work for Pinkerton at the end of the war. After your wounds healed, you became very good at tracing a suspect and . . ."

"It's not work that I'm proud of," I whispered and then cleared my throat. "Nothing you would want talked about at a family picnic. And nothing that I'd care to pick back up."

"Hear me out. It may be that you can help put an end to the killing. In January of '63, troops from the Sixty-Fourth North Carolina rounded up and executed more than a dozen old men and boys from an isolated place in Madison County called Shelton Laurel. I sent Agustus Merrimon to investigate, and what he discovered would seize up the blood in your veins."

"But that was three years ago."

"Three and a half, but people up there have long memories, and they believe in an eye for an eye. It may have been this massacre or it may have been something else, but if the killings don't stop, the violence will spread."

"Is it possible that somebody is doing all this—for that very reason?"

He looked at me long before answering. "Yes, it's possible. It's what I fear the most. That's why I want you to go down there. That's why I want you to go home."

Before I left, I said I would consider it. He wrote me out a list of the local men whom I could trust, including his friend James Patton, who owned the Warm Springs Hotel, and the sheriff of Madison County, who had fought under the Vance brothers in the war. We agreed that I might pose as a Federal pension examiner to cover my activities. Then we shook hands again; although, this time I was ready for that crushing grip.

What Zeb Vance told me about the troubles in Western North Carolina didn't convince me to travel South. The truth was that I was sick of city stench and desk work. I needed to feel the heat of the sun again and breathe new air.

*   *   *

WHEN THE DRIVER paused to rest his horses at a place called Barnard, Lyman was still asleep and snoring like a farmer. I got out to look around. The late afternoon sun was bright on the river. The smell of rain was in the air, and there was a breeze stirring in the trees. It didn't look like home exactly, but I did feel a faint tremor of recognition. A crowd of blue jays was debating in a tall poplar beside the ramshackle store, which seemed right somehow. The crossroads of Barnard was close to where most of the deaths had taken place. It was also where I was to meet the clerk of court in order to set up shop for pension and disability interviews. Mr. Patton might be expecting me at the Warm Springs Hotel, but I saw no reason why I shouldn't strike out on my own and see a little of the country.

So when the driver came out of the store after a few minutes of socializing, clutching a twist of dried tobacco in his hand, I asked him to throw my trunk off the stage.

"You for certain?" he asked with a frown. "In case you ain't noticed, you precisely in the middle of damn nowhere." He had spit on the twist and was sawing at it with a rusty clasp knife. "And, son, you don't exactly look nor talk like you're from around here."

"Looks can fool you," I said.

CHAPTER THREE

W hat in hell you mean the war is over?"

The tall, swarthy man leaned in toward me, close enough that I could smell the sour stench of sweat from his body. The sun had gone down at Barnard, and I was pretending to share my jar of brandy with two local men behind Goforth's Store. Taking just a sip as the jar went round, intending to see what they knew about Yankee veterans being killed off.

"Hell yeah, what you mean?" The other man was short and round, running mostly to fat, and had an impressive amount of hair growing out of his ears. They were cousins, or so they said.

"Boys," I said. "Have you no newspaper in this left-back corner of the world? You Rebs surrendered a year ago this April. In a place called—"

"Shut up." The tall one punched me gently in the chest with the jar.

"Not over around here," the other one said. "Be careful with that damn jar," he added to his cousin.

"Ignorant Rebel savages," I muttered.

"Hell did you say?"

"Ignorance is savage," I said more clearly.

"Damn right." The short one nodded emphatically.

"Company B, Sixty-Fourth North Carolina," the tall one added helpfully. "Fought for the . . ." He gestured at a man in a dark suit of clothes seated on a plank bench against the back of the store. The man on the bench shook his head ever so slightly at the tall cousin, and I noticed a long gray mustache under his hat brim. Say no more, his gesture seemed to convey.

"Are you a goddamn Yankee?" the short brother asked suddenly. "Surely to good God you are not a goddamn Yankee."

"Surely to good God I am," I said pleasantly. I was growing tired of the cousins' entertainment. It seemed to me that the third man, the man lurking in the shadows, knew more of what I needed.

"Why hellfire, look at that," the tall cousin said, gesturing with the jar to my right, toward the river. Years before, I might have fallen for the trick, but I was no longer the greenest recruit in camp.

Assuming I was gulled, the one built like a tree stump leaned over to pick a rock up off the ground, and when he did, I kneed him as hard as I could in the side of his fat head. He grunted and staggered backward.

The tall one took a swing at me then with the half-empty jar, but he'd been drinking while I'd been sipping and he missed the end of my nose by a foot or so.

On reflex, I reached into my coat pocket, where during the last year of the war I had always carried a derringer for just such as this. But I had brought nothing South, not even a knife.

"Son of a . . ." the tall one muttered and threw the jar at my head. I ducked under and came back up with my fists to the ready. As drunk as they were, I figured for a fair fight. I had both the cousins squarely in front of me, both starting to edge away, but I realized I had lost track of the mustache in the hat. Maybe he'd already retreated, I thought, just as something hit me in the back of the head hard enough to buckle my knees. There was numbing pain and then the slick, hard ground flying up at me.

CHAPTER FOUR

I t felt a lot like waking up in the field hospital in Fredericksburg, and for a fogbound moment, I wondered if I was back there. I wondered if I'd been shot in the back of the head.

"If you ask me, he looks like shit," a voice said suddenly. A boy's voice.

"Shut up your cursing, Sammy. He may hear you . . . And now that you stirred him up, we'll have to do something with him." This a girl's voice, or a woman's.

"Roll him in the river," the boy suggested. I could hear water rushing by, not far away. "Let the fish eat him."

Together, they propped me up sitting, the strange red-haired woman carefully tying the arms of my coat around my waist, for it turned out that I was naked. I realized suddenly that the broad, slow run of the river was only ten feet away, the sun glimmering on its surface searing my eyes.

As they worked to bring me up, they could see that my hand was mutilated. "The war," she said, and the boy nodded.

I could feel crusted blood and sand on my neck and shoulder, and when the woman ran her hand through my hair in search of a wound, she found a nasty lump behind one ear.

"Mister," the boy said. "You done had way too much to drink."

I shook my head violently side to side and then immediately groaned. "No!" I licked my cracked lips. "No. Son-bitches bush-whacked me. In back of the shtore."

"Was you naked when they hit you?" the boy asked skeptically.

I felt my two hands again running over my chest, my stomach, my legs, searching for my missing clothes. It was comical, I know, and the woman laughed, which lit a slow fuse of anger inside me. How many men were stripped naked on the battlefield and never woke at all?

"Shtole my clothes," I muttered, half to myself. I touched my naked stomach again. "Shtole my watch too, thamn it." The words were coming out twisted from the pain in my head.

As the boy in turn laughed at me, the woman knelt and dipped the hem of her skirt in the river and, after wetting my lips, began to scrub away at the blood on my neck. "What's your name?" she asked. "If you intend to live, you'll need a name." She nodded at my trunk, broken open in the bushes close by. Apparently, she meant for the boy to locate some clothes.

"Jacob," I said. It felt like my tongue had shrunk to its normal size again, and I could at least say my name.

"My name is Sarah Freeman," she said, "and this is my son, Sammy. Is that all the name you've got? Jacob?"

I started to speak and then paused. "Wait," I said, searching inside my busted head for more names. Again, she had to try not to laugh.

"Ballad," I said defiantly. "No, wait." Another pause. "Ballard maybe."

"I like Ballard better," she said. "We've got a few Ballards off of Big Pine, so you might be one of them."

She rose to rinse her skirt out in the river again and then began to work away at the coating of sand on my back. "I do believe,

Mr. Ballard, that you must have crossed paths with some of the Anderson boys last night. And you must have said something to aggravate them." I was slowly retracing my wits, between the scrubbing and the talking.

"Ignorant . . . savages," I muttered.

She leaned around to look at my face. I could feel my mouth trying to smile, and this time she laughed out loud. "That would do it," she agreed.

*   *   *

SARAH FREEMAN PRETENDED to hide her eyes while Sammy helped me finish brushing the sand off my backside and climb into a spare pair of pants and an old linen shirt from my trunk. It took the boy a few minutes to locate a second boot, for it had tumbled almost into the river. Pants, shirt, boots in place, they both helped me up the bank to the roadbed, as the moment I tried to walk, the world started spinning away from me.

At one point I had to ask her to turn her back so I could lean against a tree to vomit. "Why, you throw up as neat as a cat," she said.

When we reached the road, the woman told her son to go back for my trunk. "Find everything and put it back." When the boy started to protest, she held up a warning finger. "Everything. I take it that the papers are important, Jacob."

"More important than anything else," I whispered.

"You heard him. Everything, including every scrap of paper. Pack it up and drag it down to the store."

"How'm I s'pposed to get it up the bank to the road?" the boy whined.

"Crawl and push it ahead of you," his mother suggested. "Take your time, but don't take all day."

*   *   *

AS WE WALKED ALONG the dirt track of the turnpike, she kept her grip hard on my arm. "I must have a concussion," I heard myself whisper.

She smiled. "Is that a fancy word for a knot on the head?"

I nodded and the nausea swarmed in my stomach again; no sudden movements. "Means I don't recall much."

She laughed. "Oh, I can almost tell you to the minute what happened. At least after you offered to set the Andersons straight."

"They told me the war wasn't over."

She laughed. "That's because it was after dark and they'd been drinking. Light of day, even the Andersons know the war's over. But they must have taken you for a Yankee."

"I am. Pennsylvania, I think. And Washington City."

"I thought you said you were from Big Pine."

"You said that part." Then after a pause. "I may be from there too. Hell if I know." I didn't feel sick in my stomach anymore, but I was troubled by the twisty state of my mind, and I stopped walking for a moment to try to recall. "Governor says I'm from somewhere," I offered.

"I didn't mean to pry, Mr. Ballard. I was just talking along, trying to help you gather your wits. I only meant that the boys who knocked you on the head might have taken you for a Yankee, especially if you were calling them a pack of . . ."

"Savages."

"Just so."

"Did I say they were Andersons?" I asked as we began walking again.

"No, I was just guessing. Was one tall and dark, hatchet-faced? The other stocky like, I don't know, like a barrel with a pumpkin set on top of it?"

I remembered not to nod my head this time. "Yes. Except that there was a third one too. Older man who didn't say much except shake his head at the other two. His face is one of the things I can't recall."

She looked puzzled. "Not sure about that one. But the first two are our boys. Will and Mast Anderson."

"What the hell do you think your boys might have done with my clothes?" I could hear the edge coming back to my voice, another sign of my brains settling, that and the realization that I shouldn't trust this woman.

"Traded them for whiskey. Hung them on a fence post, unless there was something in particular they wanted. Your shoes for example, if they fit. Or just left them lay right where they stripped them off you. Hard to say, but I seriously doubt if those two had a plan."

*   *   *

MY LEGS SEEMED fairly steady on the three plank steps leading up to the porch of Goforth's Store, and she let go of my arm as we walked up to the counter. The proprietor was reading a newspaper spread open on the counter beside several bushel baskets of potatoes, a broken hoe, and a fox pelt someone had apparently given in trade.

The man behind the counter was a thin, nervous creature. Sarah had told me that his name was Ishmael Goforth. Hard to say just how old at a glance, but pushing on past seventy at least. Just a fringe of colorless hair and a pair of ancient, cloudy spectacles perched somehow on a curiously bent nose. She stood patiently in front of him, waiting for him to acknowledge her.

Eventually, he looked up, marking his place in the newspaper with a thin, bony finger. "Sarah Freeman," he said, though it sounded more like he was clearing his throat than attempting speech.

She stared straight into his face without replying, again waiting.

"What can I do ye?" Finally. Satisfied that he'd made her wait.

"We've come to get this man's clothes and watch back, Mr. Goforth. I know you've got them."

Goforth twisted from the waist to look at me, simultaneously bowing his head so he could stare over the spectacles. "You mean that man there? Looks like he's wearing clothes."

"Yes, this man here. And he wasn't wearing any clothes when we discovered him. We want the clothes he started out in yesterday—before you let the Andersons get hold of him."

Goforth grunted and bent down to reach beneath the counter. Then carefully, precisely, he laid on the countertop, neatly folded:

a pair of black suit pants, followed by a shirt, a black frock coat, a worn leather belt, and even a wrinkled string tie. "Take ten dollars for the whole pile," he said, friendly now. "The underclothes was soiled. I threw them away."

I started to open my mouth in protest, but Sarah Freeman held up her hand as if to say, I'll deal with this. I could feel the blood rise in my face at the frustration of silence. Blood that made my head ache.

"Damn your eyes, Ish Goforth. You cannot sell a man his own clothes." Her voice was still conversational, but with just enough spit to be taken seriously. "And you forgot his shoes."

"How do I know they're his'n?" Goforth asked reasonably as he reached under the counter again. "Like I said, he's wearing a full suit of clothes awready." He set a pair of dusty leather shoes carelessly on top of my clothes.

"Obviously, they're—" I started, but she held up her hand again.

"'Cause you took them off Will and Mast Anderson, who took them off Mr. Ballard, who is related to the Ballards up above Big Pine. And Mr. Ballard is a friend of mine, and as such, he is a friend of Ben Freeman's." There was a vague sense of threat in the air. I wasn't sure why.

Goforth twisted again to regard me more closely. Leaned toward me again to study my face. He started to speak but apparently thought better of it, and turned back to Sarah to address her instead. "Your . . . Ben is in jail, is he?"

"Not just now."

There was a long pause, as the negotiations were apparently at an impasse.

"Well, then," Goforth said. "In that case, I only need to recover my investment. No profit. Not a penny."

"What did you give for the clothes?" she asked. Friendly again. "A quart?"

"Two quarts," he admitted. "For that and the watch."

"Well, we want the watch and the clothes. How do you expect this man to tell the time of day without his watch?"

"He can tell the time of day by the sun, the way God intended."

Sarah leaned forward, ever so slightly, but still with some threat.

"'Sides, I already sold the watch." Goforth shrugged his bony shoulders. "Got five dollars for it."

"Script?" She was skeptical.

"Silver dollars. Federal. Some stranger passing through."

"Damn it," I said, entering the fray for the first time. "That was my father's watch. His initials are etched inside the back cover."

*   *   *

AFTER SARAH FREEMAN steered me into the back room of the store to change clothes, I could hear her threatening Goforth with every sort of violence she could think of, but all he would tell her about the man who bought the watch was that he was a stranger in a slouch hat. In between threats, she must have selected two pairs of socks off Goforth's shelves and a set of smalls that looked the right size, because she cracked open the door to the back room and tossed them to me without looking inside.

After I emerged, still somewhat bemused, still upset about my watch, she steered me back down the road toward Sammy and the trunk. Both of which were visible thirty yards away.

Together we carried the trunk down to the store, one of us on each handle with the boy trailing behind telling us just how heavy it was. When I explained that I was looking for the county clerk of court, whose post office address was Barnard, she told me that the clerk, Obediah Campbell, farmed just across the river on Anderson Branch. I also needed to go to Warm Springs too, I explained to her, but for now, the clerk of court would do. She then sat with me till the miller passed by on a wagon drawn by two mismatched mules. Using money from my trunk, she hired the man to haul me and the trunk to Campbell's house.

"It's not far," she explained. We were waiting for the miller to come back out of the store. "Less than half a mile on a line, but you're not so steady on your feet, are you?"

"No," I admitted. "No, but I can sit in a wagon without falling out." She could tell I was embarrassed. "I'm afraid I can't remember your name."

"She ain't never told you her name but once," Sammy said from where he was pestering one of the mules with a stalk of grass.

"Sarah Freeman," she said. "Has been Freeman since before the war."

Meaning that she was married, most likely to the mysterious Ben Freeman, who wasn't in jail at the moment. "Well, I thank you, Sarah Freemen, for saving my—"

"Saved your ass," Sammy said, "and your trunk!"

Not knowing what else to do, I reached out to shake her hand.

"Even if I am a Rebel savage?" Her freckles bunched up on her cheeks when she grinned.

The miller came out of the store with his hands thrust down the front of his overalls and a frown on his face. Apparently, he too had been stymied by Ish Goforth.

"Not so savage," I said finally to Sarah Freeman as I turned to climb onto the wagon seat beside the miller. *Given where you come from*, I added to myself.

CHAPTER FIVE

The miller's name was Joe Worley. He was the fattest man I ever saw in the Carolina mountains. I saw larger men in the Sutlers' Corps during the war, especially toward the end when they were fattened up like hogs from lounging in their tents all day, sampling their own wares. And I once saw an enormous man operated on in a battlefield hospital for a bullet wound. He bled like a slaughtered hog when they cut into him and died before they could dig deep enough in his massive, sweating belly to find the ball.

But Joe Worley certainly was a blue-ribbon fat man. When I climbed up on the seat beside him, I discovered that he so weighted down his side of the wagon that the seat sloped dangerously in his direction. I clung to the uphill side of the seat to keep from sliding down into his lap.

The bridge across the river at Barnard was a long wooden affair, constructed out of heavy beams and floored with thick oak planks. The whole was held together by wooden pegs as big as your wrist driven into the joints. Some of the floorboards were thicker than others, and the wagon jolted hard when the wheels would strike a high spot. Each jolt sent a spike of pain through my head and wrenched my stomach upside down again. Every so often Joe Worley would turn loose of the reins with one hand and stick the free hand inside the bib of his overalls to scratch his mountain of a belly or even lower. I looked away in embarrassment. I suspect I didn't smell a whole lot better than he did at that point, but at least I knew to keep my hands out of my pants.

And he was talking, muttering mostly. After a few minutes, I realized with relief that he wasn't talking to me but to some imaginary judge and jury, accusing Ish Goforth of every sin imaginable. The refrain was "not a single damn crumb to eat," and he kept weaving the phrase into his rant. "Not a single damn crumb to eat would he give me. And me with nothing to eat since dawn. Near starving. And him saying my brothers-in-law won't have it. Won't have me running off to leave the wife. As if she would fix a dying man anything to eat. But Ish of all people. Ishmael damn Goforth, the stingiest man God ever made out of mud and blood. Not a single damn crumb to eat, and him with a jar of pickles that would choke a mule. What I wouldn't give for one of them pickles with a slab of that cheese. Running off and leaving the wife? They hell fire. She ain't never learned to cook in ten years of feedin' sticks in the stove, and Ish Goforth is too damn mighty to give a man a crumb of . . ."

He was starving. Or some tiny creature made of gristle way deep inside him was starving. The human mind is a strange thing indeed when it can convince a three-hundred-pound miller that he's been slighted over a pickle and a piece of cheese.

But I shouldn't judge Joe Worley. My own mind was still shattered like a busted jar. Many of the shards held some maddening fraction of the fight from the night before. Why had the talking suddenly turned to fighting, and who in God's name had hit me? There was the ache in the back of my head and the memory of the Freeman woman laughing, both of which left me cold.

We clattered off the end of the bridge, and I said a prayer of thanks on behalf of my head and my stomach. Joe Worley was talking to his mules, drawing them to the left out of the main road, asking them in the same muttering singsong to turn the wagon off onto a side track that bordered the river. Dusty and rutted. "Haw . . . haw!" he called to them. "We going to Obediah's house. He'll have something to eat for . . ."

In my battered brain, I began to confuse the red-headed woman, Freeman, with the men who'd attacked me. After all, weren't they all one half-starved race, with the women worst of all? All I'd ever known were Hooker's hookers, and in direct sunlight they could be as scary as a midwinter nightmare. *Hooker's hookers* . . . I almost laughed at this faded joke before I remembered what any motion at all did to my head. And as I tried not to laugh, I realized that Joe Worley had stopped talking to himself long enough to ask me a question.

"Why you keep scratching like that?" he was saying. "You got chiggers or somethin'?"

"New set of smallclothes," I explained. "From the store."

"Ish Goforth's store?"

I nodded. "The very same."

"Well, no damn wonder." And he was off again. "Ish is the hound of hell, if you ask me, and his tail on fire. And you know what he give me to eat when I asked him all sugar-and-honey, like a Christian gentleman?"

"Not a single damn crumb?"

Joe Worley started to laugh deep in his guts, and it shook the whole wagon. "You smarter than you look there, Mr. Ballard. Not a single damn crumb, and him'n me related through our wives. For whatever wife-relations is worth. Not a single damn crumb, and him with a wheel of cheese the size of a millstone. Yellow cheese from . . . Where you from, anyway?"

"Somewhere around here," I said. "I was born here and lived here till I was eight years old—someplace called Big Pine."

"Well shit, son. You're almost home."

"Tell me something then. What was the war like here? From '61 to '65, what was it like up here?"

He turned his cannonball head to study me closely, and for the first time since I'd laid eyes on him, he seemed perfectly serious. "I wouldn't go talkin' to people much about the war times," he said. "Not if you like your skin attached to your bones."

"Folks still fighting even yet?" I asked.

He turned back to his mules and slapped the reins on their lathered backs.

"They was hard days," he said. "A lot of people died . . . and not all of 'em starved to death." And then after a moment. "Them days ain't over yet."

CHAPTER SIX

J oe Worley left his wagon sitting squarely in the middle of the road—such road as there was—in front of Obediah Campbell's house. The house itself stood in a narrow yard on the right hand with all of the French Broad River to the left. There was maybe a hundred feet of fenced pasture between the road and the river, an elegant location for a house if you favor a river for a front yard.

It was a two-story, framed structure—not a cabin or anything like. It was sheathed with milled lumber, and the whitewash was fresh since the war. The large windows were filled with whole sheets of clear glass, a rarity anywhere in the South during those hard years. The tin roof was steep and painted a faded red, and someone had swept the steps leading up to the house as clean as a tabletop. The house was past its prime, but clearly the clerk of court was a significant figure in the community and a man to be reckoned with.

All this and when Campbell came down the front porch steps to greet us, he was wearing a string tie and pulling on a black frock coat. The coat was so old and faded that it was turning an odd, almost rusty color, but it was a frock coat nonetheless, and it matched his trousers. I was as impressed with his clothes as I was with his house and tried to adjust my own clothes when I slipped down off the wagon seat.

Obediah Campbell walked with a sort of half hitch, half limp, and when I first saw him coming down the stepping stones from the house to the road, I thought that maybe he'd been wounded in the war. He was so loose-limbed that he reminded you of a scarecrow escaped from the cornfield and ranging across the landscape. One shoulder was higher than the other, and his arms dangled as he walked. Everything about him seemed not quite fastened together. He sent Joe Worley around back of the house to the kitchen, assuring him that his servant would put up a poke of rations to help him withstand the three-mile journey home. And as Worley rounded the corner of the house, moving more quickly than I would have thought possible for a man his size, Campbell greeted me with enthusiasm, as if he'd been looking forward to my arrival for months.

I gave him the briefest report on my encounter with the Anderson boys and with Sarah Freeman and her son. He was appalled—"appalled, sir"—by the Andersons but much less demonstrative when it came to the woman. Her name elicited only a snort and the warning that I'd best not trust anybody named Freeman.

He sat me down in his parlor, the front room on the right. The furniture, like the house itself, suggested affluence and even some taste. I sat down in a fine cherrywood chair while Campbell went down the long central hallway toward the kitchen, intending to bring me a cup of cold water to ease my pains. As he went, he called out to someone named May June to bring my trunk from the wagon. "Fetch it in and put it in the front room upstairs." I started to rise from my chair to go for the trunk myself. It didn't seem right that a daughter should have to haul that heavy thing up a flight of stairs, but when I came to the parlor doorway, a young Negro girl slipped past and went on out the front door of the house. I was so amazed that for a moment I stared after her before returning to my chair. Nothing about the house made sense.

In a moment, Campbell reappeared with a glass of water. Given my injuries, I was hoping for something stronger, but water, Campbell said, was God's gift to a fallen world. The purest form of liquid there was and the cure for any ailment one could name. He explained that since he had been baptized some few years back— baptized by some famous man of God named Abednego Rogers— he had only ever drunk water. And all he allowed to be drunk in his house was water.

I would have given most anything for my jar of apple brandy from Alexander's Station, lost back at Goforth's Store. But all I was to get from the county clerk was water.

"I am delighted, sir, that you are here. Ever since I heard from the War Department that you were coming, I have been reckoning up a list of those who have applied for the new disability payment, and I can assure you that it will take several weeks to interview all those involved—and I'm sure more will show up once word gets out. I say weeks, sir, for the woods are full of men who claim to have been injured in the war, most of whom are as hale and healthy as I am myself."

As he talked, I noticed that Campbell's head was slightly lopsided as well as his body. Something that had happened to him at birth I imagined. If you had shut your eyes, you would have thought you were listening to a university man, but one look at Campbell suggested something disturbingly out of plumb. So I shut my eyes and listened, meaning to do him justice.

"If you are willing and your injuries allow, we will start the interviews on Monday next. I look forward to being of service to the government and to helping prevent the sort of fraud that these mountain men seem to think is of no consequence."

I opened my eyes a slit. "I mean to go down to Warm Springs in the meantime," I offered. "I need to see a man there before I start my investigations."

"You are free to go anywhere you like, Mr. Ballard, and you should consider resting a bit at the Springs, recovering from your injuries. These locals can be despicable." He jerked his head sadly from side to side at the mere thought of the Andersons and Freemans.

"Aren't you a local man, Mr. Campbell?"

"I'm afraid so. But I have a college education, and I have traveled. I don't consider myself as limited in my outlook as most of the local people. It is deeply disturbing to me to see their disregard for the rule of law."

"What you say makes sense. I was born here myself, but I certainly don't think of myself as *from* here."

He nodded gravely. "Just so. And I'm sure you're starting to regret ever coming to this benighted corner of the world. But perhaps . . ." He paused for a moment, and I realized that the young Negro woman had wrestled my trunk up from the road and was dragging it past the door. Apparently, Campbell didn't want to be overheard as she went by. He reached back to push the hallway door closed and leaned toward me conspiratorially. "Perhaps we can change your opinion. There are civilized people in our county. At the hotel in Warm Springs, you may well meet men and woman of consequence from all over our new nation. And I will also take care to provide you with introductions to a few select individuals, local men who are not so limited by their place of origin, if you know what I mean."

My eyes had closed again while he was talking, against my will this time. I was growing to like the county clerk. He seemed more akin to me than I could have expected.

"I can see just how tired you are. I believe our May June has had time to remove your trunk above. Let me assist you up the stairs so that you can rest after such an unfortunate beginning with us."

The trunk was there, though how she got it up those steep steps, I'll never know. The bed in the front room—the room that faced the river—was turned back, and the sheets were soft cotton. I waved Campbell back once I was inside and could feel sleep looming. I smiled and nodded dramatically though it hurt like fire to move my head.

When I lay down, the pillow had all the prickly softness of down, but there was something hard underneath. Someone had placed a battered metal pocket flask under the pillow. The lid was long gone, replaced by a whittled wooden stopper. When I worked it out of the mouth of the flask, the wonderful cutting smell of whiskey flowed up my nose into the farthest reaches of my brain. I glanced at the door and saw May June peeking around the corner of the frame. She stepped into full view without entering the room.

When I had first glimpsed her in the hallway, I had thought her fifteen or sixteen perhaps, but now I realized she was older, a few years older than me judging from the width of her shoulders and the fullness of her features. Her thick hair was pulled tautly back and woven into a hard braid wound on top of her head. She wore a simple shift sewn up out of linsey-woolsey, and her body seemed to be at once both muscular and womanish.

I raised my eyebrows and pointed at the flask, meaning did she know where it had come from. She grinned and then held a finger up before her lips to silence me. Then she reached into the room to pull the door shut.

*   *   *

THE WHISKEY HELPED, though I could only stand two swallows. It was clear as water, but it was like liquid smoke and fire. The very first pull made my eyes weep but did wonders for my head, sweeping the fog clean away. The second swallow hurt just as much but made me think I might live. I stopped there, afraid that a third sip might kill me. I carefully stoppered the flask back up and hid it in my trunk. There were still things I couldn't remember from the night before, but I guessed more of what I'd seen and heard would return in time. It occurred to me that I had underestimated just how ferocious this place and these people might be and that it was high time I recalled myself. High time I summoned the soldier within.

CHAPTER SEVEN

There were three places set at the table, oddly spaced because there were two extra chairs that were leaned decisively against the tabletop, each with a cloth napkin draped precisely over the chairback. I had seen this before in homes in the North, and it usually signified a son gone off to war. The chair and napkin were waiting patiently for the return of Tom or Nat or Willie.

The problem was that the war had been over for more than a year, and if the chairs were still waiting, they'd been waiting a hell of a long time. Campbell must have noticed me staring, because when the platter of chicken, a bowl of green beans, and another of biscuits had made their initial round, he spoke up.

"You may notice, Mr. Ballard, that we have two empty places at our table." He glanced nervously at his wife. "It is with some pride that I tell you, as our special guest, that this household gave two sons to the noble cause. Both joined the Confederate army early in the conflict, and I'm afraid that neither returned to us. I understand that you yourself served in the Army of the Republic, so perhaps you can appreciate our loss, now that our great nation is reunited." Mrs. Campbell had begun silently, dreadfully, to weep.

"Of course," I said. I was momentarily at a loss for words. My mangled hand twitched convulsively where it lay hidden in my lap, and I thought of my missing fingers. "I myself lost much in '62, and I assure you that I've not been the same since." Mrs. Campbell managed a watery smile of sympathy as she dabbed at her face with her napkin. "What unit did your boys serve in?" I asked.

"Allen's Sixty-Fourth North Carolina," Campbell said proudly. "Primarily troops from Madison County, some from Henderson and Polk and a few loyal men from Tennessee. They joined up early on, in the summer of 1862, right down on Main Street in Marshall. I stood on the porch of Colonel Allen's own home and watched them march out of town."

"Our boys felt a great sense of patriotism, Mr. Ballard," Mrs. Campbell added, her voice for the first time rising above a tired whisper. "We *all* felt a great sense of patriotism."

"I'm very sorry for your loss, ma'am. I am certain that—"

"We believe they both died good deaths. In the case of our oldest son, we know that he died a Christian martyr facing the enemy at Stones River." She looked at me expectantly.

My heart sank. "You've had a report from someone who was with him?"

"We received a letter from his lieutenant, who was with him on the field." Campbell was intoning these sacred words with deep reverence. "He was not afraid to die, because he had made peace with God above and was ready to ascend to his maker." He looked down almost as if in prayer.

I didn't have the heart to tell the two of them that I had written dozens of these letters, first on the battlefield and later in the hospitals. That often as not, I had written them for men who died cursing God and screaming in pain. I had heard the chaplains natter on about *a good death* so many times that it made me sick in my stomach.

Mrs. Campbell must have mistaken my silence for respect. "Both our boys were faithful Christians and true patriots, Mr. Ballard."

I thought it was time to change the subject. "I understand, ma'am, that you only drink water in this house. Out of respect for . . . ?"

Mrs. Campbell pivoted ever so slightly to face her husband, a subtle gesture of deference that she hadn't shown before. My eyes naturally followed hers, and indeed, Obediah Campbell did seem to sit up straighter in his chair. "Out of respect for our Lord and Savior, Jesus Christ. We only drink water as symbolic of our baptized state, and we keep fast days once a month, just as our Lord did in the desert."

All this personal talk of Jesus was strange territory for me, having been raised more-or-less a Lutheran, and again I was unsure how to respond. Thankfully, May June backed through the kitchen door at that moment with a pie, still hot apparently, for she carried it carefully between two folded rags. She didn't tarry, but just as she was about to slip back out the door, she glanced at Campbell and gave him an odd look.

"Perhaps you are unfamiliar with the practice of keeping fast?" Campbell said soberly.

"I know that President Lincoln called for public fasting, seeking God's blessing on the army, but I didn't know it was called for when . . . we're not at war."

"Sir, we are always at war. The great evangelist, Abednego Rogers, preaches famously on this very point. We are always at war between God and Satan, with Jesus as our general, leading us to victory."

"I hate to ask, but I've never heard of . . . Abedbug Rogers."

"*Abednego.* The reverend took an Old Testament name when he was saved at a revival meeting, even as he began his journey as a preacher and teacher of God's Holy Writ." This from Mrs. Campbell, who was getting some color in her sunken cheeks as she warmed to the topic. She glanced around the table for something to eat; apparently her passion for the preacher had recovered her appetite after burying her sons yet one more time.

"Reverend Abednego Rogers is our greatest evangelist. He has preached the Word since he was called by God as a mere boy. He was abandoned by his earthly father at a young age and raised alone in an isolated mountain cove by his mother, a Christian saint in her own right. He has preached as far away as Charlotte and Raleigh and Knoxville, Tennessee. Perhaps you have seen the broadsides— he is also known as the Shepherd of the Mountains. We believe he has single-handedly saved ten thousand souls."

This number seemed extravagant to me, but Mrs. Campbell picked up the thread of the conversation before I could express any doubt.

"What you cannot know, dear Mr. Ballard, is that you sit where he once sat. Reverend Rogers has graced our humble table on three separate occasions when he crossed the river to preach and teach. And each time, he sat in that very chair and asked God's blessing on our table and on this house."

"This chair?" Unfortunately, my raw smallclothes lay between me and holiness, and thinking of it caused my backside to itch. My evil hand began again to twitch, alive this time to scratch.

"That very chair. He once prayed for a quarter of an hour seated in that very chair, seeking God's blessing on our repast."

"Did the food get cold?"

"No, sir, it did not," Campbell said triumphantly. "There are some things that are truly beyond our comprehension."

CHAPTER EIGHT

After supper, Campbell and I sat on the porch, where he shared with me the handwritten list of Union veterans who had applied for disability. In the long summer evening, there was easily enough light to read his careful document by chapter and verse. I wanted to figure out what sort of men these Yank veterans were, as they were the same targets that were being hunted down and killed.

The listing of regiment and company by each man's name, along with his enlistment date, brought back nothing but bad memories of the despair and the slaughter, and the desire to escape at almost any cost. And now the war had come back to the men on this roster in the form of a murderer who refused to let the war die.

LIST OF FEDERAL PENSIONERS
Madison County, North Carolina
JULY 1866

James Anderson	2ND NC Mtd. Inft. C	1st mo 1st 1865
Edmund Arrowood	2ND NC Mtd. Inft. B	10th mo 1st 1863

Thomas Boon	3RD NC Mtd. Inft. B	3rd mo 3rd 1864
Abner Brooks	2ND NC Mtd. Inft. C	9th mo 26th 1864
John Brooks	2ND NC Mtd. Inft. C	9th mo 26th 1864
Nimrod Buckner	2ND NC Mtd. Inft. A	9th mo 15th 1863
Va-Na-Deer (Native)	3RD NC Mtd. Inft. D	6th mo 11th 1864
Alfred L. Dockery	2ND NC Mtd. Inft. C	9th mo 26th 1863
Jesse Fisher	2ND NC Mtd. Inft. A	9th mo 15th 1863
Benjamin F. Freeman	2ND NC Mtd. Inft. C	10th mo 1st 1864
George W. Freeman	2ND NC Mtd. Inft. C	9th mo 26th 1863
Ezekiel P. Goforth	2ND NC Mtd. Inft. C	6th mo 29th 1864
Otus Huggins	2ND NC Mtd. Inft. F	10th mo 1st 1864
Martin Alan King	3RD NC Mtd. Inft. C	12th mo 30th 1864
Isaac Kirkendall	2ND NC Mtd. Inft. B	10th mo 1st 1863
Jahew Kuykendall	2ND NC Mtd. Inft. H	10th mo 1st 1863
George W. Lockaby	2ND NC Mtd. Inft. D	10th mo 11th 1863
James Oter (Native)	3RD NC Mtd. Inft. D	6th mo 11th 1864
Andrew Pinion	3RD NC Mtd. Inft. C	12nd mo 1st 1864
James Mitchell Randall	20TH KY Infantry G	9th mo 24th 1863
Zeb B. Roberts	2ND NC Mtd. Inft. E	8th mo 25th 1864
Thomas Runnion	3RD NC Mtd. Inft. K	3rd mo 1st 1865
Asa W. Sams	5TH US Vol. Inft. K	4th mo 18th 1865
Clingman Shelton	2ND NC Mtd. Inft. E	9th mo 11th 1863
Elifuse Shelton	3RD NC Mtd. Inft. G	5th mo 15th 1864
Isaac Shelton	2ND NC Mtd. Inft. E	9th mo 1st 1863
James Shelton	3RD NC Mtd. Inft. G	6th mo 1st 1864
Henry Worley	3RD NC Mtd. Inft. C	9th mo 12th 1864

Ben Freeman's name I recognized at first glance, along with a second man in the same company by the same last name. I could feel Campbell watching me as I studied his careful list. I spoke to distract him. "You write a beautiful hand, Mr. Campbell, as neat as any I've seen in the purser's office in Washington City."

"Oh, I don't write my own notes out fair," he said, making a noise like a saddle creaking that I realized after a moment was laughter. "I have a secretary to do that once I have completed the investigative work."

I glanced up in surprise. "Does Mrs. Campbell . . . ?"

"Oh no. But when she can spare May June, the girl is allowed to work at the table by the front window in the parlor and copy out notes and correspondence. I know she's just a nigger gal, but she is also a mute, which I have always thought makes her an especially valuable secretary to the clerk of court." He paused expectantly before adding. "I have many confidential matters that I must tend to."

"Matters you don't want discussed all over the county?"

"Precisely."

"How did May June learn to write?" I asked, genuinely puzzled. Anybody who had read *Uncle Tom's Cabin*—which was just about anyone in the North—knew that slaves were never taught to read and were severely punished if they learned on their own.

"She comes from a community of free Negroes that has existed in Warm Springs since well before the war. It is my understanding that Mrs. Patton, the owner's wife, ran a school for the children of those who worked at the hotel. It was frowned upon before the war and even now, but I'm certainly glad in May June's case. She is a diligent and painstaking secretary and never questions my orders."

He seemed perfectly unaware of the irony in what he said. "How did she lose her voice?" I asked.

"Mr. Patton says that her vocal cords were damaged when she was a young child, and she can barely make what passes for a groan or a growl. She communicates wonderfully well by gesture and the occasional note, and in some ways it makes her the perfect servant for . . . my wife. And as you say, she writes a beautiful hand."

I glanced back down at the carefully drawn list. "Truly," I said. I ran my right forefinger down the neat columns twice before I spoke again. "They're almost all from either the Second or Third North Carolina Mounted Infantry. Is that right?"

"Exactly so." If I thought Campbell's tone had been somber before, when he was talking about God at the supper table, it was deadly serious now. "That's one of the things that makes me suspicious of the claims. It leaves me to wonder if these men haven't all consulted one another about the new law and decided together how they might take advantage of it."

"It makes sense," I admitted. "But I also notice that James Randall and Asa Sams are exceptions."

"Mitch Randall and Asa Sams were true Unionists. Sams died recently, in fact since that list was made. Randall is and always was a Union man. He lost an arm in the war, and it's just possible that his claim has some merit. But the others . . . pah!" He spat over the porch rail.

"How did Sams die?" I asked, trying to keep my tone as even as possible.

"Drowned in the river and washed up against the bridge pilings right down there," Campbell replied. "I watched them drag his body out of the water. Dead as a doornail."

"What was his disability claim?"

"He lost a leg somewhere along the way. Fredericksburg, if I'm not mistaken."

"I was at Fredericksburg. In fact, I was wounded there. But what in the . . . what was a man with one leg doing swimming in the river?"

"Perhaps he was fishing and fell in," Campbell said. "I wouldn't know." It was dark enough by then, such that I couldn't read the expression on his crooked face, and his tone was perfectly neutral, which caused me to wonder.

"Mr. Campbell, what do you make of all these veterans who are dying of late? I heard about it even before I left Washington City."

"Call me Obediah," was all he said.

"Well, Obediah, what do you think of these Union veterans who've been killed around here lately?"

"I do not concern myself with them." What struck me suddenly was the coldness in his voice, the lack of feeling one way or the other.

I waited. If I was right, he wouldn't be able to contain himself.

"You didn't grow up here, Jacob, so you may find this hard to understand, but many feel that those men are traitors to the true cause for which we in the South fought the war. Howsomever, I personally believe it is time to move on and leave the pain and suffering of those years behind. 'I will repay, sayeth the Lord.' Romans 12:19."

"Well, even if you leave trial by jury to the Lord, who do you *think* is doing the killing?" The moment I said it, I feared I'd pushed him too far—into thoughts he didn't care to visit.

He leaned back in his chair and, after a moment, seemed to relax in the darkness. "Why, that's really none of our affair, is it?" He rocked forward again and put one bony hand on my knee. "As far as we're concerned, I believe the war is over."

I feigned a laugh for his benefit. "Of course it is," I said easily. "I'm just here to interview the ones who are left."

*   *   *

BEFORE WE WENT in, Campbell asked if I would leave for Warm Springs the following day, and I replied that I would. I was sure they had more than water to drink in the hotel, and I felt the need to talk to James Patton, one of the few contacts in the territory that Vance had given me. It was full dark by then, lamps had been lit behind us in the house, and when we rose from our chairs, I was careful to keep the list Campbell had given me so that I could study it further.

I recall no dream from that night, the second I spent in Madison County. Perhaps because I tried two more sips of May June's tonic before lying down. The one time I rolled over onto the knot on the left side of my head, I jerked awake in sudden fear, thinking for a moment that I was again naked in a ditch beside the French Broad River. It was a relief to slowly realize where I was and that the river was thirty yards away, outside the walls and across an expanse of pasture. The water's rush was only a distant whisper.

Lying there in the dark middle watch, I thought for a moment of my nurse in Washington City, a quiet man whose full name I never knew except for Walter. When I was first transferred there from the makeshift surgery at Fredericksburg, there was a male nurse who came and went like a sad, smiling ghost. He was a great letter reader and writer, especially for the boys he favored. And he favored me. One night, when the ward was dark, and I was close to being released from the hospital, he slipped his hand under my blanket and did something to my privates that seemed to explode years of loneliness in one hot, spilling flood. I wept afterward.

I learned later that this experience probably wasn't unique for him, but it stunned me. Nothing else he ever did for me would match the eruption of that moment. And now, as I lay awake in the far Southern mountains, I found that I felt almost nothing about him or about that time and place. Thoughts that in the past might have meant comfort or even heat left me cold now. Left me all the more alone in this dark territory I'd come to.

CHAPTER NINE

Early the next morning Sam Freeman showed up on Campbell's front porch, claiming that his mother had sent him to escort me down to Barnard and to make sure I got on the right coach to Warm Springs. It seems that, having first discovered me naked in a ditch, neither the woman nor her son trusted me out on the roads alone.

As we walked the half mile down to the French Broad River bridge, I asked the boy about his mother, wondering if maybe she'd sent him to spy on me for the Freemans.

"She's all right," Sammy said. "Working to feed that pack of cousins and help Uncle Ben farm the place."

"Uncle? I thought Ben Freeman was your . . ."

"What? That he was my daddy?"

"Well . . . yes."

"Say Lord God." He stopped in the middle of the track in surprise, apparently shocked at just how wrong I could be. "I wouldn't call him uncle if he was my daddy, would I?"

"No, you wouldn't. But you didn't call him anything yesterday. And your mother only called him by name, as if to threaten that Goforth with him."

"That's 'cause Ish Goforth's got enough sense to be leery of Uncle. Uncle's got a streak of justice in him."

"Meaning what? Meaning he'd beat hell out of an old man like Ish Goforth?"

"Maybe. But worse than that, Uncle'd cut off his goddamn trade."

"Don't say *goddamn*. What sort of trade?"

Sammy stopped again to look up at me. "Uncle makes whiskey, Mr. Jake, and brandy. The brandy is supposed to be good, but the goddamn whiskey is what grown men fight over. Old Man Ish sells both—brandy out the front door, whiskey out the back."

We climbed up the short hill to the main road and started across the bridge, empty except for a two-wheeled cart drawn by a mule coming toward us from the Barnard side of the river. There was no driver, though an old granny walked along by the head of the mule, leading it with a length of plowline. It was a gentle summer morning there on the bridge, but as we drew closer, I could see that three rough-looking men followed behind the cart, and each was armed with a rifle or muzzle-loading shotgun.

We came level with the mule, plodding serenely, pulling its cart along. A human form lay in the back, wrapped in an old worn quilt. There was no smell, but the quilt was caked with dried blood roughly in the middle, where a body's waist would be.

"What's that?" Sammy asked.

"That my boy Tom," the granny woman croaked.

"Mr. Runnion, is that you?" Sammy whispered, addressing the quilt-wrapped form.

"He can't hear you, boy."

"Why not, grandma?"

"He's dead, boy."

"What happened?" I asked evenly.

She didn't turn, didn't pause, but kept walking on. The mule beside her kept shuffling, its head down, following her slowly toward the far side of the river. The day seemed to lower, the sky darken.

"He was shot in the back from bushwhack, working his own garden patch." One of the men following the cart had spoken. "Though it ain't no particular business of yours, now is it?" Two of the men continued on behind the cart, but the one stopped to study me. I could feel Sammy tense up beside me.

"It is if he's Thomas Runnion," I said evenly, "and a Union man. I'm here to interview the veterans for disability, and I know of a Runnion who fought in the Third Mounted Infantry."

The man paused to spit a long stream of tobacco juice over the railing into the river. As he turned back to face me, the double barrels of his shotgun rose till they pointed at my stomach, and I could see that one of the hammers was cocked. "That mean you a Union man as well?"

"It does mean that," I said, wondering just how bad a mistake I might be making. Sammy took a step to the side, away from me.

"Good," the man said. "Though I'd be damn careful who you say it to. Boy in the cart is the Tom Runnion you're lookin' for. He's my nephew, though he can't draw no disability now, and he ain't got no wife to draw neither." The shotgun was pointing at the bridge planks again.

"He never married?"

"Jenny died during the first winter of the war. Givin' birth. Her and the babe both."

"Who shot your nephew, Mr. Runnion?"

He paused to spit again. "If I knowed that, I wouldn't be standin' here hobbin' with you, now would I?"

"Maybe it's the same man who's been killing off the other Yanks." I could feel Sammy's eyes on me now, staring in surprise.

"Just about has to be. That boy never said an unkind word to man nor beast. Even though he rode with Kirk's Raiders, he was a . . . quiet, family-like man. What's your name anyway? I ain't never seen you before."

"Jacob Ballard."

"Ballards from Big Pine?"

I didn't know what else to do, so I nodded.

"Well, I'll tell you this, mister. When I find out who it was shot him, I mean to serve out the same treatment. An eye for an eye, a tooth for a tooth, just like in the Testament. With all that's happened lately, they's a lot of folks keep their finger on the trigger. Rebs and Yanks alike, man or woman. But nobody in his whole mind would have killed that boy in the cart. You understand me?"

CHAPTER TEN

When we came to Goforth's Store, just beside the turnpike, Sammy and I each drank a dipper full of water from the bucket on the step and then climbed up on the porch to study the hand-lettered sign nailed to the tall chestnut that shaded the store. The sign listed coaches running north on one side of a vertical line and coaches south on the other, each stage along with its departure time.

"You know which way's north, Mr. Jake?" Sammy asked quietly. We were both struck melancholy—Sammy from the thought of Runnion's corpse, me from what Runnion's uncle had said.

"That's the one thing I know for sure. It's the direction I'll be heading once all this is over." I pointed downriver toward Warm Springs, only God knew how far away.

"Once what is all over?"

"Didn't anybody ever tell you it's not polite to ask personal questions?"

"Like saying *goddamn* all the time?"

"Exactly like. So I guess that means you're going to ask me again, aren't you?"

"Once what is all over? You gettin' your pension papers filled out?"

"The pension papers. That's my only concern here. Listen, Sammy, have you got to go straight back to your mother?"

"Naw. I'd just end up in the corn rows till black dark."

"Well then, sit down here beside me. I'm going to read you off a list of names. You tell me what you know about each one."

"I'll do it if you ride me down to the Springs. I can walk back, but I ain't rode inside a stagecoach in . . . Hell, I ain't never rode in one."

"Don't say *ain't*."

"Is that less or worse than *goddamn*?"

"Much worse."

The boy thought for a moment and then sat down on the porch steps beside me. "We got a deal? I'll tell you everything you need to know—you ride me down to the Springs?"

"I'll ride you down and buy you a ticket back if you tell me all there is to know . . . without saying *ain't*."

"Down and back?"

I nodded, and we shook hands, the boy's hand not much smaller than my good right hand. Almost as big as mine and raspy with calluses.

I dug out Campbell's list from where I had folded it carefully inside a book. I noticed there were minute and very precise letters beside some of the names. Notations that hadn't been there before, I was certain, and in the same careful script as the original list itself but in faint pencil. Holding the list up into the sunlight, I could make out a tiny letter *d* beside the name of Asa Sams and what appeared to be the letter *t* inscribed beside the names of a dozen others on the list. I had to assume that someone in the Campbell house had scratched down the notes, probably May June. What did they mean?

According to the sign, we had a half hour to sit in the sunshine before the stage came along. I figured that in thirty minutes I could learn most of what Sammy knew about the names on the list. I figured wrong.

"*James Anderson?*"

"This a list of your Yankee pension men?"

I nodded. "All of them have applied for disability based on some injury or wound from the war."

Sammy grinned and nodded.

"James Anderson?"

"Lives way up in Anderson Cove. Moved up there before the war, they say, to get away from the rest of the Andersons. The slave-owning Andersons. Married one of my cousins. Works her in the fields like *she* was a slave. Mean bastard. Don't give him nothin'."

"It's not up to me. It depends on whether he can prove he was injured during the war."

"Man ain't never been hurt in his life. Not to say there ain't—isn't—a few folks who'd like to put an ax handle beside his head. Like I said, don't give him nothin'!"

"*Edmund Arrowood?*"

"Who?

"Edmund Arrowood."

"Never heard of him . . . No, wait. I think he lives down on the Tennessee line. I've heard tell of Arrowoods work at the Springs. Uncle sells to 'em. They sell to the guests. Brandy mostly."

"*Thomas Boon?*"

"Tom Boon is a bear hunter. Killed the biggest bear in these mountains before the war. Doesn't live anywhere in particular. Doesn't have much to do with people. I've only seen him once in my life."

"How did you know it was him?"

"The stink. He smells as sour as a billy goat with rotten teeth. Plus, my mama pointed him out and said to stay away from him. He has a beard most down to his waist."

"And he was in the army?"

"Why not?" Sammy said reasonably. "If there was any killing to be done, wouldn't you want a man who could shoot your eye out from t'other side of the river and halfway up the ridge?"

I looked up then and let my head turn slowly around to stare at the mountains that rose in tumbled masses all around us. It was warm in the sun, and from the north, downriver, I could hear the sound of a hawk screaming high in the clouds. It sounded like I'd come to the end of the earth.

"What's wrong?" Sammy asked. "You ain't going back on your word, are you? You said to the Springs and back."

"*Aren't*," I said absently. The hawk sounded again, clearer, more plaintive, much closer now. "Say 'you *aren't* going back on your word.'"

Sammy poked at the sheets of paper in my hand with a dirty finger. "What about the rest of 'em? Don't you want to know about them?" He stared down into the paper and sounded out a name. "Nim . . . rod . . . Buck . . . *Nimrod Buckner*. You want me to tell about him?"

"I'm not going back on our handshake, Sammy. You don't have to worry. But I have to tell you I don't believe anybody named Nimrod actually exists, not even here."

"Sure he does. He has a brother named Ninevah. Ninevah fought for the South, and Nimrod fought for the damn Yanks. They still don't speak to each other except at Christmas." Sammy glanced up at me. "You sure you gonna be able to keep up with all this? Maybe you better write out some notes or somethin'."

"Are those names from the Bible?" I asked.

"Where the hell else you think they'd come from? The Buckners go to church more than God. Ever' time you see a pack of Buckners altogether, they're going to church. They won't lie to you neither. Not a Buckner. It's not allowed."

"Well, what about this *Va-Na-Deer*. Says he's a native."

"Does that mean he's an Indian?" Sammy asked.

"I expect so."

"Well, then he ain . . . *isn't* from around here. I've never seen an Indian. Never, not once . . . Mr. Jake, I got a plan. When all these old boys come to see you, beggin' for their pension, can I hide over to the side and watch? I'd do most anything to see old Tom Boon come slouchin' in, and I'd do more than that to see an honest-to-God Indian. I could carry your papers for you or stir up your ink bottle."

*   *   *

IT TOOK A full quarter hour for the driver, with Sammy's help, to water the horses. I bought two tickets from Ish Goforth, who turned out to be Patton's agent at Barnard, and a third ticket for Sammy's return later that afternoon. Ish repeated one more time his vague description of the man he claimed had bought my watch. Something about the description still wasn't right, but I couldn't say just what.

I let Sammy be as we pulled back up onto the turnpike and settled into the ruts headed north, let him be because the boy was obviously fascinated. He leaned his whole head and shoulders out the window of the stage, half his chopped-off shock of red hair standing straight up in the breeze, exalting in the driver's yips to the horses and the crack of the whip twenty feet out ahead of the stage.

After we were well under way, Sammy dragged his head back inside and sat firmly down opposite, apparently recalled by some sense of duty, of the bargain struck. "Who's next?" he asked. "Who else you got?"

"*Benjamin F. Freeman?*"

"That's my uncle. I done certified him."

"Makes the best whiskey anywhere."

"Yup."

"So, what's his wound?" I hated to ask the question. What if Ben Freeman was a fraud, like nearly every name on the list, according to the county clerk. It was like asking Sammy to inform on his own family.

Sammy didn't hesitate. "He's paralyzed."

"He's what?"

"He's paralyzed on his right side."

"Meaning he can't move . . . what, his arm?"

"Well, mostly in the winter, he's paralyzed. Can't move his arm or his shoulder. Sometimes his leg gets stiff on him too." The boy leaned forward to whisper. "It's why he has to have me to help out with the still."

I stared at Sammy doubtfully. "Your uncle is paralyzed on his right side during the winter?"

"Yup. That's pretty much it. Some winters worse than others."

"Well, what about this *George W. Freeman?*"

"That's Ben's younger brother."

"Is he paralyzed on his left side?"

"Naw, hell no. He got hit in the face with an ax. Somewhere up in Virginia."

"He got hit in the face in battle?" Based on personal experience, I could easily imagine it.

"Naw. In camp. He walked up behind somebody chopping wood and got hit in the mouth with a double-bitted ax." Sammy held up the blade of his hand to illustrate. "You can't see it much 'cause of his mustache, but it give him a nasty harelip."

"Is *he* your father?" I wasn't sure what made me ask the question, suddenly, as if flinging it into the boy's open, freckled face that was suddenly clouded over with emotion.

"My daddy was Ben and George's baby brother," Sammy said finally. "His name was Thomas, but everybody called him Young 'cause he was the least one. Young Freeman. They all joined up the Reb army together. Ben and George got tired of it and run off. Eventually they joined up with the Yanks. But my daddy stuck it out." Sammy paused to take a deep breath, and then, as if reciting a litany he'd learned by heart, he went on. "He was captured by you goddamn Yanks at Cumberland Gap and was sent off to some place up north called Camp Douglas. He wouldn't turn coat and join the Yanks, so they penned him up there. He died on January the 3rd, 18 and 64. Mama sleeps with his picture on her pillow to this day."

Sammy stood up in the tossing coach, tears tracking his cheek, and in memory of his Rebel father tried to hit me in the face.

I caught him up easily and pinned his arms. "I'm sorry," I muttered. "I'm sorry, Sam."

The stagecoach was on the rocks now, axle deep in brown water as it negotiated one of the many tight turns where the river washed up against the steep side of the mountain itself. The horses were straining and the driver shouting. I could smell the muddy water washing almost up into the coach itself.

When a particularly rough jolt pushed us half apart, Sammy regained his seat and scrubbed roughly at his face with both hands. With one last wrenching pull, we were back on dry ground, and the horses regained their footing. The driver whistled and cursed to them soothingly.

"You got a goddamn father?" Sam asked, his voice hoarse.

"I did have. He died when I was just a boy."

"Then you ain't much better off than me?"

"That's right. And we lived somewhere around here. Some place called Bearwallow Gap, believe it or not."

"Ever-body knows where that is. Off Big Pine Creek."

"Yeah, well, when he died, my mother moved us to Pennsylvania."

"Up north?"

I nodded.

"Do you 'member him?"

"I remember his overalls hanging on the wall all that long time when he was sick. And I remember when they moved the kitchen table into the front yard and laid out his body in a pine box. I remember the rosin smell of the box made me sick."

"I'm sorry for your daddy," Sammy said after a moment. "I bet Mama could show you where he's buried."

I stared out the window of the coach. It had never occurred to me that my father might have a grave. Perhaps even a stone to mark the place and time.

"Mama might could show you where your cabin was too,"

Sammy insisted, obviously worried about me now. "She knows stuff most people . . . haven't even thought about."

I turned back to look at the boy. "So where do you and this mama of yours live? With your uncle?"

"We live on the place. We've got our own cabin up on the shoulder of the ridge across from Uncle's. That's where we sleep and Mama farms, but most days we stay down at Uncle's, for his wife run off, and Mama cooks and helps Uncle keep after all that troop of children he's got. Uncle George lives down on the creek by the road with his bunch, so we're all along in there together. They is one man, Uncle Ben's lawyer, come around lately, who wants to take Mama away from there, me too I guess, and I ain't heard her say no."

"Have we got time for one more name?" I asked.

"Yup. Maybe just one though."

I glanced down the list on the seat beside me and chose the one I'd been saving, the one I thought might be connected to the massacre. "*Clingman Shelton.*" I didn't tell Sammy that all the Sheltons on the list had the tiny *t* scribed beside their names.

Sammy glanced up sharply. "How many Sheltons you got there?" he asked.

"Four. Clingman, Elifuse, Isaac, and James. All joined up late in 1863 or '64."

"They all joined up after the killin'. Most of 'em probably fought for the Rebs early on and come home when they tired of it."

"Like your uncles."

"Yeah. But the Shelton boys all left out after the massacre. When they joined up with you Yanks, they meant business. They wasn't just hidin' out in the army. They was goin' to war to kill some folks, as fast as they could aim and fire."

The coach was passing beneath a high wall of rock just on its right side, all but scraping against the cliff face, and then suddenly the mountains on either side retreated from the river and we were onto a well-worn gravel road between fields of wheat. It was as if we'd passed out of shadowed wilderness into something I could recognize—fields and barns and then a house built out of milled lumber rather than logs. The horses began to speed up of their own accord, knowing their own barn and a pail of grain waited not far off. A hundred yards farther and the driver was standing in the box to saw at his reins. The team, long used to this passage, had already begun to climb a short incline and turn as one animal onto a wide wooden bridge out over the river. "Warm Springs," the driver paused in his humming and cursing to call out. "This is Warm Springs!"

"By massacre, do you mean the killing up in Shelton Laurel, Sam?" I asked quietly. I didn't want to spook him.

"I ain't allowed to talk about that," Sammy said and then winced. "I mean I *am not*. Nobody talks about that to an outsider. Nobody."

THE
WARM SPRINGS,
Madison County,
WESTERN NORTH CAROLINA.

HOWERTON & KLEIN, Proprietors.

HOT, WARM, TEPID AND COLD BATHS.
Readily accessible from every section of the United States, over.
East Tennessee, Virginia and Georgia Railroad, and Connecting
Lines of Rail, via Morristown and Wolf Creek, Tenn.;
By North and South Carolina Systems of Railway,
Via Salisbury, Charlotte, Spartanburg to Morganton.
And by Fine
Coaches *of the* Western North
Carolina State Lines,
to Warm Springs.

Season EXCURIONS TICKETS Sold on all Routes.
GREAT SOUTHERN SUMMER AND WINTER RESORT.

CHAPTER ELEVEN

After I put Sammy on the coach back to Barnard, I walked across the yard to the Warm Springs Hotel. I didn't know it then, but before the war, Warm Springs had been one of the premier resorts in the old South. The portico that faced the river stood on thirteen broad, round columns—one for each of the original states. It boasted over a hundred elegant rooms in matching two-story wings that ran back from either end of that long brick front. Behind that expansive portico was an elegant lobby and a large, inviting dining room. It was easily the most impressive thing I'd seen since leaving Washington City. Facing the front door for the first time, I was surprised to see that even the paint was fresh and the brass polished, despite those lean months since Appomattox.

When I approached the registration desk to the left of the wide lobby, I did what by then had become long habit. I switched my bag over to my left hand. There wasn't enough hand left to carry anything much for long distances, but by wrapping what there was around the handle, I could effectively hide it from view. Once I was up against the registration desk, I could bend to place my bag on the floor and slip the evil hand into my jacket pocket before hailing the clerk. I was as smooth as a magician on stage when it came to tricks like that, hiding the ugly part of myself.

There were several other guests standing down the way, including a very elegant woman holding a parasol and gloves. Apparently she was waiting on her mail, as one of the clerks was sifting through a pile of envelopes that had come in on the stage. Another young man, dressed just like the one sorting the mail, stepped down the way to where I stood and offered a genuine smile. He was missing a front tooth, I noticed, but his hands were clean, and he'd been well trained by somebody who knew their business.

"How may I help you, sir?"

"I'd like to register for a few days, and there may be some messages for me."

With an awkward flourish, he spun the guest book around on a revolving wooden pedestal and dipped a pen into the ink bottle for me. "Please sign your name, sir, and I'll check for messages."

"Ballard," I said. "Jacob Ballard, from Washington City, the District of Columbia."

"Of course, sir. We've been expecting you. The Laurel Suite has been reserved in your name, and I have several items for you." He reached under the bar and brought up one letter-sized envelope and a larger packet wrapped in brown paper and tied with string. The letter was addressed to me from "Mrs. Harriet Vance, Nations Boarding House, Washington, DC."

The clerk offered to clip the string on the package, and I accepted, out of curiosity as much as anything else. There was a note inside the brown wrapper and two thick envelopes. When I unfolded the note, it had one neatly printed line that read "For Expenses" and a precise signature in pencil: "Zebulon B. Vance." It hit me that the envelopes were precisely the size of federal script, two healthy bundles of cash money.

"Excuse me, sir. Did I hear you say you were from Washington City?" I caught the odor of her perfume just before she spoke. It was strong, something floral that made me want to sneeze. One gloved hand rested demurely on the bar beside mine, and I was glad that I had kept my own left hand in my pocket.

"I am. I've lived there since the war," I said.

She touched my arm ever so slightly. "Then I am so glad to make your acquaintance. I was there myself not so long ago. Philadelphia before that, you understand, but Washington City for a time as well, and I'm always glad to meet someone who brings a wider horizon here to the Springs."

I glanced up in curiosity. She had a soft, dreamy voice, not unlike a whisper, but there was something strange about it that I couldn't place at first. Her face was shadowed by a riding hat and veil, but there was light brown hair and pale skin that had been carefully protected from the sun. "I am here on a long holiday from the rigors of city life." It struck me then. She had no accent at all. Or if she did, it was not Southern. Distinctly not Western North Carolina. She, like the hotel itself, seemed dramatically out of place, dropped from the sky into a mountain wilderness.

"Jacob Ballard," I muttered. "Here on business." I have never been comfortable talking to women like her. Women of station. "Government business," I added with more force.

"Well, then, I hope your business may detain you," she said. "So that I might make your acquaintance. It would be a distinct pleasure to hear of the capital city." Her voice seemed to smile along with her lips below her veil, but her eyes were hidden. And just as suddenly as she had come, she was walking away toward the door, joining a group of men and women both, who seemed to be gathering for an excursion.

"Mr. Ballard?"

I turned back to the clerk and smiled ruefully.

"Would you like me to put that in the safe for you?" He nodded at the two envelopes of money.

I agreed and took a sheaf of notes from one and handed him the envelopes. "But tell me now. Who are"—I paused to pull the pamphlet I'd found in the lobby out of my pocket—"Howerton and Klein? I thought James Patton was the owner of this place."

The young man grinned, and I saw he was missing more than one tooth. He turned and pointed behind him where there were two rectangular wooden frames screwed into the paneled wall. The two frames were just at eye height and just the size to contain formal portraits. They were also empty. "Mr. Howerton and Mr. Klein leased the hotel for slightly less than a year, sir, from Mr. Patton. And they made a number of major improvements, including renaming it the Ithaca Hotel for a time, after some place in Greece . . . or New York, I was never sure. But unfortunately, they weren't able to . . ." He shook his head sadly.

"Make the loan payment?"

"Exactly. And so we are once again the Warm Springs, and Mr. Patton is in charge."

"Is that a good thing?"

"Of course, sir. Mr. Patton is just here, not far off in another state. And so things run much more . . ." He paused again—this time not for lack of a word, but because he realized he might be saying too much—and grinned to cover the gap. "We'll let him know you're here, sir, as soon as you've had a chance to settle in. He left strict note to let him know when you arrive."

"That's fine, but you know what I would like even more?"

"No, sir."

"A bath. A very hot bath. Is such a thing possible in this"—I waved my bad arm around to signify the hotel—"this *commodious, convenient, and comfortable* place of yours?"

"Oh, sir, there is a bath in your suite. You have one of the few rooms in the hotel with a private tub. Hot spring water still has to be carried in, but that won't take long at all. I myself will make the arrangements."

The envelope from Harriet Vance contained a short letter from the governor reminding me to have complete confidence in James

Patton. It stated that as a boy, the governor had worked for Mr. Patton at the hotel, and Patton was the most honest man he had ever known. And there would be money at the hotel as well, set aside for expenses. At the bottom of the page, there was a brief postscript from "Aunt Harriet," reminding me to be careful.

I fell asleep floating in that hot bath of mineral water and dreamed briefly of Tom Runnion, the dead man in the cart. He was trying to tell me something, but his voice was muffled by the old quilt he was wrapped in. I leaned in close to hear but could only make out echoes of lost and desperate words. It was maddening, for he wanted to say something important. He wanted to name his killer.

*   *   *

THE TEMPERATURE OF the water woke me as it cooled. When I walked back out into the sitting room, looking for the fresh clothes in my bag, the old man was there. He sat relaxed on the divan, boots up on the low table, one forefinger slowly massaging his cheek above a snuff-colored mustache. He had made himself at home and was entirely focused on the book he was reading. His hand hid the title, but it looked to be part of an expensive, leather-bound set.

"Either I'm in the wrong room or you must be James Patton," I said.

He grunted. Then, after a bit, said a word. "Jimmy." A longer pause and then, "Let me finish this page."

It must have been quite a page, because I had time to rifle through my bag and pull on fresh smalls, pants, and a shirt. I sat down opposite Patton and studied him. He was a spare man, lean in his age, with just a fringe of gray hair. Dark, sun-spotted skin. He wore well-fitted spectacles, behind which his blue eyes were clear and sharp. When he finished his "page," he marked the place carefully with a folded piece of paper and then turned those eyes on me.

"Welcome to North Carolina," he said. "Mr. Ballard, I believe, is that right?"

"Jacob," I said.

"Friends call you Jake or Jacob?"

"Jake, I guess . . ." I realized it sounded funny. "Maybe I don't have that many friends."

"Well, you got a good one in Zeb Vance. Says he's your uncle. And if that's true, then you've got family all up and down the river."

"Am I related to you?" I didn't mean it seriously, but he paused to consider.

"No. No, I'd say not. We're as Irish as can be without living in a distillery. You, I think . . . are more English—Vance, Ballard—more Scots perhaps. Way too serious a young man to be Irish. But here's the thing you need to know. Everything here is family now. Since the war, Madison County is like old Scotland. There is no social order. Your loyalty is to your clan or your family. And you, my friend, are a Vance, whether you like it or not."

I waved my left hand at him, intending to frighten the old fool, but his eyes barely left my face. "Lose your hand in the war?" he asked.

I nodded. "Fighting for the *American* army."

He chuckled. "That would be the *North* American army, I reckon." The chuckling led to some wheezing followed by some coughing, and then he put both feet flat on the floor and bent over to pull up his pants leg. He showed me that his left calf sported a horribly puckered scar where the meat of the muscle should have been, as though it had been shot clean away.

"Good God," I said involuntarily. "Were you . . . ?"

"In the war? Oh, hell no. Was too old even for the Home Guard. I tried to play bullfighter when I was a boy. Read about it in a book, and I went out to the pasture with my sister's red Sunday coat. Neighbor's bull nearly tore my leg off." He went from wheezing back to laughing then, and he had me. I was laughing with him at both of us, him with the ruined leg and me the ruined hand.

We talked on for a bit—mostly about business, for that was the heart of his conversation. Business and books—the love of one he'd inherited from his father, the love of the other from his mother.

The book under his hand was *The Odyssey*, "About some gypsy from another war who can't quite bring himself to return home."

Patton's son had been a captain in the Sixtieth North Carolina, "that would be the *South* American army," but had not seen any real action. "Walked all over Georgia and Tennessee, got bit by every kind of bug you can imagine, lost thirty pounds, and saw a lot of sights to write home about. I believe he even took up with a loose woman in Savannah for a while, a woman of some color if what I've heard is true. But the important thing is that he didn't get himself seriously shot at, except at Chickamauga for a quarter hour or so, and joining the Sixtieth got him out of these mountains."

"Was that a good thing, to get out of the mountains?"

"Yes, it was. War was personal here. Often enough it was just an excuse for people to act like animals."

"And now the killing's started all over again?"

"Seems so. Veterans like yourself finding new and curious ways to die."

"Bad for business?" I asked.

He smiled. "Word gets out, it will be. We had a spell of peace that started last spring after Appomattox and lasted till the winter. Starting in February or so, Yank veterans started dying out faster than anytime during the war. Men and even women are going about armed out of fear for their lives."

"Vance seems to think it might have something to do with the business up in Shelton Laurel."

"He might be right, hard to say. What he's really worried about is that sooner or later both sides will arm themselves and we'll end up with our own little replay of what went on in '63 and '64. I spent most of the war in Asheville, so I didn't see the worst of what went on up here, but it was vicious. Out in the mountains, people fought the war house to house, from one cove to the next, and women and children were fair game. You'll never know how glad I was that my own son was off chasing Sherman across Georgia. I figured he was safer there than he was here at home, where he's like to get shot standing on the porch."

CHAPTER TWELVE

The old man looked down at his hands, lost for a moment in reflection. "They don't like to talk about it to us outsiders," he admitted. "And I've had to fit together what I know from talking to Zeb, from what Merrimon wrote—he was the wartime solicitor for this district—and from the bits and pieces that various ones have let slip out. I've even talked to a few men who were there, though they don't want it known." He paused again, as if gathering his thoughts.

"Will you tell it to me now? Piece by piece, in as much detail as you can remember."

"It was about salt," he said. "Like a lot of things around here, it was about the most basic scraps of survival, such as water or livestock. In this case . . . salt."

"Salt was scarce?"

"More valuable than money in this part of the world. By the winter of '62, salt was kept under armed guard in much of the South, but especially here. Most mountain farmers couldn't get it, and it was the only way they had to cure meat. You could all but guarantee that a family or group of families would starve just by refusing to give them salt in trade."

"So this massacre that nobody will talk about was over salt?"

"It started with that. There was a lot of ill will, you see, between the Confederates and what we called *Tories*, or Yankee sympathizers."

"You mean the real patriots?"

"I reckon." Jimmy Patton grinned. "But patriotism was a poker game up here. In the towns, most folks were following along with Richmond and Raleigh, especially anybody with money or slaves. But once you got out into the mountains proper, people were too poor to care and too stubborn to be ordered around. Even early in the war, folks were yelling at each other in the road and setting each other's barns on fire. Most of the local boys treated the war as a lark in the beginning. Enlisted in the Southern army, nearly all of 'em in the Sixty-Fourth North Carolina, and went marching off on what they thought would be a nice, long hunting trip. Escape from hardhanded wives and screeching babies and maybe get a free rifle in the bargain."

"Same thing happened in the North," I said. "Not many actually fought for Lincoln, at least not many of the foot soldiers in the beginning. We were just out to see the world."

"Well, once the local boys got their fill of officers and saw just how bad the food was, they came home. They no more thought they were deserting the cause than you would if you skipped preaching on Sunday morning to go fishing. One man I know who walked home from Virginia told me that the army smelled too bad for him. Said he believed winter camp was the worst stench God could imagine."

I looked away for a moment. My own memories of the smells made my guts draw up. "I can believe that," I admitted.

"So by the fall and winter of '62, there were a lot of Madison County boys back home and some of their wives damn glad to see them. Of course they were deserters in the eyes of some, but Raleigh is a long ways off. And when the Home Guard did get out and start looking around, first for plain old deserters and then later for any able-bodied man they could conscript, they knew there were places they best not go."

"Best not go because . . . ?"

"Because they'd be outnumbered. Because the population had turned and would fight back. Shelton Laurel was one of those places."

"Is Shelton Laurel much of a town?"

"Oh no." Patton laughed. "Farthest thing from it. It's a long, winding valley cut through the middle by the Laurel River. Not an hour's ride from here. Not twenty families up there now, but during the war, it was where you went if the Home Guard was after you. And it was easy to get to Tennessee from there if you wanted to join up with the Yank army."

"Meaning there were a lot of outliers and bushwhackers hiding out up there?"

"You know there were, and them living in peace with the Sheltons, share and share alike. In particular, a lot of boys from the Sixty-Fourth North Carolina who'd walked off after a few months or a year and were planning on making a life back home. Shelton Laurel was the perfect place for the outliers, as you call them, to sit out the war because they could come and go from one end of the valley or the other when some politician would get riled up and send regular army troops in there to clean them out."

I thought I saw where he was going. "But they didn't have any salt, did they?"

"Just so. The store owners in Marshall refused to sell or trade them any. Much of it was just personal rancor, and the natural superiority of someone who lives in a frame house with a carpet over someone who lives in a cabin with a dirt floor. But along with everything else, it was enough."

"Enough to stir things up?"

"That's one way to put it. Enough such that one night in January of '63, right after New Year's, forty or fifty men came down out of Shelton Laurel and raided Marshall."

"The county seat?"

"Yep. And the center of what you might call the Confederate sentiment in the county. They broke into the warehouse where the salt was stored and loaded it up by the bushel basket, they broke into a store or two for coffee and such, fired off their weapons sufficient to scare all the women and children, and when one Confederate officer home on leave ran out to stop them, they managed to shoot him as well. Man name of Peak, broke his arm with a musket ball."

"And they call that a massacre!" Having seen the acres of carnage in a real battle, it was hard to prevent the sarcasm in my voice.

"Oh no, that was just the prelude to the massacre. While the Shelton Laurel boys were helling around in town, they broke into the home of Colonel Allen, the commanding officer of the Sixty-Fourth."

"Which means the commanding officer that some of them served under before they deserted." I was beginning to see a pattern. "Insult and injury—turn and turnabout. One of those feuds you read about in the penny papers."

"Yeah, some of those boys must have served under Allen, and if you knew Allen, you'd know he was an ugly man to deal with. Turns out, once they were in the house, right there on Main Street, the sight of all Allen's polished furniture and rich possessions must have enraged them. They broke into every room, threatened his wife and scared his children. Just about all they took were clothes and blankets—which is understandable—but two of his little children were sick with the scarlet fever and died a week or two later."

"And Allen blamed them for killing his children."

"Well, of course he did. And they died at the worst possible time, after the Sixty-Fourth had been ordered into Shelton Laurel to put down the insurrection and quiet the countryside. Truth be told, I'm a father, and I can understand why the man lost his mind. But it wasn't Allen who gave the orders later on."

I could see it all taking shape, like a giant hand closing into a fist. Exactly the confluence of forces that made men hate and kill each other. And I could feel my stomach rise into my throat at the thought. "What kind of fool would have been stupid enough to order local troops into the area to deal with a local insurrection?" I asked.

"Apparently a fool named Henry Heth, general stationed over in Tennessee. Claimed later that he told Keith, Allen's lieutenant colonel, not to bring back any prisoners if there was a battle, but he never told them to kill anybody they could catch."

"So, the Sixty-Fourth went into Shelton Laurel in force, regular army troops?"

He nodded.

"What percentage of the Sixty-Fourth were from Madison County?"

"At least half."

"Men from Shelton Laurel?"

"If they hadn't all deserted by that point. And at the very least, men from close by who were related by blood or marriage to the folks they were after—and who knew them well."

"Jesus God."

"It gets worse. Near as anyone can tell they marched into Shelton Laurel in two columns, one from the North out of Tennessee and one from down this way. It was the middle of winter and iron cold, snow on the ground, and even though the outliers were shooting at them from the tree line up and down the valley, they couldn't catch anybody that remotely resembled a fighting man, deserter or no."

"Of course they couldn't. Regular army troops on the move are hard to miss." Then a horrible thought hit me. "They didn't round up and shoot the women and children, did they?"

"No, but every account I've ever read or heard says that as they came to a farm, especially if it was known to belong to a deserter or a Tory, they would torture the women to make them tell where the men were hiding."

"How do you mean, torture?"

"They would throw up a noose over a tree limb, put it around the woman's neck, and then pull it tight till she was dancing on her toes, strangling. Then after a bit, right before she fainted away, they would let her down again and ask her politely where her husband or son or brother was hiding out. One woman, an old grandma, they whipped with a birch rod while she was hanging by her neck."

"You know why they did that, don't you?" I asked.

"To make the women talk?"

"Yes, and I expect they did, some of them. But I imagine that Keith—you say his name was Keith—must have hoped that the outliers would see their women being tortured and come out of the trees to save them."

"I never thought of that." He paused as he looked at me in a strange way, his eyes speculative behind the lens of his spectacles.

"So the women gave up where the men were hiding?"

"No. No, they didn't talk. Oh, they gave up a few bushels of salt and some blankets, but none of them gave up their men. You may underestimate just how angry and how tough these women are. The granny woman they hung and beat till she bled, she apparently went crazy and they've had to care for her at home since, but she didn't do a thing but spit on them and tell them to go to hell."

The sun had passed beyond the range of the windows in the room, and it was growing dark there where we sat. It felt as though the Shelton Laurel wind and snow had blown ghostlike into the hotel room. "Well, then, who did they massacre?"

"Oh, they caught up a few men and boys as they went up and down the valley—fifteen or sixteen, accounts vary—and by the third day, Lieutenant Colonel Keith had them in custody."

I must have had a premonition, for suddenly I could smell the rusty iron stink of blood in the room. "Any of them have to do with the thievery at Marshall?"

"A few maybe, say four or five, but it's impossible to know. The fact that they let themselves be picked up makes me think not, at least not for most of them. The soldiers told them that they were to be taken to Knoxville to be tried for marauding and bush-whacking. That night, two escaped. I've talked to one of them, a young boy named Johnny Norton who works here at the hotel, and as you can imagine, he's haunted to this day. Of the ones that were left, three or four were old men, three or four teenage boys, one just thirteen, and then maybe four or five of 'em fighting age. The next day, as they were marching back up the valley, Keith halted the column, had five of them kneel in the snow and ordered them shot. Five and five and then three. They begged for their lives, but Keith wouldn't listen."

"Where was Allen? Busy burying his children?"

"Apparently so. Or maybe he just conveniently absented himself, knowing what Keith planned to do. James Keith was the man in charge, and most accounts say he stood over the prisoners and ordered them shot without time to pray."

My shattered left hand was shaking uncontrollably. Indeed, my whole arm was twitching up to the shoulder, but I guess that Patton knew just how grim was his story, for he didn't seem to notice. "Usually the way it happens," I whispered. "Usually the way it happens is that somebody refuses. One or two will refuse to fire, and the officer, the son of a bitch in charge, tells them to give up their weapons and join the prisoners. That happen here?"

"It sounds to me like you've seen something similar," Patton said kindly.

"I saw deserters shot in the army," I said. My eyes seemed to blink of their own accord. "I was one who refused to fire."

"Obviously you're still alive," he said quietly. "You must have done what you had to do."

"I did. Or seemed to. The three boys we were to shoot had dug their own graves and were standing beside them. After the captain threatened to dig one for me, I fell back in line. When the command came, I fired over their heads. I've never told anybody, but I knew one of the boys well, and I fired over their heads."

"Well, it was just as you say. Keith threatened to shoot anybody who wouldn't fire. And some of those boys in the Sixty-Fourth must have done what you did because they say that it took two volleys at least once on that day, but eventually they killed them all. Five plus five plus three, to make a total of thirteen. I hear tell of a fourteenth occasionally, but most say thirteen. Rolled them into a shallow trench they hacked out of the frozen ground and threw some dirt and leaves on them."

"And you're sure they weren't combatants?"

"Three or four may have been deserters, but neither Keith nor Allen ever claimed that. And at most, four or five may have been involved in the raid on Marshall, but that was never proven either."

"So you're telling me regular army troops under the direct, line-of-sight command of a commissioned army officer rounded up civilians, including boys too young to serve, and shot them dead beside the road?"

Patton seemed to have aged ten years. As sharp as he was, he wouldn't meet my eyes. "Yes, that's exactly what I'm telling you. Does it cause you to hate the South all over again?"

"No. No, it doesn't." I was being honest. "This doesn't sound like the war, at least not the way I saw it, and I saw the devil at large, pawing upon the earth. No, Mr. Patton, this feels more personal than that."

"What do you think it did to the men who fired the shots?"

"You think that because I . . . the men who fired the shots will feel guilty for the rest of their lives. Or worse . . ."

"What could be worse?"

"They'll spend the rest of their lives hating the men they shot. The thing about war, Mr. Patton, is that you learn to hate what you're shooting at. It's the only way to survive with your mind in one piece."

"Call me Jimmy," he said. "I'm mostly a self-taught man, Jake, but I believe the word is *parricide*. Family killing. These men mostly all knew each other. Related by blood, maybe, at some distance . . . It enraged Zeb. He almost went crazy because he knew that Abe Lincoln himself couldn't have come up with something better designed to turn the local people against the Confederacy. Plus, these were his people, the ones who were shot down. Not his people by blood, the way you are, but the people he grew up with. As soon as he heard the reports, he started screaming for Keith's court-marshal."

"It do any good, Vance screaming?"

"No, no it didn't."

"Army cover it up?"

Again, he looked at me strangely. "Why do you say that?"

"It's what armies do. They protect their own."

"Keith was eventually allowed to resign. Hid out with his wife's family down in South Carolina. But Zeb didn't forget, and he kept the pot simmering. When the war was over, the sheriff down there surprised Keith at the livery stable, shackled him, and sent him up to Asheville on a murder warrant. Spent two years in jail by the time he finally stood trial."

And then Jimmy Patton stopped as if the story was over.

"Well, what the hell happened? I can tell by what you say that they didn't hang him." The old man still didn't speak. "Surely to God they didn't release him under the general pardon?"

Jimmy Patton picked up *The Odyssey* and opened it to his place, for all the world as if he meant to continue reading. He folded down his page carefully and handed me the piece of paper he'd been using as a bookmark. I spread it out on the arm of my chair.

NOTICE
$300 REWARD

Broke jail in Buncombe County on the night of the twenty-first instant, the following named and described prisoners, viz: James A. Keith, D. L. Presley, and W. H. Walker.

Keith is about six feet high, dark complexion, gray or blue eyes, slim of face, high forehead, prominent cheekbones, black hair and gray beard, was unshaved at the time of escaping from prison, and is the rise of forty years of age.

Presley is about five feet ten inches high, swarthy complexion, light hair, blue eyes, downcast look, about twenty-two years of age, weighs about 150 pounds.

W. H. Walker is about five feet eight or ten inches high, dark complexion, dark-brown hair and rather inclined to be curly, blue eyes, is about thirty years of age, stoutly built, and weighs about 150 pounds.

I will give the above named reward of three hundred dollars for the delivery at Asheville in the County of Buncombe, N. C., or confined in any jail within the State, of the above described persons, or one hundred dollars for the delivery of either of them.

J. SUMNER, Sheriff Buncombe Co.

Asheville, N. C., February 22, 1866

CHAPTER THIRTEEN

Y ou know," Patton said, "when I first saw you, Jake, I was not so impressed. I thought old Zeb had sent me a boy to do a man's job. What are you? Twenty-seven? Twenty-eight?"

I considered before I told him the truth. "Just turned twenty-four. What do you think now?"

"I wonder how in hell you ever became a Pinkerton. Your reputation, my young friend, is that you are cold as midwinter ice."

"After I was wounded and spent time in the hospitals, I was approached by Pinkerton's son to spy on the doctors and nurses. I didn't care what I did at that point, for a dram of liquor to dull the pain in my hand. From the hospitals, I went on to trail other suspects in the city. By the end, I was part of the hunt for the president's assassins and even helped with the interrogations. I was one of the detail that marched the conspirators out to the scaffold at Fort McNair. There are far worse things than battle, Mr. Patton."

"Maybe Zeb was right; maybe you're the man we need."

"It's not what you want for your own son, though, is it?"

"No, it's not. But then my own son couldn't do what we're asking of you."

"You'd better hope not. What you and Vance don't get about this job, this tracking down killers, is that at the end of the day, it's just war. Somebody dies. Either I get killed or the man you're after gets killed. I meant to stop with death when the war ended. In particular, I was through with killing. If I find the son of a bitch, what makes you think I won't just walk up and spit in his face. Then he shoots me in the head and you're back to where you started, except that you've got me to bury along with the others."

"I don't think you were born to die just yet. I don't think your time has come. And maybe you've got more life in you than death."

"I doubt it," I said.

*   *   *

PATTON TOLD ME just to charge anything I needed or wanted, and we'd settle up at the end of my stay. "Between the two of us, Zeb and I'll cover it," he said.

"Anything?" I asked, joking.

"Anything except loose women," Patton had replied. "On your own there, son," he added with a wink as he left me.

I swung back by the hotel kitchen, where the two women named Miss Fay and Miss Rose, who seemed to be working in easy tandem, gave me a meat sandwich and mug of buttermilk.

I wanted more than anything to clear my head and think. To let my intellectuals, sadly scrambled since the fight at Goforth's, have time to breathe. I'd only been there two days, in a place I had assumed would be as empty as the bottom of a bucket, and I was already swamped with people and their tales—some vague, some enticing, some horrific. Where in God's name had I landed? As I walked, I chewed a birch twig absently. The first picture that rose to the surface of my mind was a name. *Shelton.* There had been a half-dozen Sheltons on the list Campbell had given me. Based on Jimmy Patton's story, it made sense that the Sheltons would be Union veterans and with a gut-deep hunger for revenge. With my mind's eye, I searched back down the list—had their names been marked? They had. But it didn't factor up. If it had been Reb veterans being killed off, then the Sheltons had to line up as the first suspects. But it wasn't Rebs. It was the Yanks who were showing up shot and hung and cut to pieces, and the Sheltons looked more like targets than killers.

*   *   *

LATE THAT AFTERNOON in the hotel bar, Joseph B. Lyman approached me as I walked in. He offered to buy me a drink: "Anything, anything Jacob would like to inaugurate the evening." Even though all the windows in the bar were open, it was stuffy, and I was warm from my walk up the Spring Creek road. "Something cold," I said to the bartender, the same young man who had been behind the registration desk when I'd checked in. "What's the coldest thing you've got?" I thought of Campbell's house. "Other than water?" I added.

While he was drawing cold cider from a keg, I idly picked up a pack of worn playing cards at the end of the bar and was not surprised to see that the back of each card was decorated with the stars and bars, the faded red-and-blue image of the Confederate battle flag.

When I had my mug in hand, I sat with Lyman at a corner table, beneath one of the bear skins nailed to the wall. Open on the table was a large spread of newsprint that he pointed out to me. At the top of the first page in bold type was printed:

THE COLONIST.

DEVOTED TO THE INTERESTS

of the

WESTERN NORTH CAROLINA MANUFACTURING AND AGRICULTURAL ASSOCIATION.

NEW YORK CITY AND WARM SPRINGS, N.C.,

DECEMBER 1866

Just under the loud headlines, it was duly noted that "THE COLONIST is published under the management of the Western North Carolina Cooperative Manufacturing and Agricultural Association." And it claimed to be "Issued for the present in New York, but will be transferred for permanent location in Warm Springs, N.C."

There followed a list of people who had supposedly already subscribed to a large land purchase in Western North Carolina for the purpose of establishing an ideal community based on broth-erhood and common labor. I knew none of the names and assumed they were either a fiction or New York investors I was too ignorant to recognize. The rest of the newsprint pages were filled with lists and sketches in both pencil and ink: a rough drawing of the layout of the hotel, a drawing in a different hand of the landscape around the hotel showing the river and the half-dozen houses in the town, lists of fruit trees and farm products, arguments for and against a grain mill, a note to contact someone named H. R. Helper for a letter of recommendation.

"Don't mean to be critical," I said to Lyman, "but isn't the date wrong? December's still six months away."

"You do have an eye for the details, Mr. Ballard, something I appreciate to the fullest. This is a draft, if you will, a sign of what is to come that I'm preparing for Mr. Patton, to show him just how serious we are and just how large is our vision. We intend to print a thousand copies of the finished product for distribution in New York during the heart of the winter, when our potential colonists will most want to emigrate south."

I smiled at their ingenuity. "I have to hand it to you. Nobody in his right mind wants to be in New York in the winter." I pointed to a corner of one page. "Who is Mr. Helper? Is he to commend your project?"

"Hinton Rowan Helper, the author?" Lyman looked expec-tantly into my face. I stared vacantly back. "Mr. Helper is a famous commentator on the race issue in America and a native North Carolinian. It was he who recommended Warm Springs to the syndicate in the first place. An extraordinarily articulate man and someone who could write a most convincing endorsement for the project, especially if it involved bringing hardworking Anglo-Saxon men and women into the Southland."

I wondered to myself just what Lyman meant by *Anglo-Saxon*. Not colored? Did Rowan Helper want to displace the freed slaves before they even had a chance to settle?

He went on before I could ask. "But the question is, do you think Mr. Patton will be impressed?" Lyman leaned closer. "Do you think he will commit?"

"I think he'll commit to a certified check," I muttered. But Lyman wasn't listening. Something behind me, in the inner doorway to the bar, had distracted him.

I turned to follow his stare, and when I did I saw a woman who had just entered the bar. She had straw-colored hair arranged in a way I had never really seen before. She was wearing a light-pink gown and elbow-length, buttoned black gloves, a formal effect but somehow not intimidating. She was carrying a parasol in one hand as if she might go outside into the sun, but after a smiling glance around, she walked straight up to the bar, despite being the only woman in the room. When the bartender offered his gap-toothed grin and asked what she would like, the woman turned and looked straight at me. "I believe I'll have whatever that young man is having," she said. "It looks as cool as spring water."

Even though the woman in pink had turned and with her dark eyes selected me, Joseph B. Lyman was already half way across the room to greet her, consciously or unconsciously interposing his large frame between us. I almost laughed, for it was like watching a bear stalk a fawn. With what intent? To eat her up?

Apparently, the fawn had a mind of its own. With a mug of the hard cider in one gloved hand, she turned and gracefully side-stepped, adroitly leaving a knot of bar patrons between herself and

Lyman—and reestablished eye contact with me. She raised her mug in a mute toast, and despite myself, I followed her lead, saluting her with my half-empty mug in return.

"My dear, dear Miss Cushman," Lyman said as he maneuvered to her side. "How delightful that you've found us out—men at their plotting and scheming in this den of . . ."

"Butchered animals?" she offered, gesturing at the walls.

"Of course. Artifacts of the predator male. But will you please join us? I was just explaining our plans for the area to Mr. Ballard. The New York syndicate I represent has ambitious dreams for this little corner of nature's paradise."

"I should be glad to join you, Mr. Lyman, as long as the invitation includes an introduction to your young friend." She allowed Lyman to take her by the elbow and guide her toward where I sat in the corner of the room, beside the table covered with Lyman's plans. I rose as they approached.

"Just so. My young friend, as you call him, was just about to share his views on our plans for colonization of the Southern mountains."

That was it, I suddenly realized. That was the one word that had been sticking in my craw. *Colony*. I'd never heard it used except to describe the invasion of a superior race in heathen territory. Hell, hadn't we just fought off the British in order to stop being colonies?

Then the woman was standing beside me, and the suddenness of her approach, so silent and assured, told me who she was—that and the flowery smell of her perfume. She was the same woman who'd approached me in the hotel lobby. Here, her presence was just as astonishing. At my elbow in fact, with her gloved arm brushing firmly against my sleeve.

CHAPTER FOURTEEN

Lyman did the honors. "Miss Priscilla Cushman of London and Paris, New York and Boston, may I present Mr. Jacob Ballard of Washington, the District of Columbia. Miss Cushman is one of the finest actors of our age, specializing in the dramatic recreation of Shakespeare's female characters. Mr. Ballard is here representing our federal government in the just and proper resolution of the late unpleasantness between the states."

Priscilla Cushman set her mug on the table, took a step back to gain some space, and swept into a deep and formal curtsey, gently mocking the formality of the introduction. Having watched Washington politicians ape the manners of true gentlemen, I was able to drag my foot in similar dramatic fashion, bowing low.

"And are you to save us, sir, from all the after effects of that terrible war?" Her voice was musical, rising and falling within a single sentence. "Are you to make North America once again safe for poor, wandering troops of thespians, intent on holding a mirror up to humanity?"

Despite myself, I laughed. "Oh, I plan to do all that and more, Miss Pushman."

"Cushman. Call me *Priscilla*."

"Well, Miss Cushman, since you ask, I intend to cleanse the world of *all* evil while on my Southern tour, simply by roaming the hills, hat in hand, and speaking gently with everyone I meet."

She raised her hand to her throat as she laughed, drawing attention to the bodice of the pink dress, more intriguing lace than solid fabric. "What can you possibly do for the good of the nation here, Mr. Ballard, in this . . . this barren place?"

"Ah, Priscilla . . ." Lyman interrupted my thoughts. "You have gone straight to the heart of my plan. Suppose for a moment that you could take honest, God-fearing people from the Northern cities and transplant them into this spot, this lonely outpost from civilization." He pointed down through the table and the papers on it, apparently through the floor at the earth itself. "Transplant them here into nature's unquestioned bounty, where their Godly natures will be rewarded by nature's God? Were we to replace the shiftless, bootless native with the hardworking yeomen of the North, there would be no limit on . . ." I glanced at the young man behind the bar, suddenly embarrassed that he might be listening. "Replace the one with the other, would it not be a magnificent marriage of place and people? Nature's yeomen in the bosom of nature's bounty?"

It was a set speech, probably practiced before a mirror. And watching the young man—little more than a boy—who was studiously wiping down the maple bar top, I discovered that I couldn't listen to any more. "So, Lyman," I interrupted, "do you call it *colonization*, then, because it is the replacement of the heathen with the civilized?" I could feel Priscilla Cushman's eyes on me; I suspected she had a much finer sense of irony than Joseph B. Lyman.

Lyman somehow puffed up his chest even more, something like a barnyard rooster, I thought. "Do you not think," he continued, "that it is the inevitable march of progress from a state of feeling and appreciating less to a state of feeling and appreciating more?"

Lyman paused for effect, but not for long. He loved the sound of his own voice too much for lengthy pauses.

"Now that chance has brought us together in the backwoods of Carolina, Miss Cushman, I hope to interview *you* for my series on the *Eminent Women of the Age*. Surely you have seen the individual character studies in the *Atlantic Monthly*, soon to be collected in a handsome, leather-bound volume by Ticknor and Fields. I flatter myself that it echoes the work of Plutarch, had he been sufficiently prescient to focus on your fair sex."

Priscilla Cushman only glanced at Lyman before turning her eyes back to me. She smiled ironically. "I know your work, Mr. Lyman," she said. "But I struggle to believe that a theater woman who has lived as widely as I will appeal to your audience. But perhaps . . ." I could feel myself smiling back at her, even nodding ever so slightly. "Perhaps," she continued, "there's time enough for both. Perhaps I might answer your questions here in the bar before dinner. And after we eat, perhaps you, Mr. Ballard, might tell me more about your sojourn in the South. Over a drink more suitable than this vile cider?" She laughed as she put down her mug. And the sound was so infectious that I had to laugh as well, though I'd long ago drained my own mug, hard and sweet.

While Lyman brought out a notebook of lined paper from his bag and filled his pen with brown ink from a small, traveling ink bottle, I brought her a glass of white wine from the bar.

"Can you tell us something about your family, Priscilla, your forebears? May I call you Priscilla?" Lyman had begun, and his voice was well-oiled, humming like a machine in steady use.

"Now why would I want to do that, Mr. Lyman? I don't think about my family, and they try not to think about me."

"Well, my readers often want to know about the origins of someone special, someone of genius. They like to speculate about the source of such talent. Was your childhood one of poverty and deprivation?" Lyman asked, pen poised. "Were you raised in a cold-water flat, or even better, a tenement with no running water whatsoever?"

"Not quite," she admitted. "My grandfather did take us in after my father died. And so I was raised in a huge, dark house with little laughter and no music except what my mother and I could generate when my grandfather was not at home. The house was not poor in dollars but poor in spirit." It was a line she'd delivered before, and she hit the intonation perfectly.

Lyman mouthed the words as he wrote "in spirit."

"My mother and I would put on small-scale dramatic readings for the servants when my grandparents were out of the house. Closet Shakespeare, we called it. And one day when I was fifteen, my mother made the fateful decision that would change every-thing. She and my aunt found a way to sneak out in the evenings—one from her father's house, one from her husband's—and they auditioned for a local variety show as Romeo and Juliet. My aunt Charlotte played Romeo and my mother Juliet." Aside to me, she whispered, "Charlotte loved wearing trousers with that dagger in her belt."

"And they were caught?" Judging from his voice, Lyman had fallen prey to the suspense.

"On, no. They were too clever for that. They weren't caught. Worse . . . they were *good*. So good that there was a review in the *Boston Globe* that called them by name. Charlotte's husband threatened to divorce her, which was unheard of in polite society, and grandfather expelled us from the house like Adam and Eve from the Garden!"

Lyman was writing furiously, pausing only to dip his pen. Without looking up, he said, "So then you and your mother were forced to endure penury and privation! I knew it. All eminent women suffer for their art."

"Not quite. You will remember that I was fifteen. Mama followed another woman to Europe, a journalist whom I won't name, except to say she did the nicest things for men's clothes." She glanced at me again. "Men's clothes and cigars," she added for effect.

Lyman had stopped writing—suddenly, as if in midsentence. "The *Atlantic Monthly* won't . . ."

"I'm sure they won't, but I thought that you and Mr. Ballard might be afforded a more complete view of the time and place. I left them in New York, on the docks, waving as they boarded ship for France."

"But you were only fifteen!" Lyman exclaimed.

"By then, probably sixteen, but who's counting. What's important is that while we were in New York, I found a home at the Bowery Theater with Tom Hamblin. And I discovered my life's calling."

"What year was that?" I asked innocently.

"If I told you that, Mr. Ballard," she said dryly, "I might be revealing more than I ought. It was at the Bowery that I began to play Shakespeare. First the smaller parts of course, but eventually my face was on the posters and my name in the newspapers."

"She took New York by storm," Lyman said to me. "She was especially renowned in the great comedic roles wherein women disguise themselves as men: Portia in *The Merchant of Venice*, Rosalind in *As You Like It*. There was even a poll in the *New York Post* over whether the famous *P. Cushman* was actually a man or a woman. But then her Lady Macbeth removed all doubt. She was revealed . . ." Lyman stood with a theatrical flourish all his own before adding, "as a woman in full!"

"Having conquered New York, did you then invade Europe?" I asked, ignoring Lyman. Despite myself, I was intrigued. I felt as if I was watching a drama while seated onstage.

"London, Paris, Rome . . ." Lyman was almost ecstatic, but Priscilla, I noticed, was not swept away by his enthusiasm.

"Prague," she said calmly. "Let us not forget Prague."

"What happened?" I asked quietly. "From Prague to Warm Springs. From the capitals of Europe to . . . here?"

She paused before she answered. "The *war* happened, Jacob Ballard. I made the mistake of returning to the United States in

1860 for a special production of the Scottish play Mr. Lyman is so fond of, and I got caught. I should have left the country the day Lincoln was elected, but I was under contract, and I was too foolish to break it. By the time the run was over, Fort Sumter was old news and theaters everywhere were closing. I tried to get back to Europe but was advised to stay put until the national unpleasantness resolved itself. I was reduced to playing musicals and patriotic drivel to half-empty houses like Ford's in Washington City."

"I'm told the war is over," I said. "Perhaps it's time for a comeback."

"Perhaps," she bowed to me with just her head, again lowering her eyes submissively. "But then we survivors have our scars, don't we?"

CHAPTER FIFTEEN

There were over a hundred people at dinner that evening. You could order from a generous list of entrees. I recall chicken and dumplings, roast mutton, beef tenderloin, stewed kidneys, and a dish called pig's head with carrot sauce. The waiters brought out some boiled vegetables and delicious wheat bread, sliced hot at the table. Butter and molasses. I learned later that Jimmy Patton was fond of sorghum molasses, and it was most always on the table. There was cider if you preferred it, coffee, tea, and buttermilk. And if you were with Priscilla Cushman, there was white wine. I decided to follow her suggestion into the bottle with the fancy red label from Virginia.

There were five seated at our round table set for eight. The two others were a long-married, long-suffering couple from Charlestown, South Carolina, who were visiting the Springs in search of relief from the husband's gout. They spoke in slow, elaborated syllables that Priscilla began to imitate while we ate. At first, I thought she would insult them—Sturtzel, I believe was their name—but she was so easy and so subtle that I don't believe they ever heard her mockery. Words seemed to drop from her tongue like little spangles of light while she played with the Sturtzels, asking them about the theaters she'd played in Charlestown before the war. She was seated beside me, with Lyman on my left and the Sturtzels on her right. She all but cut Lyman out of her conversation by focusing on the old couple, and from time to time she would reach under the table to touch my right arm or hand as she made a point. She had taken the long black glove off her own right hand while she ate, leaving her left hand and arm sheathed. The effect of her gloved touch was electric when it caressed me, shooting a Morse code up my arm.

Indeed, the effect was so strong that I was almost mesmerized, and at one point she even leaned over to quietly remind me to eat. "You might need your strength," she whispered.

When dessert was served, Mr. Joseph B. Lyman attempted to reassert himself by announcing to the Sturtzels just who and what he was—and I will admit that the man got a response. They were visibly impressed with his tone and gravity. And when Mr. Sturtzel, a nicely dressed, gentlemanly man, asked what had brought Lyman so far south, away from his grave responsibilities in New York, Lyman was at once mysterious, almost coy. "I'm afraid that I'm not at liberty to discuss the business venture that brought me to Carolina, but I am happy to say"—this with a dramatic pause—"that finding Miss Cushman here has given me the opportunity to interview her for the *Atlantic Monthly*. Do you know that august periodical, sir?" He didn't give Sturtzel time to reply. "As part of my series on the Eminent Women of the Age. I believe we may continue our interlocution after dinner in the lobby of the hotel, and you might attend, if Miss Cushman doesn't object."

"Of course not," Priscilla Cushman said. "I have an appointment with Mr. Ballard for a walk in the park immediately following dinner, and I'm afraid I will need our constitutional to gather my wits, so perhaps we could continue our conversation in half an hour. In the lobby, did you say?"

"In the lobby, ma'am. Where we may take refreshment as we please and talk without interruption."

*   *   *

ONCE WE HAD ESCAPED outside to the porch, I could feel as well as hear her take a deep breath.

"And so are you an eminent woman of the age?" I asked.

"Eminently bored. That much I will admit. Tired of the Ly-man and his questions."

"Aren't you promised to him in half an hour. To be delivered to the lobby . . . ?"

"I didn't promise."

"You said—"

"Mr. Ballard, will you ever . . . *ever* ask me to call you Jacob? Must I get down on my knees on the front porch of this institution?"

"But you said—"

"I lied." She had stepped in front of me to stare into my face. Appraisingly, I would say. Or pleadingly. With her, who could tell?

"Call me Jacob. You lied?"

"Jacob, I'm an actress. I lie for a living. It's what I do. Of course I lied. Do you think I want to spend the rest of the evening with Lyman for God's sake?"

She had me; I laughed out loud. "I hope the hell not. Can we go for our walk now? The walk you keep claiming to have promised *me?*" We took one step forward. "So, Miss Cushman, how will I know when you're lying to me?"

She pivoted in front of me again. Again, almost as if we were dancing to some music only she could hear. "That, Jacob, is easy. If I'm looking at you. No, not just at you. Looking into your eyes . . . yes, like this. If I'm looking into your eyes, then I'm telling the truth. If I'm looking away, you won't know one way or another. If I'm avoiding your eyes, if you can't make me look at you, I'm almost certainly lying. That's how you know."

I stared into her dark-brown irises, black in the fading light of evening. They were guarded, however, not bare as before. "Are you telling me that you cannot lie to my eyes?"

She stared straight back into me. Without blinking. "That's what I'm telling you. I can't lie to your eyes . . . And Jacob?"

"Yes?"

"Can we please go?"

"Go where?"

"Anywhere. Off the front porch for a start. I don't want us to stand here staring so long that you make an honest woman of me, and I get trapped by that buffalo Lyman."

*   *   *

AFTER A STROLL by the river, we circled around through the trees to a spot where we could see the side porch of the hotel across fifty feet of lawn. I had a key to the outside door of the Laurel Suite, and I thought I could just make out the door under the overhang of the porch. Even though it was July, the evening had settled, and it was cooler under trees. The light was waning from the air.

"We could wait till after dark," I whispered.

"The bugs are eating me," she whispered back. "We have to run for it."

"You can run in that . . ."

"That what?"

"Costume?"

"Fast enough," she whispered. "Have you got the key?" And although we'd been playful enough before, there was a hoarseness in both our voices. For some reason other than Lyman, some unspoken reason, neither of us wanted to be seen.

I could feel the key, along with the wooden disk it was attached to, in my pants pocket. I nodded, and she was gone.

I followed across the dew-slick grass. She wasn't what you would call running, but she was as quick as a hare. Again, I was struck that she almost floated, so silent and graceful was that swift gait. I struggled to keep up and finally just ran, so that we arrived together at the side steps. We were up and then to the door, and I realized I'd never tried it from the outside.

It was times like this when I loathed my bastard hand. I felt in the dimness for the keyhole and then struggled to manage both knob and key.

"Let me," she whispered. "I'm used to it." And she gently eased the key out of my hand. She didn't flinch, I admit, when her fingers brushed my scars, and she had the door open in a flash.

We were in and the door shut behind us, and it *was* as if we'd escaped. She reached behind me to turn the bolt and, with all the ease of a pickpocket, slipped the key back into my jacket.

"I'm sorry I took it from you," she was still whispering. "I'm sure you would have had it in a trice, but then, it's your first night here."

"I only have one decent hand," I whispered, following her lead. "I'm not what I once was."

"Not at all. Seems to me I've seen two strong hands." She reached up and put her palm flat on my shoulder and left it here, a gesture both comforting and, beyond that, intimate. Someone, a maid perhaps, had lit a lamp at the far end of the parlor from where we stood. Despite the light, it felt to me as if we were in a hidden place, just the two of us. And though our breathing slowed, my pulse did not. I was sure she could feel it surge beneath her hand, and I blushed at the thought.

After a moment, she took mercy on me, and turned to walk to the couch in the center of the room. From there, she surveyed the furniture and the few books strewn on the table. Pictures on the wall of some classic ruins, tall columns rising into empty air.

"Jacob?"

"Hmmm?" I was suddenly hot and was taking off my jacket.

"It's a beautiful room. Do you mind if I sit for a while before I go? I'm afraid the Lyman . . ."

"Might still be lurking?"

She nodded, her eyes suddenly gleaming. "With his antlers and his wit," she said. And then after a pause. "Perhaps you might even offer me a drink." She sat down on the couch and seemed almost visibly to relax.

"Are you really an actress?" I'm not sure where the question came from; perhaps I was just stalling because her touch had unnerved me. But I did look directly into her face, remembering what she'd said earlier.

She didn't look away. "So, *you're* going to interview me now?"

"I have some very good brandy. Yours if you tell me the truth."

I had brought a jar of Freeman's apple brandy to my room when I dressed for dinner, and I found not one but two glasses in the cupboard. When I came back to the couch, she took her glass gratefully and pointed to the chair directly across from her—just where I had sat earlier when talking to Patton.

I sat, but she didn't speak, rather sipped from her glass and then stared down into its rich depths.

"Are you really an actress? Is Cushman really your name?" For reasons I couldn't have named, I was pushing at her now, trying to gain some distance from which to regard her.

She sat on—close, silent, still. And then, decisively, as if she'd found something in her thoughts that she was looking for, she drank again from her glass and set it on the low table. She held up one finger as if to tell me to be patient, rose and walked behind the couch into the shadows at the far side of the room.

I will never forget what happened next.

CHAPTER SIXTEEN

The stage was set. I was in the middle of the parlor room, seated in a well-padded chair with a low table in front of me, and on the other side of the table a couch faced me. The lamp was behind me on the mantle. Beyond the couch was the darkest part of the room, but I knew there was a chest that had glasses and decanters on its top. I couldn't remember what else was in the shadows. Perhaps a chair.

Suddenly, a voice—at first I didn't realize it was hers—spoke ever so slowly, and in the deepest possible female register:

The raven himself is hoarse
That croaks the fatal entrance of Duncan
Under my battlements.

The tenor and power of that voice was so strong that I felt my flesh creep, and my glass trembled in my good hand.

Then she—whoever she was—emerged from the shadows. She had undone the top two or three buttons on her dress and loosened her bodice, so that her neck and chest were bare down to the top of her breasts, which heaved with the effort of that voice. Her hair was down as well, about her face and shoulders, a thick brown tide of hair. The figure strode forward with a slow, majestic purposefulness, just to the back of the couch.

Come you spirits
That tend on mortal thoughts, unsex me here,
And fill me from the crown to the toe top-full
Of direst cruelty.

Her hands were clutched together below her waist such that her shoulders knotted and her fingers turned white with the effort, and suddenly the hands turned inward against her belly and slowly slipped upward over her body as her voice intoned the words. I would never have believed what I was seeing, but her hands—her own hands—slid lavishly over her breasts and up to her throat to grasp her open collar.

Make thick my blood;
Stop up th' access and passage to remorse,
That no compunctious visitings of nature
Shake my fell purpose, nor keep peace between
Th' effect and it.

With the next words, her voice lowered yet again, almost into a hiss, and she pulled her dress down off her shoulders, baring herself to the waist and cupping her own breasts in her hands as she leaned forward toward me over the couch.

Come to my woman's breasts
And take my milk for gall, you murd'ring ministers,
Wherever in your sightless substances
You wait on nature's mischief.

I am sure I had stopped breathing, and my blood pooled in my veins for a long moment. Then just as quickly, she twisted away, covering herself again as she stared at me over her shoulder.

Come, thick night,
And pall thee in the dunnest smoke of hell, . . .

Sinking lower and lower until only her face was visible above the couch, frightening in its intensity, her eyes black in her skull.

That my keen knife see not the wound it makes,
Nor heaven peep through the blanket of the dark
To cry "Hold, hold!"

And her face sank beneath the back of the couch as if into a lake of water or fire. There was a long moment of unnatural silence, as if her voice, full and rich as cannon fire, had stunned the air.

Almost as if on cue, there was a frantic knocking on the outer door, and if I was holding my breath before, I swallowed it then. Louder knocking! Followed by an angry voice. "Ballard! Ballard, goddamn you. Are you there? It's Lyman, and I'm looking for Miss Cushman. She's not in her rooms, and I'm worried that something's happened to her. Ballard, if you're in there, answer, damn you!"

Priscilla popped up from behind the couch and, clutching the front of her dress together, fled noiselessly into my bedroom. I stood and tiptoed just close enough to the hall door to be sure the bolt was thrown. When I saw that it was, I followed her, not as quickly or quietly as she, but I was sure Lyman couldn't hear me from the hall. And somehow, I did manage to pick up both our glasses and the jar of brandy.

Once I passed through the door, she pushed it shut and bolted it behind me against the monstrous knocking, still knocking on the outer door. I remembered just enough of the room to bump forward to the one bedside table and set down the jar and glasses, having spilled a good deal of the brandy down my shirtfront.

Then she was behind me, her arms around me, her lips against the back of my neck. She was laughing silently, if such a thing was truly possible, laughing at the uproar and the locked doors.

"I feel like I'm in a play," I whispered; although, she was holding me so hard I could barely breathe. "Like Duncan trapped in Macbeth's castle."

"You are, you fool," she whispered back. "Captured within my battlements."

I tried to face her, and she relented just enough to let me turn within her arms. In the dark I could feel her hair wild around her shoulders, her dress barely together at all above her waist, her lips against my neck. "Didn't Duncan die?" I muttered into her hair.

"Always and forever, he died," she said dreamily, more slowly now. "And trust me, he loved it each and every time." This as she nipped me, in the hollow at the base of my neck. Bit me and kissed the bite as if to wound and heal at once.

I picked her up and threw her on the bed. My hand—my left hand and arm—could have torn her dress from bodice to hem, so mad was I for her. Somehow, she had shredded years of distrust and distaste, and I was sixteen again, chasing a neighbor girl into a Pennsylvania haystack. The bed, the haystack—there was a strenuous wrestling, twisting, biting—and it was only later, when I tried to recreate it all in my mind, that I realized she was fighting just as hard to pull off my clothes as I was hers. And she was much better at it. After all, she had two hands and she was more experienced by far.

My body was wanton, was taut, was *harsh* with wanting her. I was shocked, for it had been years since I had felt anything like this boiling flood of sensation.

"My God," she said, later, when we were both sprawled in the twisted covers, spent. "Are you always like that?"

Only half conscious, I let the truth slip out. "I'm never like that," I said. "With anyone."

At some point just before sleep, I got up and pulled the sheet and blanket free and tossed them straight again over the bed. When I did, even though the light in the room was shadowy thin, Priscilla turned away from me. And in that briefest instant, I realized she was different than I had supposed, heavier perhaps, older certainly. But I didn't care. Surely she could see that I didn't care. I was still in shock from the response she had wrung out of me.

*   *   *

LATER IN THE dark and twisted depths of the night, I returned to that field hospital in Fredericksburg, where they treated the boys dragged off that bloody hillside. I lay not in a wonderfully soft hotel room bed with Lady Macbeth but *on a hard, cold wooden tabletop. My uniform blouse was wadded under my head and a bloody sheet thrown over me. Two Negro men were tying my arm to a plank, and a man I had never seen before was standing behind them drinking from a flask he held in one hand; in the other was the bone saw, already red with some other bastard's blood. The flask came down, and he spoke in a harsh whisper. "Chloroform?" he asked the empty air. "Done gone, boss . . . Been gone, boss." And I begged and begged for my arm. Tried to raise it, but it was already lashed down. Chop off the fingers, I said. But leave me a hand. Please, God, you can manage just one hand. And God said if I leave the hand the fever will destroy you. Please, God, please. And almighty God shrugged. God laid down his bloody saw, wiped his own hands on the edge of the sheet, and picked up a heavy, double-edged catlin. And God said let his hand be held down on the plank. "What hand, boss?" What's left of it, God said. Wiped the catlin on his coat sleeve and bent to his task. The glorious labor of destruction. I could hear the horrible keening sound of prayer . . . screeching in my throat . . .*

She woke me with shaking, harder and harder, and then slapping me. Coming up, I thought at first she was God Almighty with his knife. That I had died to this earth. But no, no, I was only waking to first light. On earth, not as it is in heaven.

Priscilla Cushman was dressed and sitting serenely on the side of the bed. Demure, every button perfectly in place up to her chin. Her hair woven back into its perfection. "Were they going to take off your arm?" she asked quietly.

"My hand," I said. "The way they did in those days—neatly at the elbow."

"But you talked them out of it, didn't you?"

"I begged," I said. "I begged and he relented. I regret it to this day."

"You wish he'd sawed it off then?" she said, the amazement creeping into her voice.

"Oh, I wish I'd died," I said. "So much less pain."

She stood and turned to look through the doorway to the outside windows, measuring the advance of early morning. After a moment's reflection, she stepped to the dresser where my few possessions lay. "Do you have any money here in the room, Jacob?"

"In the top drawer," I said. "Why?"

She opened the drawer and felt under my one spare shirt. Held the thin sheaf of bills to the light and counted off several and tucked them into the waist of her dress. Returned the excess to the drawer.

"Do you need money?" I asked.

"Yes, I do," she said. "Besides . . ." she nodded her chin ever so slightly at the bed and said, "I don't perform miracles of the dramatic art for free."

CHAPTER SEVENTEEN

You know he done stammered since he was a boy," Miss Fay said to me when I asked her about Johnny Norton.

"Stuttered," Miss Rose corrected her. "Word is *stuttered.*"

"I like to say *stammered*, Rose. Don't sound so—"

"Why?" I interrupted. The two were fixing a powerful midday meal in the hotel kitchen, and they expected Johnny himself at any moment, to help serve. "Why do you think he stutters . . . or stammers?"

"Do you need a reason?" Miss Fay asked.

"His father is mean as a rattlesnake," Miss Rose said. "Devil himself ain't in it, how mean that man . . ."

It was then that Johnny walked in from the dining room and both women hushed. Miss Rose stopped chopping cabbage and cut a thick slice of roast beef and laid it between two pieces of bread. She held it out to Johnny and nodded at me, where I stood by the outside door drinking a mug of coffee.

"Go on," she said. "Take the man his sam-wich. I ain't got time to mess with you *or* him right now."

Even so, Johnny hung fire looking around for one of the girls who wasn't busy. Miss Fay pushed him gently from behind. "Go along, Johnny. He won't bite. He's one of the good 'uns."

When Johnny approached the door, I withdrew to the porch, forcing him to follow. When I took the food, I smiled and nodded at one of the rocking chairs.

"I'm awful busy in the kitchen, Mr. Ballard. I don't know that—"

"I spoke to Mr. Patton, Johnny. And he said it was all right for you to talk with me. I'm down here to interview Union veterans who might apply for disability payments, and I'm trying to get a feel for the job I've got out ahead of me."

Johnny collapsed into the rocker with some sense of relief. "Well, sir. I expect you got a big job ahead of you. They's a lot of men come home sick or shot up. I ain't . . . I mean I *haven't* got a disability, but I know a lot of 'em that does."

"Do you draw a pension?" I asked with my mouth full of sandwich.

"Yessir. Five federal dollars a month. Mr. Patton banks it for me along with my pay. I'm savin' up to buy some land up home."

I smiled. "Up in Shelton Laurel?"

"Yessir. That's where my family lives. But I don't have much notion of workin' for my father. He's a hard man, and he hangs on to what land he's got."

"How old are you, Johnny? Can't be much over twenty."

"I'll be twenty-two come September. My name's in the Bible for September the 10th, 18 hundred and 47."

He was only two years younger than I was, but at that moment, I felt like an old man by comparison. "How old were you when you joined up?" I kept smiling reassuringly as I sipped my coffee. I wanted him to relax and talk as easily as ever he could despite his stammer.

"Well, sir, I walked over the mountain to Erwin, Tennessee, on my sixteenth birthday. September of '63."

"Told them you were eighteen, did you?"

"Yessir. That won't hurt my pension none, will it?"

"Lord no. I'd have done the same thing. I ran off from school early in the war just to see the world."

"I never did see much, myself. Saw a little dab of Kentucky. Least, the lieutenant said it was Kentucky. Saw a lot of that damn Tennessee. Near froze to death in Tennessee."

"How old were you when the Sixty-Fourth came up into Shelton Laurel and rounded up the men and the boys?"

"Well, let's see. I was fifteen, I guess, for it was in Jan . . ." Johnny Norton froze in midsentence. "I don't favor to talk about that. I mostly try forget about all that."

"Somebody's been killing off men up and down the river, Johnny."

Johnny nodded, almost spasmodically, and mouthed *yessir*. Swallowed hard and then spoke aloud. "I mean, yessir. Most folks around here know about that."

"Who do you think is doing it? Some soldier boy don't know the war's over?"

He shrugged and looked down at his feet miserably.

"Johnny, look at me. I came here to help. And I think what's going on may have something to do with the killings in Shelton Laurel. Can you tell me about it?"

"Maybe you ain't noticed, but I don't talk so . . . good. Not when I'm scared. I don't tell things so easy like you." The boy's hands were clenched in his lap, and his shoulders shivered with the strain.

"I know how you feel. Sometimes, even now, I hear cannon fire in my sleep, and then my bad arm shakes so hard it wakes me up."

He looked up, and I held out my butchered hand for him to examine. The boy whistled. "That's a bad 'un, sure enough," he said.

"You help me, I'll help you. I'll help you with your pension and your land. Besides, I think you may know something about what's going on and don't even realize it."

Johnny Norton looked down at his own hands clenched together in his lap. After a moment, it sounded almost as if he was humming to himself. I leaned forward in my own rocking chair, and when I did, I realized that the boy was whispering. I reached out to the arm of his chair and ever so gently set it to rocking, hoping that the motion might help. The sound through the open windows of the women working in the kitchen covered up some of his voice, but leaning forward till our heads almost touched, I could make out what he was struggling to say.

"It was my job ever' day in the winter to haul hay to the cattle in the upper pasture. I used an old sledge and a mule to haul the hay. I was at the barn forkin' up my second load, when them Rebs came marchin' by on the road. Right there beside the barn, they beat me with their rifles, then took me up an' tied me to a line of men and boys they had caught. Took the mule too."

"Did you tell them you weren't a soldier?"

"I tried my best, but my words got all tangled up, and I couldn't. I couldn't get none of it out my mouth."

Johnny was still rocking, rocking.

"They done a crazy thing then. They tied us up in two long lines, and they made us walk along each side of the road."

He was gesturing with his hands, and I realized he was trying to show me something about the order of march. I whispered in reply, "Some of the Rebs walked between you as you went down the road?"

He nodded.

"You were shielding them from the woods. Probably some of the officers. Allen? Keith?"

The same frantic nodding.

"Both?"

"That first day, both of 'em. They 'as givin' each other hell and yellin' at us ever' time one of us stumbled. Or fell. It was freezin' cold, and the soldier boys had taken our coats and hats, but that Keith didn't give a . . ."

"A damn? He didn't give a damn."

"Naw. And long 'bout dark, we come to Aunt Judie Shelton's place. Taut log cabin part, way up the valley. They tied us to a tree in the yard, while they bi . . . biv . . . in the barn."

"Bivouacked in the barn?"

Again the violent nodding. "Allen come out after a bit, and he told us that we was to stand trial in Knoxville. That's over in Tennessee where they was a lot of Rebs in camp. And then he mounted up and rode away. Back down the valley. After it was black dark, that Keith . . . he come out and cussed at us. Said our mamas and sisters was whores and told us we could roast on a spit in hell, and one of the Sheltons yelled out at least we wouldn't fuckin' freeze to death. They beat him for that. 'Bout midnight they untied us and locked us up in that cabin. Give us two pones of bread to split between us, and we busted up some chairs to burn. Old Stobrod Shelton said like as not, they'd shoot us all the next day. When he heard that, Pete McCoy climbed out a window, busted one of the guards with a chunk of stove wood, and run off. Joe Wood tried to follow him out, but they flung Joe back in."

"Who else was there, with the Rebs? You must have known some of them?"

"'Sides Keith?"

I nodded gently.

"Officer name of Nelson, 'nother one name of Robbins. The Campbell boys, they was there. Henry Sale. Marsh McKamey. I don't know who all done the killin', but they was all there that mornin'."

Nelson, Robbins, Campbell, Sale, McKamey—I repeated the names silently to myself.

Johnny was still rocking, still nodding. But slower now, in a gentler rhythm. "How did you get away?" I whispered.

He made the strangest gasping sound, and for a moment, I thought he was crying. But no. No, he was laughing. Quietly, as if to himself. "Why, there was a rope-and-rail bed in the back room," Johnny said. "And when they come for us the next mornin', I hid under the bed."

CHAPTER EIGHTEEN

I found Patton in his office that afternoon, sitting at his desk behind a stack of four huge ledger books, which a clerk was showing him by turning the pages over one by one. Patton waved at a chair on the other side of the desk. "Give me a minute. Having a look at last month," he said, his eyes never leaving the pages as they turned. "Month of June," he added. Patton was wearing a tie and vest; there was a suit jacket hanging on the back of his chair. He was massaging his cheekbone with one long forefinger—a characteristic gesture—when abruptly he stopped to point at a ledger entry. "Garrett is that far behind?" he asked.

The clerk nodded and bent to look more closely over Patton's shoulder. "Three months of cigars and haircuts, three months of running up a tab in the bar."

"That's a considerable bar tab," Patton said.

"Perhaps the major, he drinks to forget," the clerk offered.

Patton guffawed. "At that rate, he should've forgotten everything he ever knew."

"Was your Garrett a major in the Sixty-Fourth?" I tried to keep my tone perfectly friendly even though I was turning an abrupt corner.

Jimmy Patton considered for a moment. "Yes. Yes, he was. Served under Allen and took Keith's place when he was dismissed from service." Patton looked up at Reevis. "Matthew, perhaps you'd better give Mr. Ballard and me some privacy. I promise I will go over all of the books before morning, and if I have any questions, I'll ask them just after breakfast here in my office."

After a pause, during which Patton marked his place in the ledger with a turkey feather, I pushed on. "So your Major Garrett served under Allen and Keith. Was he there . . . in Shelton Laurel?"

Patton shook his head. "Guarding a bridge against Kirk's Raiders somewhere in Tennessee. Claims he would have stopped it had he been there, and you know, it's just possible. He's a big man, though he's run to fat since the war."

"Too much liquor and cigars?"

"Too much chicken and dumplings. Ever notice how some of you boys couldn't get enough to eat, once you were drummed out of the army and could tuck in?"

I nodded. "Half the Army of the Potomac has done nothing but eat since last summer. Starvation is a mean master."

Patton nodded. "Was John Norton able to tell you anything?"

"Told me that you've been helping him out since he came to work for you. Banking his wages along with his pension. Told me the name of some of the men who were there when the Sheltons were shot."

Patton looked up in surprise. "You recall who he said?"

"*Nelson, Robbins, Campbell, Sale, McKamey,*" I said, ticking the names off from memory. "At least they were there that morning, when the thirteen were marched off down the road toward Marshall. Out of sight of Judie Shelton's cabin, I imagine, was all Keith was after, and out of sight of whoever had been watching from the woods during the night."

Patton mused. "Nelson was a cavalry captain, if I recall correctly. Was killed in battle later on, which frustrated Keith, because he claimed that Nelson would have cleared him. Robbins I've never heard of in relation to this. Campbell probably means one or both of Obediah Campbell's sons."

"What?" I thought of the two chairs leaning against the table at the county clerk's house. Two napkins folded carefully in place on the chairbacks, waiting for the return of the missing boys. "You mean the Campbell across the river from Barnard, the clerk?"

"Yep. Obediah Campbell is James Keith's brother-in-law."

"Wait . . . How?"

"Mrs. Campbell was a Keith before she snagged Obediah at some sort of church meeting years ago. They both know better than to talk up the connection now, since Keith is a fugitive from the law, but I have always wondered if the Campbell boys were there. One of those boys was crazy mean, they tell me."

"They were killed during the war? Mrs. Keith-Campbell is still in mourning."

"Yes. One in a Yankee prison camp and one at Stones River."

"So much for having complete trust in my host, the county clerk."

"Well hell, son, I'm not for sure you can trust anybody in this whole countryside till you know their allegiance. Campbell is a rabid Confederate, for example."

"Can't trust you?"

Patton laughed. "You can trust me . . . But I will tell you this."

I raised my eyebrows.

"I wouldn't confide in Miss Priscilla Cushman if I were you. She strikes me as a busy woman."

I nodded. "Don't plan to," I said.

"Is there anything else you need before you head back up to Barnard?"

"I need a weapon," I said. "Something I can defend myself with or . . ."

"Or do harm to others with?"

I nodded again.

"Rifle?"

"No, something I can carry in my pocket. Something deadly. I would have brought something with me, but I gave up my weapons when I quit the Pinkertons."

"I'll see what I can do," Patton said and shrugged. "I don't know why I didn't think about it sooner."

"Be glad you didn't," I said. "Be glad it isn't part of your daily meditation."

*   *   *

AS I WAS leaving Patton's office, I met Joseph Lyman at the door. He was dressed impeccably, smelled of sweet cologne, and carried a cardboard portfolio that must have contained his newsprint and maps. When I glanced back at Patton, the old man had pulled on his suit jacket and was approaching Lyman with a businessman's intent—smiling, welcoming even. Lyman nodded curtly as he squeezed by me in the doorway.

*   *   *

I HAD MY own ideas about that evening. I was headed back upriver the next day, expecting to begin the pension exams on Monday morning, starting with the scarecrow, Campbell, and his weeping wife. And with May June, who—maybe because she couldn't speak—seemed to know everything. And if I was right, and she had placed the initials beside the names on the list, I would find out what she was trying to say.

My head still ached from the fight at Goforth's, and so my plan, my avowed plan, was to take it easy that evening. Perhaps take some supper at the kitchen door and then sit outside the ballroom to listen to the Charles Porter Orchestra, fresh from Philadelphia according to the broadside tacked up in the lobby. Everywhere you looked on Patton's porches were rocking chairs, so there would have to be one strategically close to a ballroom window. A cigar maybe . . . Major Gentry's expense account had given me the creeping lust for a smoke. A cigar with a little brandy would help me think about the puzzle pieces that had dropped into my lap so far.

Rather than going in to supper at the appointed hour, I visited the bar and ordered a jar of Ben Freeman's apple brandy from Johnny Norton, my friend again after the morning's tension. Miss Fay and Miss Rose gave me a plate of mutton roasted with some new potatoes and the wild onions they called ramps. I enjoyed my supper on the side porch just outside the door to my own room, where an inquisitive sparrow visited with me for the odd crust of bread I might share.

I ate up my mutton while it was hot and then tore the last scrap of bread into small bits for the bird. I went inside to get the list of federal pensioners out of my bag and sat in the rocking chair with my brandy, sipping comfortably, while my eyes roamed down the list. In talking with Sammy, hearing the boy's stories woven around and through the names, I had begun to feel my way into the place and into its people. The stories and the way Sammy told them reminded me of the sound of a creek running over rocks, laughing, meandering, deepening here and there into a pool of meaning. We had only gotten as far down the list as the Freemans before somehow slipping into the world of the Sheltons and the horror of the killings, a horror so real that it froze even young Sammy's tongue. I took another sip of brandy and looked back up the page to the names that followed the Freemans.

The names seemed to be speaking in a sort of pattern or rhythm.

GOFORTH
KING
KIRKENDALL
KUYKENDALL

LOCKABY

OTER

RANDALL

ROBERTS

The two Kirkendalls were obviously the same name, probably written down at different times by different clerks. Somehow, I knew the error wasn't May June's but had arisen somewhere else, perhaps in the men's halting efforts to spell their own name. Which meant in turn that Oter was likely Otter, given the low booming of the French Broad just at the edge of hearing.

How would Sammy tell these names? And if May June could speak, what would she add to the chorus? This was a poem I couldn't read, but I suspected that Sammy's and May June's and Johnny Norton's voices heard together could decipher the text. I looked again at the faint notations beside the names. Campbell had said that the one-legged Asa Sams had drowned a week or two before, and there was a tiny letter *d* inscribed beside his name. So *d* means dead. Asa Sams is dead. Then what must *t* mean? Target? But if May June had scratched these notations—for the more I studied them, the more convinced I became that the script matched the rest of the list—then how in the hell did a Negro house servant know they were targets? And targets of who or what?

I took another sip of brandy. Detective work called for brandy. My mind shifted from one slowly spinning wheel to another. A wheel named Revenge. Since midday, Johnny Norton's testimony had haunted me. There had to have been nearby witnesses to what had happened on Shelton Laurel or there wouldn't be so many odd details floating around—shot in groups of five without time to pray. Brother, cousins, a father, a son of the men who had been executed. Someone watching from the woods when Keith gave the order to fire. There was the other man who, according to Johnny, had escaped: *Pete something or other, not Shelton.* Odds were that he was related to the Sheltons somehow. It would make a perfect kind of sense for somebody to be trailing the men who had pulled the trigger on those thirteen men and boys. But the problem, I reminded myself, was that it wasn't former Rebs from the Sixty-Fourth North Carolina who were getting themselves hung and drowned and otherwise killed. Vance must be wrong. The massacre was three and a half years back, and if it had anything to do with the killings that were going on now, the connection was dim and distant.

Sitting there, I realized that I had been taken in by this twisted knot of a problem, just the way that Vance and Patton must have hoped I would be. Men were dying for no good reason, except for some lacerating hatred left over from the war, and I had wasted two days recuperating at Warm Springs when I should have been walking in the killer's footsteps, whistling his death march. I knew that I'd be on the stage to Barnard in the morning, and I knew that I had the advantage. He didn't yet know I was after him.

CHAPTER NINETEEN

Priscilla Cushman found me where Johnny told her I might be—on the side porch in my rocking chair, listening to Charles Porter and the boys through an open window. There was a row of chairs similar to mine farther down the porch.

She stopped beside me. "You're not dancing," she said. "I'm disappointed."

"Never learned," I replied evenly and raised my brandy jar in salute. "Just a Pennsylvania farm boy," I added.

She glanced down and saw that my jar was a third empty. "Oh, I doubt you're just a farm boy," she said. "You strike me as someone who would never quite say who you are."

I nodded and smiled. "What I think about you as well."

She stepped closer, and I could feel the full effect of her presence. She hadn't touched me yet, but the gesture was waiting in the air. "May I sit down?" she said in the soft, carrying way she had.

"Of course." I sat my jar on the floor and rocked up and out of the chair to my feet, feeling my way through the brandy and conscious of how awkward I must seem to her. I lifted the closest rocking chair and sat it down beside my own, facing both chairs out toward the darkening yard. I motioned for her to sit.

She bent at the knees gracefully and sat her jar beside mine. "Reinforcements," she offered.

We rocked comfortably together for a while—she, composed but quiet.

After a bit, I broke the silence. "What in the world are you doing here?" I asked. "Warm Damn Springs, North Carolina? There's no fit audience for your talents for a thousand miles."

"To which talents are you referring?" Slightly suggestive but still her tone was quiet, demure even.

I felt myself smiling. "Any of them, I expect, but I mostly meant your dramatic talents. Shakespeare's male and female characters." I bent and picked up my jar.

She didn't hesitate. "I came here with a Philadelphia banker whom I met on tour. He had promised to fund a full-scale production of *Hamlet* in New York. Edwin Booth as Prince Hamlet. This was to be a trip south to discuss the particulars. The rest of the cast and so on."

"What role were you auditioning for?"

Even though she was sitting beside me, outside the direct range of my vision, I could easily imagine how she stifled a smile. "Ophelia," she said.

"Aren't you a little . . . ?"

"Don't even say the word," she interrupted me. "On stage, age is strictly a matter of talent . . . Besides, Ophelia is a hell of a lot more fun than Gertrude. Gertrude is a ninny."

I offered her my jar. "What happened?"

"To the banker?"

I nodded.

She took a sip before replying. "Oh, his wife showed up. Unexpectedly, or so he said. Wife showed up with grandchildren in tow. I have to say, it's damn embarrassing when your paramour's grandchildren suddenly appear on stage."

"You don't like children?"

She laughed outright. "No. No, nor wives."

She handed back the jar, and I sipped before asking. "How are you going to get back to New York?"

She leaned forward and looked sideways at me. "Well, now, that's the question, isn't it? I was rather hoping that you might be interested in traveling north and that you might enjoy a bit of company. Wouldn't that take you back closer to home, and don't you find the company of an interesting woman one of the finer things in life?"

I shrugged. "I don't know much about the company of interesting women."

"But surely to God you don't mean to stay long in this part of the world. You who have an envelope full of federal dollars in the hotel safe. And I would certainly be worth your investment. I can play any woman you'd like or even a boy if you're so inclined. Young or old, I am as you wish me to be."

I shook my head to clear the thoughts she was conjuring up. "I came here to do a job," I said finally. "I promised my uncle I wouldn't leave until it's done. And while there are parts of your Lady Macbeth that render me damn near speechless, I have unfinished business that keeps me here."

"Business for your uncle?"

"Yes, and for me too. At any rate, I intend to finish that business before the situation gets any worse."

"What sort of situation is it?" she said easily, conversationally.

I ignored her question. Instead I asked, "What about that Reb general dancing in the lobby? Seems like a general should have some payroll potential that you could take advantage of."

She laughed again. "Braxton Bragg? That old gristle? He has more headaches than a milk-fed virgin."

"Don't tell me you didn't consider it."

"Of course I did. But just briefly. He's headed in the wrong direction, back to Arkansas or some such province, and he looks like a squirrel."

The jar went back and forth companionably for a few minutes.

"Would you like to dance?" I asked.

"I thought you never learned."

"Didn't, but I figure if there's a woman in North America who can lead, it's you."

She rose effortlessly, her pale gown shimmering in the dusk. "Of course," she said and curtsied with the deep, formal—ironic—grace of the day before.

Before I rose to meet her, my left hand reached into my watch pocket and took out the folded bills it had secreted there. I leaned forward in the chair and watched my hand tuck them into the waist of her dress, exactly where I'd seen her secret my money twelve hours before.

"My, my," she said. "I believe this dance is all yours."

*   *   *

OUR COUPLING WAS once again furious, unrepentant, and raw. At one point, I confess that I found my hands—both good and evil—wrapped tight around her throat and she trying to push them away. "No," she whispered. "Not that. Not that, soldier."

*   *   *

SHE FELL ASLEEP before I did, and I was left alone to reflect. Almost in shock, really. What in God's name had she called out of me? Something full-blooded, no doubt, but beyond that—angry, violent, grasping. She was reawakening in me the long-fallow desire for her sex, and it was a rough and desperate birthing.

It seemed to me as I lay there that I had given up women during the same dark time when I had forsaken intelligence work. I grew so sick of shadowing a forlorn suspect through the nighttime streets of Washington City, just as I grew sick of pursuing a woman, any woman, who seemed to me just as forlorn, just as lonely. Just as suspect. I grew tired of being a shadow in someone else's life. Someone who would end up dead, like as not.

My dreams were no better when I finally pulled up the blanket of sleep. I was in that barn, but this time, thank God, not as a patient. But as a nurse, the butcher's assistant. I knew this because my dream hand was already mangled, and I was there to help chop up the next brigade of boys. The saws, large and small, were arrayed on the top of a hay bale covered with an old quilt. Retractors, forceps, catlins, and scalpels. Coils of harness scavenged from the barn, for use in restraining the patients, often the best they could do when the morphine and the chloroform ran out. Within the dream, I was not afraid that I would be cut, but even so, I wanted to run away, to somehow escape all the knives, all the scalpels, even if escape meant death. Then the surgeon walked into the barn, limping with fatigue. He looked at me out of red-rimmed eyes and asked with eerie, pulsating slowness, *"Are you ready to begin?"*

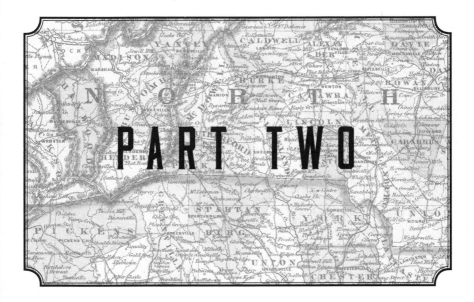

PART TWO

CHAPTER ONE

Since boyhood, I have been fascinated with maps, no matter the kind: real or imaginary, old or new, near or far distant. In fact, the farther away the territory, the more attractive the map in my young eyes. I would pore over the globe at the Lancaster Lending Library until my dirty fingers began to blacken the continents on the far side of the world. I was still a boy at eighteen when I ran away to war, and most of what I wanted was to visit the faraway states I had seen only on paper.

That Sunday morning, Jimmy Patton had spread a map of Madison County over the accumulated papers on his cluttered desk. This particular map seemed at once alien and yet vaguely familiar. When he put his finger on the small river town designated Warm Springs, the sinuous line of the river suddenly came to life, running like a curved blue string in either direction. He oriented me as he pointed with a pencil.

"When you left Asheville, you were headed northwest up the river valley. You caught the stage here, at Alexander's Station. From there you were on the old Buncombe Turnpike past Marshall, Barnard, Stackhouse, and down into the Springs."

"What happens if you keep going?"

"North another five miles you come to Paint Rock, a huge cliff beside the river, and beyond that, you're in Tennessee, where the people are short, savage, and bald-headed."

I glanced up to be sure he was joking. He was poker-faced, so I assumed he was.

"How far does your stage run?"

"To a little town called Greenville, Tennessee, which nobody would ever have heard of except that President Andrew Johnson was born there."

"Where's Shelton Laurel?"

He traced a blue line that ran north and east from Warm Springs and was labeled the Laurel River in tiny print. It was not so far away, but there was little to suggest a road between here and there.

"Can I make a copy of part of this map?" I asked.

"Do you want to go deeper into the country?"

I nodded. "In a manner of speaking. I don't imagine that I can find the killer unless I can recall what life here is truly like. Become one of the family again, so to speak."

He nodded, and in a few minutes' time, I sketched my own copy of the territory while bending over the table in his office.

As I worked, I noticed the corner of Lyman's "Colonist" sticking out from under one side of the map I was copying. I paused long enough to tap "The Colonist" with my pencil. "You know you can't trust that carpetbagger," I said.

Patton snorted. "I was knowing that first time I laid eyes on him. Question is . . . why do you care? Being a good Lincoln man and a veteran of the true cause?"

I had to smile. "I don't know what I am, truth will out, but I am damn sure what he is. And I don't like the way he talks about the people down here."

He patted me on the back. "Draw your map, son. And don't worry about that cock robin. I've got my eye on him, and I'm not nearly so young in business as he imagines."

"Speaking of strange birds, what do you really know about Obediah Campbell?" I asked. "Other than the fact that he's Keith's brother-in-law?"

Jimmy leaned back against his desk and massaged his cheek while he considered for a moment. "The thing that strikes me is how much Jesus he carries around in his pocket. He's a fairly well-respected clerk of court, in part because he claims to be well educated and doesn't seem to pick sides. In part because he prays at the opening of every session of court and always has a Bible ready to hand. There's a lot of mountain folk who love to have the Lord right up front of any business, legal or otherwise. Especially the women."

"And it's real, do you think, this faith of his?"

"Well, now, who's to say? I don't particularly care for what the mountain people call *hollering,* meaning the sort of preaching that intends to scare the hell out of you and generally does. And I don't much trust a religion that struts itself down the middle of the wide road, but still . . . I doubt if, underneath it all, Campbell is the true Barabbas let down from the cross."

I finished the last lines of my map.

"Before you go," he added, "there's one other thing you asked for." From his desk drawer, he handed me a .31 caliber Colt pocket revolver. During the war, we had called them cap-and-ball pistols because each of the five cylinders had to be loaded with powder and ball. In battle, I had never carried anything more elaborate than my Springfield rifle, of course, having risen only to the rank of corporal before Fredericksburg. And after, during my time with Pinkerton, I carried a single-shot derringer. But when Patton asked me if I knew how to load his pistol, I said yes. He handed over not only the pistol but also a leather case that contained a shot mold, a powder flask, a wad of small cloth patches, and a paper packet of primer caps. The weight of the case suggested there were plenty of balls already pressed and ready for firing.

"Are you sure . . . ?" he asked.

"Oh yes," I said. "I've never used anything just like it, but it looks simple enough, plus I handled a lot of weapons over the last five years. And now I have one more question. Campbell has a house servant named May June . . ."

He nodded. "Her last name is Washington. I know her family from the hotel. She was married to a young man who went North to join your colored troops and disappeared during the fighting."

I pulled the list of disability applicants out of my pocket and showed it to him, along with the faint notations beside some of the names. "How would she know who is being targeted, even before you or me?"

He paused to consider. "For years, there was a freedman named Joseph who worked here in the stables. He was the best man with horses we ever had. Well, whenever I had a question about this place I couldn't answer or a mystery I couldn't solve, I'd go down to the stables with a couple of cigars and we'd talk. And more often than not, he would tell me what was going on. At least, he would tell me if he thought it was any of my business."

"What does that have to do with May June?"

"I'm saying that May June and the other colored folks around here have a telegraph all their own. They know things we don't because they live in a different world, overlaid with ours but different. When old Joseph died, I felt like half my understanding of this place went into the ground with him."

*   *   *

I HAD A fellow traveler on the afternoon stage upriver, a neatly dressed guest from the hotel who was leaving after a stay of several weeks. He was a slight man, dressed in a sober, neatly brushed suit of brown cloth. Curiously, he owned one blue eye and one brown eye and had the habit of closing one or the other while he was talking. When I said I was a disability examiner from the government, he smiled.

"Is that funny?" I asked.

"Seems we're in the same business," he said. "I'm a Methodist minister."

"I don't understand."

"I was a chaplain in the war. Army of Northern Virginia for three years. And I reckon every man who served—North or South—is disabled. Myself included."

"Every man?"

He tapped his chest gently. "Wounded in the heart," he said, "or the head. So I reckon I'm a disability examiner myself." He smiled ruefully. "With only Jesus for my surgeon."

"What wounds are you and Jesus cauterizing and amputating?"

"Why, guilt I suppose. Or fear." He considered for a moment. "Mostly guilt."

"Why guilt?"

"The guilt for having survived when so many died. Or the guilt for coming home half-destroyed."

"Not the guilt for what we did?"

"Oh no. The guilt for what we've become."

I smiled back at this quiet, blinking man. "How's Jesus doing in this hot weather?" I asked. "How are you and him making out with your surgery?"

"We're trying our best to bind up the wounds," he said, "but it's a big country."

CHAPTER TWO

My afternoon at Campbell's was uneventful. For supper there was cornbread and some potatoes baked in the kitchen fireplace. The potatoes had been in the cellar since the previous summer, and even Campbell had trouble eating his. Apparently May June went home to Marshall on Sunday, and the quality of the cookery declined precipitously. Mrs. Campbell was not in evidence, and Obediah confided that she had been struck down with a sick headache after church and would likely not appear that evening.

Before I climbed the steep stairs to my room, we agreed that once we commenced in earnest the next day, May June would be available to take dictation as needed. Campbell asked if I wanted him to sit in on the interviews. I told him that since they would often involve medical issues, and I might have to actually examine the men's bodies for signs of infirmity, it wouldn't be appropriate. "But rest assured," I said, "that when I need a witness to certify a formal statement, I'll call you in. That way you can hear the gist of each man's statement and advise me privately if you think he's lying."

"Excellent plan. Excellent." You could tell he liked the role of secret advisor, and so we parted on good terms for the night.

In my room, I sat for a while and sorted the various forms and documents that I'd been given to use in the interview process. I discovered that while I'd been down in Warm Springs, my clothes had been unpacked from my trunk and carefully put away, and my best suit coat had been brushed as well as hung in the closet. I could not imagine Mrs. Campbell negotiating those stairs and taking such care. It had to have been May June. I still had the flask, transported carefully to the Springs and back, but as it was empty now and with no evident means of refilling it, I went to bed cold sober.

I woke sometime after midnight and got up to open the window. As I stared out, my eyes began to adjust to the sparse bit of moon and starlight. There was a thick fog that had crept up from the river, rising as far as the road and even drifting in wisps up to the house. I was shocked to see a figure below me standing on the steps leading up from the road, half-obscured in the mist.

The summer air was warm and humid. There seemed to be a faint but marked odor creeping into the house that I hadn't smelled there before—like hogs almost, but worse. I felt a well-water chill creep up my back. The figure was slight, and as I watched, it stared up at me from a thin and very pale face. I had the queerest sensation that, for the first time in my life, I was seeing a ghost. Not just any ghost, but a ghost that was looking back at me. I flinched from the wild look on its face. His face or hers? As my rational mind woke up enough to claim some privilege, it whispered silently to me that what I was seeing was a woman, lost and forlorn. The ghost's lips parted ever so slightly in the moonlight, and I thought I heard a hissing, keening curse.

Then its hat was back on, and the figure turned to slip silently down the steps and away, into the river mist. I shivered, but not from any war memory.

I hurried downstairs and out the front door as quietly as possible, not wanting to wake the house or warn the intruder. The pistol was ready in my right hand, even if I would be firing at a ghost. Assuming I had surprise on my side, I eased down to the road where I glimpsed footprints in the soft ground at the fence, and beyond, a faint trace through the dew-soaked pasture grass. I followed almost at the run, hoping to catch whatever it was before it disappeared. Soon though, the trail vanished into the shaggy pasture, and even the moonlight gave nothing away. I stopped and stilled my breathing to listen, but excepting the sluicing of the river, it was eerily quiet. Nothing. No sign, no sound.

When I gave up and made my way back to the road, I studied the size of the boot print in the soft earth. It was small, so small that I measured it with my hand rather than compare to my own shoe. And again I wondered if the figure I had seen was man or woman. I knew from childhood that a ghost could fire a gun or ring a church bell, so I supposed one could leave a footprint if it chose.

Something was rotten in this place I had come to, the hands on the clock and the pages from the calendar ripped off. Whatever it was seemed half buried in the minds of those all around me and yet still out of my reach. It was late before I slept at all. There were too damn many spirits here, it seemed to me, more people dead than alive.

*   *   *

THREE MEN WERE standing in the front yard the next morning. All wore beards, one down almost to his waist, and two wore hats. The longest beard was holding what looked like a long rifle from another age. There was a smaller figure sitting on the steps to the road, a smaller figure with shocking red hair. Sammy Freeman, had to be, and my heart lifted. He held fiercely to a burlap sack beside him on the step. May June had come out to the porch, and after a moment, began to poke my arm impatiently. When I looked at her, she raised her hands together up to her chin as if she were praying and then pointed to the left, farther down toward the bridge. There was a man and a woman walking toward the house, the woman possessed of a large goiter swinging loose under her chin like the pendulum of a clock. The man strode along proudly upright, with a towering shock of white hair and an equally white beard halfway down his chest. I would have thought of St. Nick, but the face was thin to the point of emaciation.

"Jesus God," I muttered.

Beside me, May June made a funny coughing sound, and I realized she was laughing.

"Who?" I whispered.

She shook her fist in the air and made as if she was shouting.

"A preacher?"

She nodded.

"That . . . what's his name . . . Rogers?"

She nodded. Looking me straight in the face, she winked and then slipped back into the house, shutting the door quietly behind her.

Before I had time to call out to Sammy, Campbell burst through the door. His wild gesticulations reminded me just how like a puppet he was, with taut strings jerking him in different directions. "We are blessed," he gasped. "We are blessed by the great apostle himself. God's own shepherd of the mountains."

I was anxious to visit the privy. "Is he applying for disability?" I asked, trying to edge around Campbell to the door.

"Of course not, you . . . Of course not. He's here to visit my wife. He was traveling down the turnpike, and when he heard that she was ill, made a special detour to comfort her."

I ducked under Campbell's upraised arm and into the hall. "Praise the Lord," I said over my shoulder.

Coming back, I took my own detour around by the side of the house. A deep, singsong voice hummed through an open window, and when I glanced in, I saw Mrs. Goiter and Mrs. Campbell kneeling at the feet of the prophet, each clinging to one of his hands while he prayed. They were both swaying to the rhythm of his words. I had never seen anything quite like it, even during the great camp meetings in the army.

I eased down to the road by the garden path and so came round to the steps from in front. I could hear Sammy singing to himself, something about Cock Robin. Singing so naturally in his own voice that it was almost as if he weren't singing at all but just breathing with words.

> . . . *says the sparrow,*
> *With my little teeny arrow*
> *I killed the robin O.*

> *Who saw him die?*
> *Me, says the fly,*
> *With my little teeny eye*
> *I saw him die.*

I wanted to hear the rest of the song, but Sammy noticed me and stopped. With barely a pause, he said, "I thought you was in the house." He nodded backward with his head. "Preparing to judge on those old boys in the yard."

"We haven't started yet. What are you doing here?"

"Don't you 'member . . . ? I'm to be your lieutenant. Sharpen your quill and such."

What I had forgotten was how like a banty rooster *he* was. "Did I say you were to be my assistant?"

"Hell, no. But I said it, and you didn't counterdict it. Which amounts to the same."

"Do you expect to be called Mr. Freeman or just Sammy?"

"Sam. Sammy sounds like a kid."

"What's in the sack, Sam?" I asked.

"How much you gonna pay me?"

"Who said I was going to pay you? Anything for me in that sack?"

"Ten cents a day. I'll bring my own dinner."

"Dime per day, then. Shake on it. What you got in your sack? More than dinner, looks like."

"Mama sent along some dinner for you and me both. A jar of brandy for you, which I . . . ain't allowed to touch. And a note for you."

Dear Mr. Ballard,

Sammy says he is to come to work for you while court is in session. Where he got the idea you are holding court, I'm not sure, but he claims he is to be your assistant.

By Wednesday, I expect you will also need a home-cooked meal, so I am inviting you up to the farm for supper. It would be a pleasure to hear a new voice up here.

Sincerely,
Sarah F.

I folded it carefully, put it in my pocket, and started up the steps with my jar.

"Hey, Jake," he jumped up to follow.

"Yeah?"

"What are my goddamn duties?"

*   *   *

THE THREE MEN in the yard had been joined by a fourth, who turned out to be a curious passerby. I nodded as I went past, and they mostly just stared. The one with Methuselah's beard and the long rifle had retreated to the sycamore in the side yard, but the others were front and center. And I noticed that two of the three who were left were also armed, so when I carried the letter and the jar of brandy up to my room, I put my own pistol in my coat pocket. Seeing that perhaps my clients knew something I didn't, the weight felt good tugging at my coat.

*　　*　　*

IT TOOK SOME doing that first morning to sort things out, but here's the way it finally worked. Sammy's post was outside under the sycamore, where he built himself a comfortable seat out of chunks of unsplit firewood. Oak, or so he said. When I glanced out later to check on him, I noticed that the old-timer with the beard was showing him the antique rifle. Once I began to ask questions and get answers out of the first candidate on the list, I realized that May June might as well stay right there in the parlor unless one of the men had to disrobe. So she set up at her usual work table by the front window where she could see to write. I took one rocking chair and the applicant took the other. We talked to three men that first day, and in between each one, I spoke briefly with Campbell, who abused each of the three for one reason or another, and I talked at some length with Sammy—or rather, Sam—who retold the details he'd shared on the stage.

Just before Edmund Arrowood—for he was the first candidate—came in, Abednego Rogers came down the middle hall with his follower to leave out the front door. The great evangelist himself only nodded gravely and intoned "Bless your good work, my son" before passing on his way. The goiter woman, however, glared at me as if she saw some devil in my face. I had Campbell's Bible in my hand because I was about to swear in Arrowood so he could give his testimony under oath.

"I am glad to see you have found refuse in God's Holy Word," she said, with acid on her tongue.

"Yes, ma'am." I smiled sweetly. "I hear tell of a Barabbas who puts in an appearance somewhere in here." I shook the Bible at her. "I wonder, could you tell me who he is?"

"Who is Barabbas? Why, I suspect he just might be your own self," she said and marched on after her prophet.

317.350
Edmund Arrowood
Co. B. 2NC Mounted Infantry
P.O. Barnard, Madison Co, NC
Barnard, NC July 16/66
Hon. Commissioner of Pensions,
Washington, DC

Sir, the claimant in above entitled case has applied for disability based on the loss of three toes on his left foot and four toes on his right foot, which loss he claims occurred in the line of duty during the winter encampment of 1864–5.

Under cross-examination by myself, he described the conditions by which he suffered severe frostbite while on sentry duty and subsequent loss of his toes to the surgeon's knife. After checking with several sources in the local community, I can find no one who has anything critical to say of Arrowood excepting that he walks with a limp, which is worse in winter than in summer. The store owner and station agent at Barnard recalls that he had this limp when he returned from the war and has suffered from same continually since that time.

Significantly, Arrowood claims that this injury limits his ability to work his farm because he is unable to walk or even stand for long periods of time. This has forced him to seek other means of employment.

I hereby recommend that Edmund Arrowood be awarded $10.00 monthly disability pension to be mailed to his attention, P. O. Barnard, Madison County, North Carolina.

Very respectfully,
J. I. Ballard
Special Examiner

In the official correspondence, there followed lengthy transcripts of Arrowood's testimony in response to my questions, including details like the doctor's name who had cut off his toes and the name of the town in Kentucky where it had happened. Enough to document his case for the hired men in the pension office. We would transcribe dozens of these claims in the coming weeks.

In any narrative, though, much is left unsaid. In Ed Arrowood's case, we did not report to His Honor the Commissioner that Ed's other means of employment included moving both apple brandy and white liquor from the Freeman farm on Anderson Branch to the Warm Springs Hotel, where it was sold both over and under the bar, as required. Nor did we report that before he left he told us a joke to be used next time I ran into the Mrs. Loudermilk, which turned out to be the goiter woman's real name, herself a staunch Southern patriot as well as a good Christian warrior.

"Who's the stretchinest man in the Bible?" Ed asked me just after I told him what my ruling would be. May June covered her ears.

I shook my head. "Don't know. Who?"

"Abraham. It's recorded in holy writ that he tied his ass to a tree and walked up the mountain."

I figured that alone was worth ten dollars a month. Plus, the man did have a horrible limp.

James Anderson I rejected out of hand when all he could produce was a powder burn on his face he claimed was the result of his having fired his Springfield so many times in anger, defending this great nation of ours. By the enlistment records, he couldn't have been in the army more than four months and that at the very end of the war. Even May June looked skeptical at his testimony, and I remembered what Sam had said about his ways. He left with a shrug of his shoulders and a few choice curses, including one involving a dead mule that I had never heard before.

That left only the infamous Thomas Boon to be interviewed.

Boon together with his rifle smelled so rancid that I interviewed him on the front porch, with the window open behind me so that May June could take down dictation from inside the parlor. Tom Boon was seeking a disability payment for the loss of his right eye. Boon's eye was barely open at all, and from what I could see when he pulled the lid up for me, it was as if the orb was made of bloody fog. The problem with his testimony was that he really couldn't remember when and how it happened, and there was no objective proof that it had happened while he was on active duty. My gut told me that he was not lying, because the money just didn't mean that much to him. And so it was on instinct more so than reason that I marked him down for a payment.

Partway through the interview, when we took a break for May June to rest her hand while Boon and I shared a dipper of water, he explained the smell. "Bear grease," he said. "I keep a smear of it mixed with beeswax in the butt of my rifle." The gun, Boon explained proudly, was a .41 caliber Mathew Gillespie made for his father in the first half of the century, and was nearly as long as Boon was tall. To that day, he still favored a flint because it was more dependable than a percussion cap, and he showed me the grease box in the stock that held the mixture he had described. He used it to lubricate the cloth patches that held the ball in place when he loaded. And so the rifle smelled about like what you would expect rancid bear grease and beeswax to smell like.

When I asked him if he'd carried it in the war, he nodded. "I was there to do rifle work," he said simply. "Why wouldn't I carry one I knew how to handle?" He told me how many Rebs he had shot with it before he lost his eye; it is a number I don't care to record. Suffice it to say that it goes with the near impossible numbers of bear and deer he also named. The man was a walking death warrant.

When we were done, and I had offered him a five-dollar-per-month disability payment for his eye, we shook hands. May June had his testimony ready shortly thereafter, and he signed with a shaky X over his printed name.

"Are you as good with your left eye as you were with your right?" I asked, walking with him down the front steps to the road.

He shook his head. "No. No, but I'm good enough to get along. If I can see it, I can generally make a hole in it."

"Would you be interested in doing a little hunting for me?"

He turned his head slightly to examine me with his good eye. "What sort of creature you after, Mr. Ballard?"

"Whoever is murdering the Union veterans around here."

"Not interested," he said after a long moment. "I'm done with that. I don't care for the smell of human blood anymore. My own or anybody else's."

"He might come looking for you," I said and immediately regretted it, for Thomas Boon was not a man to be threatened.

"If he does, he won't find me to home," Boon said easily and started in a loose-limbed stride up the road, in the direction I had seen Sam and his mother take. But then he turned to look back one last time. "Tell you what, though," he said and nodded, his long beard bending in the breeze. "You better be careful your ownself if you intend to go around asking about them murders. My old mother used to say that if you call up the devil, he's like to appear."

"When he does appear, I mean to deal with him," I said.

He paused. "I will do this for you," he said eventually. "If I spy your man in the woods, enough to be certain of him, I'll send word."

CHAPTER THREE

The following morning, Benjamin Franklin Freeman himself appeared. Sammy's uncle Ben in the flesh. He turned out to be much more than a famous distiller and bootlegger. Among other things, he turned out to be a master storyteller, such that his deposition went on for pages, by far the longest I would send back to the Honorable Commissioner of Pensions. A brief sample of my conclusions suggests the cleverness of the man.

There are two issues that cloud his petition for relief. The first is that it is difficult to determine whether or not his "feebleness" was contracted during the period of his service, and the second has to do with the possibility that his physical problems may be the result of having contracted syphilis either during or just after the war.

Direct evidence as to the innocent or guilty contraction of such a disease is impossible to obtain, for the reason that those who could know the facts could hardly be relied upon to tell the truth, if disposed to talk at all. The former wife, Harriet Freeman, is by all accounts a lewd and profligate woman, who is much given to the lie. I did not, therefore, attempt to take the wife's statement.

Claimant himself is a little over medium height, spare, thin, and skin of a very dirty yellow for a white man, but I discovered no weakness of mind, but on the contrary I thought him unusually shrewd in his own case. He readily answered all questions but always prefaced the answers with numerous introductory and explanatory remarks. He has the appearance of a man having dyspepsia and liver disease very badly. He lives in a very rough, sparsely settled community. After making close inquiry of every reliable person I could find near him and in Marshall, where he is well acquainted, I was not able to find anyone who knew and would say anything against him, except that he was a little eccentric in his talk or manner or both at times. But no one would say they knew of any misconduct or bad habits of the man, except a young man, who has been in this place only a short time, said he thought he saw him once or twice under the influence of liquor. All the old citizens remember that claimant and his wife had trouble when he came back from the war, but which was to blame or what caused their troubles not a single one would tell if they knew. I think claimant discloses enough in his own deposition to show that there was at least a possibility that he may have incurred syphilis from some other source than his wife, and also enough to satisfy any one that he is not entirely abstemious from the use of spirituous liquors or alcohol.

Claimant is a great talker and spins yarns, but I could not find a man who knew him that would say he could or would not believe him under oath.

"Not entirely abstemious from the use of spirituous liquors!" In all likelihood, Ben's liver was pickled. "A great talker and spins yarns?" The man could have entertained a courtroom full of judges for hours at a time. He didn't even blink when later he described threatening to cut his wife's throat—as if he were describing paring an apple rather than an artery. Even May June was mesmerized by the stories he told.

At midday, we ate under the sycamore, while a congregation of crows above called for our scraps. Ben Freeman, his nephew Sam, and me. I had not allowed Sam anywhere near the house while I was interviewing his uncle, and I was glad of it because I had Freeman strip down so I could examine his emaciated frame and—based on what Campbell had said—ask him about syphilis. Even so, Freeman's appetite was not the least affected by the tales of blood and disease he had just told. He ate easily, mostly with his left hand.

This infuriated Campbell, who asked me twice to come into the house and dine like a Christian. I put him off by saying I needed to continue the interview we had begun that morning, as Freeman could testify about the other pensioners as well. We ate salt ham and biscuits from Sam's mother and a couple of small red apples each. Freeman called them June apples and said he only grew them because they would serve for a midsummer run of brandy. On this day, however, we did not live by water alone, for Freeman had his own jar from this first run, which he shared with me.

"When will the rest of the petitioners come in?" I asked Freeman at one point. "Yesterday, there were three men in the yard ready to be interviewed, and the only one we sent away mad was James Anderson."

"He was mad when he got here," Freeman said with a grin. "I believe he was born in a fit. Married my oldest daughter, James Anderson did, but I haven't any use for him." Sammy nodded solemnly.

"Still doesn't explain why you're the only pensioner who showed up today."

Freeman paused to consider. He had a long beard, as did most of the mountain men on that side of the river. Hung down to the top button of his vest, thick and brushy, brown mostly with some rust spun in. It made for a strange contrast to his yellow skin. When he finally spoke, he emphasized his words by waving his pocketknife at me, the knife he was using to pare an apple with his left hand as he clutched it in his right. "You know some of our boys have been waking up dead lately," he said. "Men who thought the war was over and now are coming to find it close on 'em again."

I nodded. "I hear Alan King was shot down just in the last few days."

"Alan was bushwhacked from the woods while walking home from his mother's house after Sunday dinner. Some neighbors walking along behind saw it happen. But he isn't the only one. You know that."

Again I nodded.

Freeman lowered his voice. "Well, a number of the boys who ended up fighting for the Union don't like to come here to Campbell's, especially since dying seems to be the order of the day." He nodded at the house behind me. "Tom Boon ain't afraid of nothing that walks the earth, so he came along yesterday, just to get the lay of the land. And I come along today to see just what kind of queer bird you might be. See if you could be trusted, so to speak."

It took me a moment before I fully digested what he was saying. "You mean I might be part of what's going on . . . ? The hell you say!"

He grinned. "Well, now that I got to know you, I can see how simple that sounds, but we had no way of knowing, did we? Men getting hung with their own plowline, drownt in the river fully clothed. It's got to be a regular shambles around here. And you show up in the middle of it, not having been seen for ten or fifteen years."

The look on my face must have shown just how ridiculous I thought it all was.

"I know Sarah pulled you out of the ditch, and Sammy thinks you're his new boss man, but the men up in the coves still aren't entirely sure. They'd like it better if they didn't have to come here to interview."

"What is it about Campbell?" I too was whispering now. "I know both his sons got themselves killed for Jeff Davis, but I haven't seen any other sign."

"I don't know," Freeman admitted. "It's an odd thing. The second boy died at Camp Douglas, like my brother Young . . ." He reached one calloused hand over to grasp Sam's shoulder, held it briefly. "I hear tell that Mrs. Campbell tried to throw herself in his grave, to be buried alive with him."

"So it's Mrs. Campbell scares the people off, the Yanks anyway? She is a stranger, I admit."

"She's part of it. They're both rabid Secessionists. That and a number of the boys wasn't sure about why you were born here but left out. Went off to some far-distant land." He waved his knife airily above his head.

"Won't his fault," Sam said stubbornly. "I done told you."

"My mother took us to Pennsylvania when my father died. Long before the war. She got tired of fighting rocks and snakes for every scrap." I realized even as I said it that I had heard this explanation as a boy, mixed with tears often enough.

Freeman laughed and nodded. "Can't blame her for that. Some days seems like there's a rock under every snake."

"Who's doing the killing, Ben? I know you and the others have a thought. There can't be that many angry Rebs still burning a fuse for the war?"

"They's more than you might think. I expect it hurts worse when you lose." He paused to consider. "My guess is there's enough angry Rebs in these woods to drum up a whole company with a taste for vengeance. Enough such that those of us who might make a target have trouble narrowing down the search. We've started blaming it on a ghost."

I glanced over at the steps leading down to the road, the spot where I myself had seen something. "A ghost?" I said skeptically.

"I know. I know how it sounds. But shitfire, you just got here. We've been asking around and looking behind this for months now, and so far, nothing. If we thought we knew, we'd have laid it to rest long before now."

I remembered Ben Freeman's talent for revenge. Marital and otherwise. "What about Keith?" I asked. "He escaped from jail a while back. He seems like he's mean enough."

"James Keith? Major in the Sixty-Fourth?"

I nodded.

"Son, I tell you now—he's more than mean enough—and him claiming to be a doctor." Freeman shook his head sadly. "Son of a bitch killed more than he ever thought to heal."

"Well? What about him?"

"Problem is nobody's seen him anywhere down in the country for two or three months. His wife's gone to Arkansas, or so they say. And while this may look like wilderness to you"—he gestured up at the mountains on both sides of the river—"it would be awful hard for somebody like Keith to hide out for months on end without being seen. They's too many still owe him a debt from that business up on Laurel."

"A killing debt?"

"That's the kind I had in mind."

*   *   *

UNLIKE TOM BOON and several other applicants we interviewed that summer, Benjamin F. Freeman wrote a beautiful flowing hand—with his paralyzed right arm, of course. And when he signed his name, even May June was impressed.

We were finished with his deposition by midafternoon, and I walked partway up the road toward Anderson Branch with Freeman. He carried a fine muzzle-loading shotgun that he had left wrapped in a burlap sack under the sycamore during our interviews. Sam walked along as well, even though he had informed us that he was to spend the night with me, protecting me from the ghost. Apparently, he liked the notion of a ghost even better than that of an assassin.

Freeman stopped in the road and glanced back at the house. "What have you got for armament? You being a Yank yourself, and asking ever-body you meet about the killings ain't exactly the safest way to comport."

I pulled the pocket pistol that Jimmy Patton had given me out of my coat and showed it to him.

He nodded. "Get good and close with that thing if you mean to do some damage. You got the munitions for it?"

I nodded and pulled the leather case out of my other pocket.

"Let's us and the boy go down here below the road where nobody can see and fire off a few rounds—warm up the barrel on that thing and see if it'll actually throw a bullet."

The pistol was a five-shot revolver, the word "Colt" stamped into the metal above the trigger guard. It had a fancy octagonal barrel, maybe four inches long, with a small sight at the end, which was all but useless. Each cylinder had to be carefully filled with a given amount of powder, and then a ball wrapped in a round cloth patch was rammed in to compress the charge. All that part of the process I was used to from my Springfield, which had misfired in the least bit of weather. But instead of a ramrod, the revolver had a three-inch-long brass lever under the barrel. You rotated the loaded chamber to the bottom position and then pulled down several times on the lever to ram the load tightly into place where it would remain, dry and ready to fire when you cocked it and pulled the trigger. Then you repeated the process four more times, once for each chamber. The final step was to prime each of the five nipples on the rear of the cylinder with a small cap, like a tiny fuse.

Freeman loaded and fired it, and then I loaded and fired it. Even Sam took a turn. We shot at a piece of newspaper fixed to a handy birch tree beside the river. I surprised Freeman and amazed Sammy by shooting the target to pieces.

Freeman laughed. "Well, remind me never to gainsay you when you're armed." And then he stepped closer for a private word. "And if I were you, I'd go armed from here on. Reload when you're sober, and check the damn cylinder every morning. If you ever think you might get serious with that thing, replace the caps before starting out. Nipples on that thing as finicky as any woman."

CHAPTER FOUR

After supper and a walk by the river, I climbed up into my room to think about all I'd seen and heard, struggling to trace a line of evidence that would point at some culprit lurking close by that I was too much the outsider to see. It was hot, even this close to dusky dark, so I stripped down to my smalls and sat back to consider. But before I had a second sip of brandy, Sam was in the room, jumping up and down on the bed and then launching into his own rendition of "Froggy Went a Courtin'."

When I finally got Sam calmed enough to sleep, I made him lie down on a pallet of blankets on the floor.

"Jake?" he whispered, just before dozing off.

"Hmmm?"

"I want to see a dead body. If you come across any while you're here."

I jerked. "You what?"

"I want to see a body. I seen lots of dead squirrels, rabbits, chickens, even helped bury a mule, but I have never been let close to a regular old human. When Aunt Fonie died, Mama wouldn't even let me look in the casket."

"You don't know what you're saying."

"How many dead bodies did *you* get to see? In the war, I mean . . ."

"Hundreds. Hell, thousands."

"Swear to God! How many did you get to touch?"

"Hundreds, damn it. I already told you hundreds."

"How many did you kill?"

"None of your goddamn business! Now go to sleep."

He was smiling as he drifted off.

What I did not tell him, then or ever, was about the burial details. Our brigade was ordered in five days after Antietam, where we threw dozens of blackened corpses into shallow trenches, trampled them down into the ground, and then threw on just dirt enough to protect them from scavenging hogs. Once, I had watched while exhausted soldiers from an Ohio regiment threw a dozen Rebel corpses down a farmer's well to save digging their graves. Nothing I ever saw, not even the hospitals, was as bad as the burials.

*   *   *

EARLY THE NEXT morning, I stood yawning and stretching at the front window of my bedroom, staring down at the road and the river beyond, watching the mist rise up from the water.

Someone had discarded a parcel of old clothes in the road, just at the foot of the stone steps leading down from the yard. A parcel of old clothes that began to look vaguely like a human form stretched out on the ground. The bundle of clothes was streaked with dirt as if it had been washed in muddy water and baked in the sun. I threw down the quilt I had wrapped around me, pulled on my pants, and jammed the pistol into my pocket. I hopped while pulling on my boots, without bothering for socks, and then leaped down the steep stairs.

I pulled the bolt and threw the door open, taking time even then to hold it from slamming against the wall so it wouldn't wake

Sam and the Campbells. Jumped down from the porch and on down the stone steps to the road, where I knelt. Let it be a scarecrow, I thought, or an old man asleep. Let it be a drunk, anything but what it smelled like.

The bundle of clothes had a head.

The head was cocked at an impossible angle to the clothes, and there was a piece of frayed harness that led from the head on up the road to where it was broken off. Or not broken, but cut off sharp by a knife.

I rolled the bundle over—it was too heavy—and it became a man. The hands were tied cruelly behind his back and his neck was broken. The harness was looped around his neck and had been pulled tight with ferocious force. The skin that was left on the man's face was a mottled blue. His crusted, black tongue was sticking half out of his mouth, and without a second thought, I stuffed it back in and tried to leverage the jaw shut. The jaw was raspy with two day's growth of beard and already stiff. It would not close and the tongue flopped out again.

The dead man's hair might have been brown or black, hard to say under the dirt. *He was dragged*, I whispered to myself, *dragged behind a horse.* His clothes were torn half off, and pale flesh was showing through, marked and torn red by gravel and dirt. *Dragged for quite a ways.* The smell was dried blood and mud and something worse—the beginning of decay. He had that gagging hospital smell once the arms and legs had begun to pile up.

His shoes and socks had been removed before he was forced to run behind the horse. I crawled on my knees down to examine his feet. It was then that I saw that one foot—his right foot—was missing all but the big toe. The other foot was missing the three middle toes. The feet were bruised and bloody from recent events, but the toes had been cut off long ago.

I stood up ever so slowly, my hands stained with dried mud and blood. Caked with rot.

I felt another person close by and looked up. Leaning over the corpse was May June. Barefoot, her hand stretched out, almost as if to touch me as she was gawking down at the dead man.

"Why in the hell?" I whispered. "Why in hell would the son of a bitch leave this on Campbell's doorstep?"

May June straightened and shrugged her shoulders. She hadn't yet pulled and braided her hair that morning, and it was wild around her head.

"He means it for me, damn it," I said, answering my own question. She nodded.

"He knows I'm after him," I muttered. "And this is his answer." She was still nodding.

Hell on earth, I thought to myself. "Bring me a knife and a blanket," I said aloud. "A knife and a blanket and then go back and keep an eye on Sam till I can get the body into that barn." I gestured at the large hay barn perhaps twenty yards away, in the pasture by the river side of the road.

She was turning to go when I reached out and grabbed her naked arm. "I don't want Sam to see him," I said, recalling the night before. "Too young for this." Still I held onto her elbow. "And then we'll have to see about finding Mr. Arrowood's family."

She raised her eyebrows at the mention of a name. I pointed with the pistol at the corpse's mangled feet. Her eyes followed the gun barrel and she saw the missing toes. The words she had written to my dictation only two days before flowed unbidden through my mind: *I hereby recommend that Edmund Arrowood be awarded $10.00 monthly disability pension to be mailed to his attention, P. O. Barnard, Madison County, North Carolina.*

As soon as she was up the steps and gone, I did what I had dreaded from the beginning. I knelt again in the dust beside Arrowood's body. The legs of his pants were stiff with dried blood, but there was no blood in the dirt under him, which meant he'd bled out before he was left there in the road. I carefully unbuttoned his trousers and pulled them down enough to see that he'd been stabbed twice in the lower belly. The iron stench of blood was almost overbearing, even from a wound that was hours, perhaps days, old. Even as a mangled corpse, Ed Arrowood had a lot to say about his killer. And the first message he had for me was that whoever had gutted him had done it coldly and calmly when he was still alive and then forced him to run behind a horse or a mule while the blood flowed. Forced him till he could run no longer and so was drug to death.

I had fastened up Arrowood's trousers before May June returned, suddenly embarrassed for him and for the rest of humanity.

Using the butcher knife, I carefully pried loose the harness embedded in his neck, severed the noose, and then peeled it gently out of the swollen flesh. She had offered to help me with the body, or at least I assumed that's what she meant by standing by, but I sent her on back to the house to keep Sam at bay. "I'm used to this," I told her coldly. "I've done something like it a dozen times."

I stretched out the blanket on the grass and gravel and then rolled Arrowood up into it just like rolling up a soiled carpet. I tied the piece of harness around the middle of the blanket roll to keep it from coming loose when I picked it up. I wiped the knife clean on the blanket and laid it on the stone step, where I wouldn't lose it in the grass. Then I stood the whole up on one end and bent to pull it onto my shoulder. The body was stiff, so it was like carrying lumber, and I was reminded again of hospital work—and of burial detail.

Once Arrowood's body was deposited in the barn, I walked slowly back and forth along the road. In the dry summer dust, you could clearly see where the body had been dragged from the direction of the Big Pine Road and the river bridge. The body itself had erased most of what could be seen of hoofprints right up to the point where it had been left to rot. Farther up, in the softer ground under the trees, were what might have been the hoofprints of the killer's horse—unshod and stamping in place. Nervous horse then, rather than stolid mule. Beside the hoofprints were the footprints of its rider, two perfect imprints from where he had dismounted before cutting the harness and abandoning the body. The prints appeared to be from a pair of small boots. I measured them against my own hand and saw that they could easily be those of the ghost I'd seen on the lower steps at midnight. Were they a woman's prints? Now every instinct recoiled at the idea. The rider had stabbed Ed Arrowood and then drug him deliberately to death over the rough and stony road, and that didn't sound like a woman.

I knelt in the soft ground to study the boot tracks for more detailed marks like a bent nail or worn heel, and I thought again that I smelled hog waste.

It was then, kneeling there in the dirt, that I heard the hard, flat pop of a musket being fired from up on the ridge behind Campbell's house. There was the sickening buzz of a ball close by my head and the slap when it hit a tree behind me. It was a tune I knew only too well, and it made me so angry that I disobeyed four long years of training and instinct to stand straight up in the road rather than diving into the dust.

The ridge above was quiet and still in the yellow summer sun, not even a puff of smoke to be seen above the trees. "Goddamn you," I yelled, so loud it tore in my throat. "Come on out of there, Goddamn it, and show your face." But I knew it was pointless. And I was left to wonder if he'd meant to kill me and missed or if he was just offering a further warning. But one thing I did know—I knew the ghost carried an Enfield rifle.

CHAPTER FIVE

Later that morning, John and Abner Brooks appeared in the front yard of Campbell's, come to be interviewed. Ben Freeman had apparently given me his blessing, and they thought it safe, especially as they traveled down from the head of Big Pine together. I met them there, in the yard, before they came up onto the porch, and took them across the road to the barn. Sam was still furious with me for not letting him see the body and was lounging despondently on the porch steps teasing a wooly worm with a twig.

The inside of the barn was cut through by bars of dusty light that shone between the logs. It smelled from generations of corn and hay. I had laid Arrowood's body on a wide chestnut plank across two sawhorses, and the flies were already buzzing close in the thick air. When the Brooks brothers came in, I untied the piece of harness and pulled open the blanket to show them what had happened. When they saw the body, both men turned almost in unison and spit over their shoulders. They knew Arrowood's sister,

John and Abner allowed, knew where she lived with her own family across the river.

"Will you go tell her what happened?" I asked. "So they can come for the body."

The brothers glanced at each other nervously. I had seen that look before, most often the night before a battle.

"Go together," I said. "I'll stay here with him."

They were still deliberating when another figure darkened the barn door. A short man with a long black beard stepped out of the light onto the dirt floor of the barn. He reached out to shake my hand. "Nimrod Buckner," he said, with a shockingly deep voice for so small a man. "Freeman boy on the porch says you got one of ours laid out in here."

"Ed Arrowood," I replied and nodded at the body. "Dead in the road this morning, right in front of the house."

Buckner took a brief look at the body before turning away. "Startin' to stink, ain't he?" he said pleasantly.

We all stepped outside into the sun, and I pulled the barn door closed behind us.

"Who's goin' to tell Mamie?" Buckner asked.

"We was just considering," Abner Brooks said, "whether it was safe."

"It ain't," Buckner rumbled. "But it's to be done regardless." He stared up at the brothers for a long moment. "Shit on you boys," he said. "I'll go." He turned to me. "You Ballard?"

I nodded. "Jake."

"You keep an eye on Ed till I can locate his sister?"

I nodded again. "Can you send word to the sheriff?" I asked.

He nodded briefly. "I'll pass along the news down at Goforth's, and somebody'll carry it to Marshall. News like this here rides a fast horse."

Buckner turned on the Brooks boys, who were already edging into the road. "You boys need to get right with God," he shouted suddenly as they began to march quickly away. He turned back to me and winked. "Them boys a walkin' through the valley of the shadow," he offered, "and they ain't right with God."

*   *   *

OBEDIAH CAMPBELL HAD been strangely absent during the morning's proceedings, keeping to the house even though there was a corpse in his hay barn. But when I went in at midday, he was waiting in the parlor. Sammy had disappeared, with May June in the kitchen, or so I hoped. She had left my shirt on the porch rail, and I pulled it on over my smalls and tucked it into my pants before going in to treat with Campbell.

He had taken his customary chair on one side of the fireplace, the chair I usually sat in to interview the applicants. Automatically, I sat opposite, as if I myself were appealing for official relief.

"I understand from my servant that you have placed a dead man in my barn." Campbell's voice was noncommittal, steady even. His head was cocked to one side as it usually was, and for a horrible moment, it reminded me of Ed Arrowood's twisted neck.

"I didn't have any other handy place to put him to get him out of the sun, Obediah. And his family should be here to get him this afternoon."

"I understand. My only concern is the effect that all this strain will have on my wife's health. She is somewhat frail, you know. Having that boy in the house upsets her as well."

"You mean because of your . . . the ones you lost?"

"Yes. That's right. There are times when I think she still expects them to show up for supper."

"I plan to take Sam home this evening, and I'll leave him there if it will help."

"Thank you."

The frustration from that long morning had been rising up in my throat. The man in front of me seemed fully capable of floating along as if people all around him weren't dying, as if the evidence of violent death wasn't lying on a plank in his own barn. "Who's doing this, Obediah?" I blurted out. "You know this county as well as anyone. You must have some thoughts on the matter!"

"Who's doing what?"

I mastered the desire to shout at the man, the man that Sammy called a bullfrog walking. "Murdering Yank veterans. The last one of which was dropped off in your front yard, in case you missed the newspapers."

Campbell seemed to reflect. "I'm glad you asked," he said softly. "Because I think I know." As he had once before, during our first conversation, he turned and pushed the door to the hallway closed.

Despite myself, I leaned forward.

"In the army, men had to deal with truly horrible conditions, did they not? They had to witness the carnage of war, even in the Union army?"

I nodded. "Worse than anything you could imagine."

"And in a sense, they themselves were reduced to something less than human. Something less than civilized."

"That was my experience," I admitted.

"And in those hateful conditions, often they grew to hate one another. The men to hate their officers and to hate one another."

"It either brought them closer together or pushed them far apart."

Campbell stood and walked over to May June's table under the window. He picked up two sheets of paper off the top of one of the stacks and handed them to me before sitting back down. It was the annotated list of disability applicants.

"There's your killer."

"What?"

"I believe that one of the men on that list has gone mad. From guilt as well as the horrible experiences suffered during the war. And he is methodically destroying the men he served with."

"Why do you say guilt? What guilt?"

"Why, from betraying his country, of course. The guilt of betrayal."

"Betraying what country?"

"Jacob," the clerk said slowly, as if lecturing a particularly stupid child. "When the Southern states withdrew from the Union, as was their long-established right, they formed a separate country, a Confederacy of independent, sovereign states. North Carolina was one of those states. As such, any man from this region who fought for the North was a traitor to his country. I would not like to say this in public, because feelings here still run very high, but I have always thought that the men from here who deserted and fought for the North must feel a horrible sense of guilt to this day. And . . ." Campbell leaned forward in his rocking chair before adding, "one way to ease a guilty conscience is to punish those like yourself. I believe your killer is on that list, or will be when May June adds the names of those who have applied since you arrived." He leaned back and smiled a triumphant, if crooked, grin. "And in a sense, this is the playing out of God's will, isn't it? Evil consuming evil, doing our work for us. It's as if a great cleansing is taking place, as I believe your Mr. Lincoln himself said."

"So you think it's a Yank veteran who's killing off other Yanks out of self-hatred."

"That's right. And very well put, I might add. Jacob, these men out of the mountains were little better than savages before the war. You and I have the benefit of education, the civilizing influence of a society beyond fiddle tunes and cornbread. Surely, in these past few days, you've begun to see that you're dealing with the lowest social class imaginable, human beings barely above the level of their own livestock. Is it any surprise at all that under the pressures of war these men would fall to murdering each other?"

"What about the law, Obediah? Aren't you an officer of the court?"

"I am an officer of the court, and I cannot condone anything illegal, but the men who've died of late are nothing but trash from the hills who didn't have the courage to do their duty. 'He that troubleth his own house shall inherit the wind.' Proverbs 11:29."

I realized with a shock that even a few short weeks ago, Campbell's depiction of the mountain people as half-crazed savages might have made sense to me. Convinced me even. Now, though . . . *He may be crazier than his wife*, I thought and looked down to hide a smile. *And that's saying something.*

After a moment, I looked up again. "If you wanted to put a stop to the killing, Obediah, how would you go about it?"

Campbell didn't hesitate. "If it were me, I'd let God's will work itself out. Just as I believe it should work itself out in my own life and that of my family."

"Did the Reverend . . . Rogers teach you that?"

"Yes, he did. Abednego Rogers is the apostle of our Lord and Savior, and he interprets the mysteries of the Bible for those of us who believe. He sees the Lord's hand in the horrors of recent years."

I made a mental note to visit with the apostle. Hear him preach if possible. "Yes, but if you *wanted* to stop the killings, what would you do?"

"If I was Jacob Ballard and I was charged with stopping the murders, I would . . . I would keep right on doing what you're doing. I would keep right on interviewing the pensioners and let the murderer come to you."

I thought of the figure I had seen standing on the steps. "Even if it meant that the murderer showed up on your own front porch, hat in hand. What about you and Mrs. Campbell?"

"Oh, my wife and I are safe, Jacob. We're protected . . ."

"By the Lord," I finished the thought for him. "Why did you say that I was *charged* with stopping the murders, Obediah? I'm here to interview pensioners."

"Isn't it obvious, Jacob? Apparently, these men *are* dying, but truthfully, you are the only one in a hundred miles who cares."

"Oh, I imagine the victims care," I said evenly in return. "I haven't met a Yank yet who was so guilt ridden that he wanted to dance behind a plow horse with a noose around his neck."

*   *   *

ED ARROWOOD HAD been such a gentle and funny man that I expected the same from his sister Mamie. Something soft, something caring in response to her brother's death. But when she arrived that afternoon with a wagon drawn by a team of mules, she wore a sun-faded bonnet pulled low over her face and showed less emotion than if she'd been picking up a load of hay. *She's been expecting this*, I decided as I helped load the body in the back of the wagon. *Expecting it for so long that it's a relief it finally happened.*

Rod Buckner was still with her, having gone and returned, and in addition, he had recruited another man to help with the body. "Nin Buckner," Rod said to me by way of introduction, once the body, still wrapped in its blanket, had been shifted to the wagon bed.

"Your brother, Ninevah?"

"The very same."

"I thought you two never spoke to each other on account of the war."

"We don't speak," Nin Buckner admitted. "Lessen we have to."

"And this here seemed like a case of have to," Rod finished his brother's thought.

*   *   *

LATER THAT AFTERNOON, when I was ready to start up the mountain with Sam, I took a last trip to the privy and stopped at the water bucket on the way back into the house. As I stood on the porch, drinking from the dipper, Mrs. Campbell came out the back door and passed by as if I wasn't there. She was carrying a covered basket over one arm and kept walking up through the back pasture. *She doesn't even see me*, I realized.

I could hear Sam behind me through the open kitchen door, chattering away at May June like a mockingbird. It had to be May June, as Sam would never have gone on like that at Campbell. The odd thing was that Sam would pause from time to time as if he was caught up in real conversation. There was no second voice—after all it was May June—but it felt as if Sam was pausing to listen in between his own words, taking turn and turnabout.

A small cloud of passenger pigeons passed suddenly overhead, cooing at each other to hurry, pulling along an updraft to gain the top of the pasture and the trees beyond. The breeze had picked up, tossing the leaves first and then the tree branches in the yard and then up the pasture to the height of the ridge. I saw dark clouds the color of a bruise looming over the river, and the smell of rain was in the cooling air.

I walked up to the rail fence just beyond the privy. The fence separated the narrow backyard from a grown-over pasture that lay against the steep side of the ridge. I could see Mrs. Campbell climbing with a stolid, determined stride up a faint trace through the pasture. A place deep inside my belly said to follow her, said she was leading me to something I needed to see. After only a moment's pause, I followed.

But instead of trailing the old lady straight up through the pasture where she could have turned and seen me at any moment, I followed the fence itself up to the right, where it ran closest to the trees. After a few moments of hard walking through thick, waist-high weeds, came the shadow of the trees, and now there was a slight break between the fence and the woods. I kept climbing, glancing from time to time over my left shoulder, where Mrs. Campbell's head and shoulders were still visible as she climbed. She was steadfast, eyes forward, like the good Christian soldier that she was. I was short of breath but from fifty feet away, she seemed not to be straining at all—just climbing with a fey intensity.

My instincts seemed to whisper that she was taking me to something important. The thought flickered. She was, step-by-step, leading me to someone.

I struggled through a thick patch of blackberry briars and then found myself almost upon her. I paused and held my breath while she carefully climbed over the rails at the upper end of the pasture and then stepped lightly along a path that ran straight on into a flat glade of shorn grass. I worked my way as quietly as I could up the flank of the hill through a dense copse of oaks and then paused behind a worn gray boulder.

It was the cemetery, the Campbell family cemetery by the looks of it because there weren't more than a dozen graves inside a small yard encircled by a wall of stacked field rocks. She was kneeling beside two identical grave markers, the newest in that patch of ground. From her peck basket, she took a bundle of flowers and divided them equally between the two stones, between her two sons, and then, oddly, took out a packet of something else wrapped in a cloth. She laid the packet between the two markers. Those were cruel times, and I had known bereft mothers do far stranger things than leave gifts for their dead.

I had thought that she would lead me to her brother, James Keith, the man who'd ordered the executions at Shelton Laurel. Someplace beneath thought, I'd connected him to the killings and Mrs. Campbell to him. When she began quietly to weep and pray over the graves, I slipped away back down the mountain. She had taken me to someone all right—to two men dead and gone. Unless it really was a ghost that was abroad in the land, she hadn't offered up any answers I could use.

CHAPTER SIX

Sammy and I walked most of the way up Anderson Branch in a summer shower, sudden and drenching. He wore the slicker, much too big for him, and I wore the hat, in our first sad attempts to stay dry, the result being we both were soaked through and laughing at each other. As we topped a rise in the road, little more than a trail along the creek by then, the rain slowed into a drizzle. And as the mist began to burn off, Sammy stopped me to point out the various landmarks of the Freeman farm, folded back into ridges now alive with running water and swirling mist.

The head of the cove was surrounded by steep, cultivated fields. Anderson Branch ran down just below us on our left, through a fenced pasture of perhaps two acres. Grazing peacefully beside the water was the biggest bull I had seen since leaving Pennsylvania, massive head down in thick grass, its long tail whipping at the flies annoying its back. Huge and shaggy such that it looked like something out of myth, Zeus come down to graze in some lost hollow in the Carolina mountains. In the same pasture were two smaller oxen, one standing asleep on its feet in the newly rinsed sunlight and the other dozing on the ground in the shelter of a lone apple tree. It seemed to me that the land was at once old and yet new and bright, rinsed clean in the spangled light.

Just where the branch appeared through the trees at the top of the valley, stood a ramshackle cabin with a pale sheen of smoke at the chimney. Uncle George Freeman's house, according to Sam. Farther to the left, up on the flank of the ridge, chimney and smoke just visible from the trail, was Ben Freeman's cabin. It had been built after the final separation from his wife, the infamous Aunt Harriet—meanest damn woman in Madison County—again, according to Sam.

"Where's your mother's place?" I asked.

Before he could answer, there was a sudden deep baying from the cornfield just above us, and then immediately after, Sam was all but bowled over by a red dog, whining and jumping up to lick his face. He was knocked down on his knees in the trail, stroking and hugging the dog, who obviously knew him.

"Fate," he kept calling the dog, who after a moment turned her attention to me.

"Lafayette, meet old Jake Ballard," Sam whispered happily to the dog, who was regarding me with deep hazel eyes. "Jake, meet Lafayette the coonhound, though she's a god-awful coonhound."

Fate stepped forward and pushed her nose against my knee. I knelt and rubbed her long, floppy ears and ran my hand down her back, ruffling her coarse fur. If her face hadn't been so keen, it would have been sorrowful the way all hounds' faces are sorrowful, but Fate was the most intelligent of God's creatures: too smart to be sad except at the very last extreme.

"She's mostly redbone," Sam said proudly. "Born to hunt, but she was the runt of the litter, and only Mama wanted her as a pup. Now she's worthless, Uncle says. Won't hunt because she won't leave Mama's side, tame from sleepin' in the house."

She had the thick chest and long, straight legs of a dog bred to run, and she truly was a rich, deep chestnut. Thin in the hips and belly, both tail and head high and sharp. "Is she a good watchdog?" I asked. "For you and your mother?"

"I guess so," he said, puzzled at the term. "She watches every-thing. And she won't let you near the house unless we say so."

"What happened to her nose?" I asked, pointing at two puckered scars on her muzzle.

"That was a copperhead snake," a voice said, not Sam's. "Wanted to spend the winter in the woodpile under the eaves of the house, and Fate thought different. She tore down half the stack to get at it."

I looked up from where I knelt in the trail, and there she was—Sarah Freeman—in shade from the waist down but from the waist up gleaming russet in the late afternoon sun. "And the snake?" I asked.

"All we found were pieces," she said. "Four and five inches long, just enough to know what kind." She laughed. "And Fate's head swelled up like a pumpkin."

*   *   *

THE DOG DANCED around as we walked up the path through shoulder-high corn on both sides, corn green and thriving in long, curving rows.

From somewhere down below came the distant squeal of a fiddle being played, slowly, thoughtfully even, as if the fiddler was working out his line. I paused to listen, trying to catch the tune, and when I did, Sarah noticed the questioning look on my face.

"That's George," she said. "He likes to sit on the porch with his fiddle before supper. Loosening up his strings, he calls it. Talking back to the day."

"Sounds like old Ireland," I said, whispering so as not to drown out the faint, plaintive notes.

"Why Ireland?" she asked.

"There was a drunk old Irishman in Pennsylvania, where I grew up," I said. "A fiddler. His name was Patrick O'Brian, and the drunker he got, the sadder the sound. Till he got so drunk, it turned happy again."

She laughed. "Would you like to hear him play up close?"

"With all my heart," I said, feeling suddenly the haunting memory of childhood.

"Well, then, Saturday night it is. Saturday night on Big Pine. Up at Worley's barn, not so far from the church." And after a pause. "Do you dance, Mr. Ballard?"

I had a sudden flashback to the Warm Springs Hotel and Priscilla Cushman standing before me on the porch. "Not so well," I admitted.

"I can show you, Jake," Sam offered. "I been practicing on my own for the next chance I get with that little Anderson girl."

*   *   *

SARAH FREEMAN'S CABIN sat just over the top of the ridge and down into a slight hollow on the far side. Not large by any measure, perhaps twelve feet by twenty. But there were two floors, not just a loft. Below, everything was open—a large rock fireplace, a table and four fine ladder-back chairs back against the wall from the door, and in the corner farthest from the fire, a bed neatly made and covered by a scrap quilt. "I am sinfully proud of those chairs," she admitted as she showed me about. "All done by Asa Buckner, one at a time over the years, each one bought in fair trade. And if you behave yourself, you will be allowed to sit in one."

I started to ask in fair trade for what, but Sam led me up the ladder to the second floor to show me his bed, which stood at one end, lower under the slanting eaves of the roof, and at the other end of the loft, a . . . I wasn't sure.

"What . . . ?" I whispered to Sammy as I pointed.

"It's my loom, Mr. Ballard," she said from below, my first reminder that everything said in Sarah Freeman's house could be heard by all within. "I'm a weaver, don't you know."

I must have still looked confused because Sam took me by the arm and led me to a trunk that was pushed up under the slant of the roof, hard against the long poles that supported the wooden shakes. He held his finger over his lips for silence and, without moving the trunk, carefully lifted its lid a few inches. He pulled out a folded piece of cloth and handed it to me. It was rough to the touch.

"What are you two up to?" Sarah's voice from below. "Too quiet up there!"

I carried the weaving toward the only window in the room, which was open behind the loom. I let it unfold without allowing it to touch the floor. The cloth was rectangular, perhaps three feet by five, a rich brown with one broad yellow stripe and one broad blue stripe across each end. The threads at each of the long ends were tied off and cut, left as tassels soft to the touch.

Sammy was tugging at my arm. When I looked at his face, he was mouthing a word, but it was difficult to make out.

"Cover-up?" I said aloud, guessing.

"Coverlet. If he's got any sense—which I wonder—he's saying coverlet." Sarah had climbed the ladder into the loft far enough so that her head and shoulders were above the floor, and she was staring at us, amused.

"You're telling me you made this?" I said.

"What do you think I traded for the chairs?" she asked.

*   *   *

TURNS OUT SARAH cooked most evenings for Ben Freeman and his brood, and she and Sammy would eat supper at his cabin a quarter mile away over the ridge. Her plan for that particular day was for the three of us to walk over to Freeman's, so she could set the meal in train. We then would walk back to her place to eat, carrying our supper in a bucket. "Except for that," she said, nodding at a Dutch oven that was resting on her hearth, close enough to the banked fire to stay warm. "That can stay here."

"Where'm I gonna eat?" Sammy asked, staring at the oven.

"With your cousins who love you," his mother said absently, glancing along the walls at the dried plants that hung there.

"Don't love me worth a shit," he whispered to me, low enough so that she could ignore it if she chose.

She did not choose. She reached back and slapped the side of his head. "Enough of that," she said, still looking for what she wanted.

Sammy didn't hesitate even to rub his head. "Why can't I eat with you and Jake? I can carry the bucket."

"'Cause, Jake—Mr. Ballard—and I have business to discuss," she said, "that you don't need to hear." She turned decisively. "Come on. I'll find some fresh jewel weed as we go."

Jewel weed turned out to be a waist-high plant that was growing along the pasture fence by the creek. Medium-sized green leaves in profusion with small orange blossoms at the end of each stem. "Touch-me-not," she called it and set me to stripping leaves and flowers both while Fate danced around us. Sammy had begun automatically, as soon as he saw that she meant to gather it. "Ben's littlest girl gets a peculiar rash that even he can't seem to cure, but this soothes it down so she can sleep at—"

"I don't see why I have to eat with them heathens," Sammy cut her off.

"Don't interrupt your mother!" The words were out of my mouth before I had even thought them. Harsher than I would have spoken if I had stopped to think.

There was a pause in which we could hear the creek running. Sarah straightened and stared at me with her hands on her hips, grinning.

"Or what?" Sam said, defiant.

"Or I'll box your ears."

The boy, his rusty cowlick standing straight up on top of his head, started to laugh. Shaking his head, he walked off, his still-wet overalls clinging to his thin legs. "I'm goin' on to Uncle's," he called over his shoulder. "Warn 'em what sort of man Mama has brought here."

*   *   *

THE TRAIL CROSSED the creek in front of George Freeman's place, a rambling log structure with lean-tos precariously attached on three sides. A short man with a long brown mustache was seated on the front porch plucking the strings of a fiddle that he held low against the bib of his overalls rather than tucked under his chin. He was parsing out a tune, something light and fancy, studying how to bow it.

"George," Sarah called as they passed. "This is Jacob Ballard, federal examiner for the disabled. Have you got any disabilities you'd favor for him to examine?"

The edges of George's mustache rose, and I realized he must be grinning. George laid down his fiddle on the bench beside him and stood.

"My lip is crippled," he said, with a slight slurring of his speech. "Ever since I got hit 'ith an ax in the Yankee camp, I can't spit worth a damn. I had to mostly give up my twis' of tobacco, for I couldn't keep it in my jaw."

"I would have to put that down as a severe disability, sir," I said.

"Is it worth some a that federal money?" he asked.

"Yes, sir. But you've got to come down to Campbell's so we can fill out the papers."

"You goin' back down there in the mornin'?"

"If I'm released from duty." I nodded at Sarah.

The corners of his mustache raised up again. "Well, give a yell when you go by, and I'll walk along 'ith you. Safer that way." He sat back down and picked up his fiddle, and this time he let the bow strike the strings.

"What tune is that, George?" Sarah asked.

"'Soldier's Dream,' I call it. It commences with a light and hairy part." He plucked a few notes to demonstrate. "Then the battles

take holt in earnest." He bowed some deep, nightmare tones that
seemed to shake the leaves on the dogwood beside his porch.
"Then Old Soldier gets to come on back home. Minus an arm or
a leg or some damn part but still alive, thank God." Then he dove
into something fast and lively, a jig or reel that still carried along
the deep, shivering notes of battle but buried them in the run of
happier sound.

Sarah Freeman took my arm then, to lead me along farther
around the cove, with George's fiddle playing behind us.

"Did I mishear or did he say the first part was hairy?" I asked.

"I think he meant light and *airy*." Sometimes when she smiled,
the edges of her lips turned down, I noticed, while the corners of
her green eyes wrinkled in fun. "You know, like . . . like a bird."

CHAPTER SEVEN

We left them all seated around a rough wooden table, bent over their plates and bowls, with the only sounds the slurping and growling like that around the campfires of a hungry army. Ben Freeman himself saluted me with his spoon and a ready grin as we went out the door. Walking back, Sarah began to tell me about her own family, and I realized what she most wanted to tell about was the people of the place. People and relations. I was carrying the bucket, which contained a crockery bowl of stew in the bottom, a plate of the beans, and wedge of cornbread on top. "What was your name before it was Freeman?" I asked her as we walked along.

"My name?"

"Before you were married?"

She laughed. "Thought that's what you meant. I was a Ramsey, but my mother was a Hicks. The *Hicks* is what matters." She looked at me expectantly. "You don't know what that signifies, do you?"

"Not really," I admitted. "But it's not my fault, remember? I was dragged off to Pennsylvania as a shirttail boy."

"Before the age of accountability?"

"Just so."

"Well, the Hickses are singers. Singers and storytellers. Always have been as long as anybody can remember. I got this god-awful hair and all these freckles from the Ramseys, but most everything else . . . came down through my mother."

"Is she still alive, your mother?"

There was the longest pause as we walked along—past the head of the cove once again and back up the trail toward her house. A pause so long that I was afraid I'd hurt her somehow and was about to ask her forgiveness. "No," she whispered, and then she repeated herself more loudly. "No, she left us a year ago. Over a year ago actually, in the winter. Slipped away one night after a long bout. She died up home in Yancey County before I could get there."

"I'm sorry," I said. "It does sound as if she gave you many gifts. What was her name?" Making a mental note to remember what she told me.

"Margaret. Margaret Hicks Ramsey." Her spirits seemed to revive. "Which means I was a Ramsey before I married Young. But now that they're both gone, Mama and Young I mean, now I think of myself as just Sarah. Sometimes Sarah Hicks or sometimes Sarah Freeman—that's when I talk with Sam about his father. Truth be told, most of the time I'm just Sarah, though weeks will go by without me hearin' my name actually spoke aloud."

"Why is—"

"Why, there's no one to call me that except maybe Ben or George, and they hardly ever call my name. With Sammy, it's Mama this and Mama that. With Ben's tribe, it's always Aunty. Where in the hell they got *Aunty*, I cannot say."

"I . . . well, may I call you Sarah?"

"I already told you to, back at Goforth's Store, the day we pulled you out of the ditch."

"Same day that I asked you to call me Jake. Which you did

several times, saying it like you were tasting it to see whether you
liked it or not."

She laughed. "Well, Jake, come on in my house and eat your
supper. As hot as it is, we can sit on the porch, but let me dish it out
first." As I stood in the doorway of the cabin, she took down two
pewter plates from a set of shelves on the wall while she continued
to let her thoughts roam. "You heard me tell Sammy that there's
business we have to discuss." She didn't pause for me to respond.
"Well, there's something I want to talk to you about, something
about that boy. And I can't imagine you'll tell me the truth with
him and his ear to the door."

"He reminds me of me sometimes," I admitted. "I don't know
if that's a good thing."

She smiled. "Come on. I'll show you something before we eat."
She led the way around the side of the cabin and on toward a log
barn perhaps forty feet beyond. "Truth to tell, I had in mind you'd
sleep in the barn tonight. I can't imagine you want to sleep in that
hot loft with Sammy . . ."

I was shaking my head at the very thought, recalling how frantic
a sleeper the boy was.

"So it's the barn unless you want to stay with Ben and his tribe.
I fixed you a bedtick full of corn shucks, and once Sammy's up the
ladder, I'll sneak you a pillow."

We were into the barn by then, and she was pointing to a pallet
over against a stack of loose hay. There was a scrap quilt folded
neatly on the pallet, and immediately Fate ran to lie down on the
pallet with her head on the quilt. "I'll keep her in the house when
you come out to the barn," Sarah said. "Else she'll want to sleep
with you . . . But that's not what I want to show you." She led
me over to a set of shelves nailed up to the log wall of the barn,
beside a large spinning wheel set back in a corner behind my bed.
"I'm guessing you've got that cap-and-ball pistol in your pocket that
Sammy won't give up talking about?"

I nodded.

"For this evening, I wish you'd fold it into that quilt, or else put it up on top of those shelves. One or t'other. There's something on the shelves you might want anyway, something to go with your supper."

I took the pistol out of my coat pocket and folded it into the quilt on top of the bedtick, and then I ran my hand down the length of the high shelf till it struck what felt like a jug. Carefully, I pulled the jug toward me with one hand and caught it with the other. It was heavy, and there was a shaved wooden stopper jammed tightly into its mouth.

"It's the real thing," she said. "The wicked brew that keeps Ben Freeman and all his relations with a few dollars for the necessities. And I figured you might rather have that than spring water with your supper."

"Will you have a sip with me?"

"Maybe. I have to cut it with honey or blackberry juice. With me and liquor, it's most always maybe. But here you are, and I don't have much else except water and buttermilk, and Sammy says you've been living off well water at Campbell's, so I thought you might like something to lay down the day."

I unstoppered the jug and breathed in the fumes that rose from within. I fought the urge to cough—it was that strong. "You think I might need more than cornbread to ease the day?" I asked.

"Well now, it's the best cornbread you'll ever eat," she said as she turned back toward the house. "But even so . . . Come on and sit down. Bring one of my good chairs out on the porch where it's cool."

"Aren't you going to sit?"

She smiled. "Why, I guess I am. Bring two chairs then."

*   *   *

AFTER SETTING OUT the chairs, I found two mugs on the shelf and poured an inch of the white liquor into each. True to her word, she stirred a dollop of honey into her mug. She gave me a plate piled high with stew and green beans, a chunk of cornbread with butter resting on top. I watched her carefully, unsure if she might bless her food, and waiting on her to begin. She nodded and smiled. "Tuck in, Jake Ballard. It's getting colder by the minute."

It was delicious, I have to say. Better than the food at Patton's Hotel, better than anything I'd had in a long time. The beef had been boiled tender but was strong to the taste and went well with the potatoes and onions. The cornbread was not sweet, but the outside was crisp and the inside chewy. The beans had just enough fatback in them to make me even hungrier as I ate.

But as ravenous as I'd suddenly become, I noticed that she had no beef on her own plate, only the potatoes and onions with her beans. "That won't do," I muttered around a mouthful of food.

"Hmmm?"

I swallowed. "That won't do—for me to eat the meat and you not." I held my plate out toward her, meaning to share.

"There's more in the bowl by the fire." She paused. "It's just that I knew that calf. Sometimes I'm troubled to eat animals I knew well. Pigs and such."

"How about chickens?" I asked, amused.

"Oh Lord," she said. "A chicken has no mind. The only thing it's good for is eggs. A crow, now—a crow is a smart and playful bird. But a chicken!"

I extended my plate toward her one final time, offering.

"Eat up your beef, Jake Ballard. It's rare enough we have it."

She did not pick at her food, Sarah Freeman, but enjoyed it fully, and I realized just how hard she must have worked that day. Both here in her own house and at Ben Freeman's.

"It's delicious," I offered. "Every bite."

She nodded and smiled. Suddenly quiet.

The evening was setting down in front of us, dusk pooling in the stand of pines in front of her cabin. I noticed a firefly or two, twinkling among the shaded limbs.

I set my empty plate on the floor beside my chair. "You said you were a Hicks," I offered. "And a singer. Would you sing something?"

"If you hear me out about Sammy," she said, "why then, I might.

There's a blackberry cobbler in that Dutch oven, still warm I hope. If you agree to my plan about Sammy, you might earn yourself a song with your cobbler."

"What about Sam?" I said. "Is something wrong?"

"No, nothing's wrong with him like that. He's not sick, I mean. Here lately, I think he needs something I can't give him. He misses his father."

"I think I know what you mean," I offered quietly. "When I asked him about his father in the coach on the way to Warm Springs, he tried to hit me."

"Well, I swan. I never . . ."

"He was crying."

"He doesn't cry. At least not in a long time," she said wistfully.

I held my tongue.

"He's only ten years old, but he's trying to be a man—and he needs a pattern."

"The pattern for a man?"

"Yes, someone to follow after. So while you're here, I wish you'd let him spend as much time with you as possible. I don't know how long you'll be here and I don't know how much you even care for the boy, but it would certainly mean a lot to him. When you told him you'd box his ears, he lit up like a lantern."

"What about his uncles?"

"Well, they've each one got enough children of their own so that they can hardly recall their names. Ben does pay attention to Sammy because the boy's good around the still, but Ben also spent nigh two months in jail last winter, which brought his devil of a wife sniffing back around. And once George comes in from the fields, he does little else but play music and sing to himself."

"Not so much of a pattern."

She shook her head. "No, even if they are kin."

"What about the lawyer that wants to take you and Sammy away from all this? He won't do?"

She leaned back in her chair, and if it hadn't been dark under the roof of the porch, I would have sworn she was blushing. "What do you know about that?"

"Sam says that he's the first man who's climbed that hill that you haven't turned away with a gun barrel."

She had to laugh. "His name is Pharaoh Breese, and he's reading law with his father, the one who handles Ben's various legal tangles. Pharaoh was with Young in the Sixty-Fourth. That's why I first bothered to listen to him. And he claimed that Young asked him to care for me if something happened."

"Was he at Camp Douglas?"

"Sammy tell you about that too?"

"Yes."

"Turns out Pharaoh wasn't at Camp Douglas. He somehow wasn't at Cumberland Gap either, when Young and the rest were captured by you damn Yanks."

"So he wasn't anywhere close by when Young might have named him for his substitute?"

"That's the conclusion I came to. But I'll tell you where he did mean to be."

I glanced through the door at her bed.

"Just so. Right through that door and into bed. And the man can talk. I'll give him that."

"How far did he get?"

"Well, I don't know that's any of your affair, but the truth is he only got as far as the steps. I made him speak his piece from the front yard." She seemed to laugh at the memory. "He wants to take me to Asheville and set me up as a lawyer's wife."

"What about Sam?"

"He didn't mention Sammy till he saw that Asheville didn't make such an impression. Then he seemed to take notice that I had a son in the bargain and began to discuss his future as well. I turned him away, but I will say he is a pretty man with a thick, full beard, and he swore on his mama's Bible that he would return to the fray."

"Carries his mother's Bible, does he?"

"The memory of it. He seems to hold the memory of her Bible more sacred than the woman herself. And I would have to admit that Asheville might offer more of a future for Sam. For me and for Sam."

"So while we're waiting on Pharaoh to reappear with a better offer, you want me to make some sort of pattern for Sam."

"Yes, I do. I can tell Sammy's getting restless. I'm afraid he's too smart to spend his whole life up here."

"Aren't you afraid he'll get hurt if he goes along with me?"

"Why would I be afraid he'll get hurt? He knows most of the men you're interviewing already."

"He didn't tell you about Ed Arrowood?"

"Only that you wouldn't let him see the body no matter how he begged. But Ed Arrowood isn't your problem to do with. He belongs to the sheriff if anybody. You're just a nice, harmless man who's here to hand out pensions. You read and write for a living instead of breaking your back in a damn cornfield all day."

"I wish you might be right. I wish that was all I was here to do. Just like I wish I had two hands and a kind heart."

She stared at me in the growing dark. Her hair was a muted-rust color now, but the spray of freckles still stood against the skin of her face, and her eyes—well, her eyes bore into me. "What are you here to do, Mr. Jacob Ballard, from the far off capital city?"

"Jake. I wish you would call me Jake. Truly."

"What are you here to do, Jake?" Her voice, at least, was softer, if not her eyes. Her eyes had shaded to a deep Irish green in the growing dark.

"You're right about the cornfield, but not about the other." I paused. Somehow sitting there with her felt obscurely like home—like some place I'd been before, a long time ago, perhaps in a dream before the war. And by God, I had made it further than Pharaoh Breese. I was on the porch. "I'm here to find out who's killing Yank veterans and put a stop to it. Zeb Vance sent me."

"I'm guessing I'm not supposed to know that, am I?"

I shook my head no.

"Meaning you don't want me to tell anybody else, do you? Not even Sammy?"

"Especially not Sam. He would want to help, don't you see."

She leaned forward in her chair and put one hand lightly on my knee. Stared now into my face, her lips parted in concentration as she studied what she saw there. "Are you sure you're the right man for this, Jake?"

"Sorry to say that I probably am." I hesitated. "I refused when Vance first asked me, but he talked me around to it. And now that I'm here, I see what has to be done."

*　　*　　*

WE ATE HER cobbler off our same plates, wiped clean after the first course. The cobbler, she explained, was from blackberries she'd picked herself the Sunday before. As we ate, I noticed that she sipped from her mug between each bite, as did I.

"The fireflies in the thick branches of those pine trees are quite beautiful," I offered at one point.

"Hemlocks," she said. "And we call them lightning bugs." And then after a long pause and another sip. "And yes, they are beautiful, I grant you."

*　　*　　*

WE SET OUR plates beside us on the floor and sat sipping from our mugs, the liquor reaching down, taking root deep inside. After a moment, she said, "This is a song I used to sing to myself after Young was killed . . . to remind me of what it felt like when he was alive. To help keep him alive in my heart." After another sip from her mug, she began slowly, quietly to sing, as if it was as natural as breathing, there in the gloaming light.

Jack went a sailing
with troubles on his mind.
To leave his native country

and his darling dear behind
 Sing ree and sing low,
 So fare you well my dear.

She dressed herself in men's array,
And apparel she put on;
Unto the field of battle
She marched with men along.
 Sing ree and sing low,
 So fare you well my dear.

She paused for a moment and then let her voice out a notch. The words came louder, faster—sweeter.

Your cheeks too red and rosy,
Your fingers too neat and small,
And your waist too slim and slender
To face a cannon ball.
 Sing ree and sing low,
 So fare you well—

"Eee-Yaaa!" At just that moment Sam cut loose with his version of the Rebel yell from right beside the porch. "What are you two doing, sitting out in the dark?" My heart almost stopped, and his mother threw her mug at him.

He was proud that he'd managed to slip through the woods and come up right beside us without either of us hearing a thing. Only Fate had sniffed him out as he crawled by the barn, and he had shushed her by whispering in her ear and feeding her some cornbread crumbs. Together, dog and boy had crept up almost to our very feet before he screamed out, and she barking along with him.

*   *   *

THEN THERE WAS all the evening work—milking the cow, putting up the chickens, throwing corn to the sow and her litter. In between helping Sammy and petting Fate, I slipped the jug back onto its shelf in the barn.

Once, as I carried firewood into the cabin, I glanced at Sarah's carefully made bedstead in the corner of the room, Pharaoh Breese's target. The quilt was pulled tight over the mattress, and the palm-sized tintype of a soldier boy was propped against the pillow. Young Freeman, no doubt, slowly turning his wife's bed into a grave.

When I passed her in the yard, me with an armload of firewood and her on the way to the springhouse with a pail of fresh milk, I asked how the song ended, but she only smiled and shook her head.

There was a time by her fire, warm against the cool evening air, and because she asked, I read aloud from one of her books, Jane Austen as I recall. She attentive to every word, Sam beginning to nod off. And at chapter's end, the two of us all but pushing the boy's sleepy weight up the ladder to the loft.

She walked out to the barn with me, carrying one of the two feather pillows from her own bed, claiming she wanted to see the sky one last time before sleep. As we walked, she pointed out the rising moon, tangled in the branches of an ancient oak that stood sentry up the ridge. At the barn door she handed me the pillow, and as she did, she grabbed my hand by accident, my left hand.

She didn't let that hand go immediately, as horrible as it was, but shook it gently before dropping it. Somehow, they fit together ever so briefly, those two hands, as the wind threw moonlight shadow across the barnyard.

"He'll want to go with you in the morning," she said quietly.

"I know."

"And I think he should," she was leaning close to whisper. "You might just need him."

"What about his mother? What does she need?"

"I gave up on needing things two years ago, when Young was killed. That part, the needing and wanting part, was torn right out of me."

"Well, what about that lawyer man? Pharaoh, for God's sake? What about him?"

"I haven't made my mind up about him."

"You can't spend your whole life a widow. Sleeping with a ghost makes for an empty bed."

I could feel her stiffen, and for a moment I thought my tongue, loosened up by liquor, had gone too far.

"I'm older than you are," she said. "It's not easy for me."

"Well hell. What are you? A hundred and ten?"

She laughed. "Close to . . . I'm twenty-seven."

"My Lord God. That's not old by any calendar. You must be lonely as a cloud up here."

"I am," she said finally. "But I don't know any other way."

"The fighting is over. By my count, Young died over two and a half years ago, and it's probably been much longer since you actually saw him. Maybe it's time we all gave up the war."

"It's all still real to me," she whispered and reached out to squeeze my mangled hand again, ever so gently, before turning back to her own house, her own cold bed, leading Fate along with her to the cabin door.

It was only as I lay wrapped in the quilt, burrowed down into the corn shucks, that I began to wonder why in God's name I had told her the truth about myself and what I was there to do. What had I gained in return, if anything? What could she teach me about this place that would help me track the killer?

Or had I betrayed my sworn duty for a smile and a piece of a song?

CHAPTER EIGHT

I believe that I first started walking in my sleep because of the hoods. After President Lincoln was killed, when we brought the final eight conspirators to the Old Arsenal to await trial, Stanton ordered that each had to wear a canvas hood twenty-four hours a day. They were manacled at the wrist and ankle and then shackled to a seventy-five-pound iron ball. A canvas hood, padded an inch thick with cotton wadding, was lowered over their heads and tied tightly at the neck, leaving only a small hole for breathing and eating. Those of us who guarded them decided to leave only the woman, Mary Surratt, unhooded, and eventually even Stanton relented in her case.

But the rest spent their last days in the sweltering heat with their entire heads shrouded, and I was not the only one who thought that if they weren't crazed before they were hooded, they became so as they waited. The inside of the hoods must have been slick with spit and sweat, eventually with blood as the raw skin scrubbed away. And the inside of their heads? Only God knows what the inside of their heads were slick with.

After the trial and executions, I began to sleepwalk, often dreaming that I was marching out to that scaffold at Fort McNair, only that the hood was drawn tight over my head and I was the one gasping in the blind, choking air.

*   *   *

ON THIS NIGHT, though, I woke without screaming, standing just outside the door of Sarah Freeman's barn in my socks. Though it was summer, my feet were cold. The only night sound was that of peep frogs in the trees and the gentle blowing of her plow horse in its stall. I woke on my own and—strangely—not panting aloud, not scared half out of my wits by prison dreams. Just a lonely man standing in his socks, staring sleepily about him at a mountain cove. And it was quiet, so quiet there except for the peepers, that I could hear the creek running far away.

Sarah had told me that after the word came down to her that Young was dead, she set about farming with a furious vengeance, almost as if she were doing his work as well as hers, as if proving with her own sweat that he was still alive. Even during the war, when there were no men who could be trusted and Sam was too young to be of use, she had plowed with that same horse now behind me in its stall, had fought back against the wilderness by continuing to plant crops all the way out to the fences she and Young had built before the war. She farmed partially to keep from losing her mind and partially to keep the land itself in heart. To keep it awake for some future day, when the sun would again shine down on green rows. Here now was that same farm breathing easily in the moonlight, resting after its day's labor.

I was beginning to realize that in the Southern mountains, the old ways hold sway in the night, when people lie asleep, and the tide of nature itself rises iridescent and resplendent. The moon and stars sweep through the sky, and all is as it should be, undisturbed by the hooded insanity of man. So it seemed to me as I stood there, half asleep, half awake—half inside the barn and half emergent in the world. The owl screeched to its mate in the woods, and I stumbled forth.

The moon was a brilliant half of its full circle, and I realized deliriously that I was too stupid to know whether it was young or old, waxing or waning. Still, even at half ebb, its light was enough to bathe the barnyard in quiet, pooling silver. I paced out slowly beyond Sarah's cabin, where she and the boy lay wrapped in sleep. Beyond the cabin and barn, I came to a stacked rail fence that marked the border of her yard and the beginning of her pasture, the falling away of the land into the cove that lay below. The land that was neither Ben's nor George's but hers alone.

What I saw there woke me fully. In the pasture, those moonlit four or five acres, there was a flock of sheep—some kneeling asleep, some cropping the close grass, but all a ghostly gray in the moonlight. Leaning against the fence, I realized that I had walked forth armed for danger, my pistol in my whole right hand. But there was no danger, only the peaceful dozing and grazing of sheep. Standing there, I was surprised to feel myself breathe without gasping and see without weeping.

*   *   *

SHE WOKE ME at daybreak. Humming as she worked in the barn. Even before I opened my eyes, I could hear her voice, humming softly with a few words here and there as the tune seemed to require. I recognized the love song from the night before.

"I didn't know you kept sheep," I said quietly, still with my eyes closed.

"They mostly stay down by the creek where it's cool during the day and graze in the upper pasture at night. I didn't know you wandered in your sleep," she continued. And then more loudly, in a daytime sort of voice, "Did you have a nightmare?"

"You saw me?" I asked, opening my eyes, blinking at the early morning light, streaked yellow and brown in the barn. She was perhaps ten feet away, bending to pick up a chicken egg out of the loose straw.

"Fate heard you and whined, and when I went to the window I saw you walk by, looking most forlorn, I must say."

"I do walk in my sleep sometimes, when I dream of the war. By the time you saw me wandering, though, I think I was awake."

"Well, sometime if you were to tell me the worst of the dream, then you wouldn't have to suffer it anymore."

"This is a war dream, a butchering dream." I sat up slowly and stretched my back. "Do you really believe that telling it to you could take it away?"

She looked down, for once quite grave. "I tell very few people this, Jake Ballard, for as you can imagine, I don't want it generally known. But yes, I eat dreams."

*   *   *

WE ATE AT the small table. Biscuits and eggs scrambled up with pieces of the stew beef from the night before. Coffee for us, Sammy allowed only fresh milk.

I brought up the dance that Uncle George Freeman was to play for on Saturday night. "Am I still invited?" I asked, Sammy watching our faces as he chewed.

"Maybe," she said without a smile. "With me it's always maybe."

And then we marched down the path through the corn to meet Uncle George, with Fate prancing, leading the way.

He was standing under a maple tree where the path met the road by the creek. He had what appeared to be his military issue Springfield and a faded leather haversack over his shoulder.

We joined him, and suddenly Sarah asked, "Are you partial to riddles, Jake?" For some reason, her mood had shifted and there was a lilt in her voice.

I nodded. "I was the champion of Lancaster County," I said. "Never yet was the riddle I couldn't factor."

Her eyes, I noticed that morning, grew bigger when she laughed. "Well then, you may come back when you can answer this one."

"If I name the answer here on this ground, I will come back for

Saturday night," I said. "Being as I am a dancing man."

"Hot damn," George said and grinned horribly.

"*As I went around my whirly-go-whackum,*" she said with her hands on her hips.

"*There I spied old Bo Backum,*
And I called out Lafayette Lackum,
To run Bo Backum out of my whirly-go-whackum."

I was half lying about being the riddle champion of Lancaster County, but only half. I'd heard a version of this one long ago, from my mother, it seemed to me. I squinted at Sarah, who kept a perfectly straight face. With riddles, it always pays to watch the face, and when Sarah had "called out Lafayette Lackum," she had glanced down at the dog, who was listening as intently as the rest of us. So there was one clue, one she meant for me to have.

I had a brief, fleeting memory of the sound of my mother's voice saying "whirly-go-whackum." I was still staring at Sarah's face. Her lips, I noticed, were the same dark-brown, berry color as the freckles on her nose and cheeks. Her mouth twitched, as she was trying not to smile. "Whirly-go-whackum" I knew was her corn patch or corn-field, but what the hell was "Bo Backum"? Something on a farm . . . something that tore up the corn . . . something that rhymed.

"He's done," Sammy muttered. "He don't know for . . ."

"As I went around my corn patch . . ." I said to shut Sammy up so I could think. Sarah nodded and winked. I could swear she winked, though it was as quick as a raindrop.

"As I went round my corn patch,
I saw that old hog tearing it up.
I called for my good dog, Fate,
To run that old hog out of the corn."

"Hot damn," George offered again.

Sarah laughed. We all laughed. "Saturday then," she said. "Come early and we'll all walk up Big Pine together. Sometimes George will play us a tune as we go along."

And then, as George and Sammy started down the dirt road

toward Campbell's, she said more gently, for my ears alone, "Bring Sammy home on Friday if you like. And if it is the nightmare that destroys you, you may tell it me."

*   *   *

"IS THERE SUCH a thing as a dream eater?" I asked George Freeman as we walked along. It was still early, and the pasture grass was soaked with dew.

"Well, of course they is," he said. "They is fire eaters and sin eaters. And they is dream eaters. Surely you hear'd of fire eaters in the army?"

I nodded slowly as we walked. "A man or a woman who could suck the fire out of a burn. Time I saw it done, the man was a corporal in the Fifty-Third Illinois. He whispered some kind of magic words down into the burn and drew the fire out with this breath. We were laughing because we didn't believe it, but the burned man swore it was healed, and the next day, the corporal had blisters on his lips and he could only drink cold water for a while after that."

"Those words are the potion," George explained. "That's what the fire eater knows that the rest of us don't, usually as it's been passed down from one generation to the next. Passed down mother to daughter or father to son. Up here where we ain't got much for a doctor except what Ben prescribes, there's such as that gets practiced more than you might expect."

"What does a sin eater do?"

"Well, now, that's more complicated. You might see a sin eater at some special church meetin' or at a big revival like the one that's brewing for next Sunday down at the river. Hear tell that man Rogers is gonna save a hundred souls on Sunday, with some of the lesser preachers babtizin' folks as he calls 'em out, and they's usually a sin eater or two lurking in a crowd like that. It's most always a man, and he will suck the sin right out of a body."

"What the hell does that mean, *suck the sin out?* I thought Jesus took care of all that."

George frowned, or at least I think he did—hard to tell at times with his mustache. "Jesus can sure work on some sin, I grant you, but sometimes a sin sticks to a man—or a woman. A man who can't quit fightin', say, or a woman who can't forbear raisin' up her skirts for everything that wanders by."

"How do they get the sin out?"

"Well, there's a good deal of prayin' and shoutin' goes on, and then the sin eater commences to speakin' in tongues, there's your magic potion again, and then he fastens his mouth on the sinful part—say, the man's throat if he's bad to drink or the woman's belly if she . . ." He glanced down at Sammy, who was listening ever so closely even as we walked along. "If she likes to you-know-what. And then there's a great drawin' of breath, and the sinner faints away. The time I saw it done, the sinner passed plumb out of mind and fell on the ground. The sin eater staggered around and had to be led away, his head lolling from side to side and his tongue hangin' out."

"Who was it, the sin eater, I mean?"

"I ain't supposed to say. That's part of the power, you see, part of the secret. Besides, if you was a sin eater, would you want sorry-ass folks lined up out your door and down the road, wantin' you to put your mouth on various parts of their bodies?" George winked at me. "Various evil parts."

Sammy made a retching noise.

"Maybe some of the women," I admitted.

"Hot damn," George agreed and tried to spit.

We walked on, past the little frame church house that Sammy and I had seen through the rain the day before.

"Is any of this stuff in the Bible?" I asked George. "Sin eating, for God's sake?"

"Well, now it might be. I can't say for certain, 'cause I can only read the least little bit. Mostly I know my Bible from hearing Sarah or Ben or one of them preachers line it out."

"Well, who is this Barabbas people keep accusing me of being? Who's he?"

Sammy sniggered.

"Why, don't you know, he's the sinner that Pilate fellow let loose instead of Jesus. That Roman general Pilate offered the mob to turn Jesus loose since he couldn't find nothin' to accuse him of, and them heathern Jews hollered, 'Give us Barabbas, give us Barabbas!' which he did."

"So Jesus went to the cross instead of Barabbas?"

George nodded, wiping at the spit that had dribbled down his chin while he was imitating the heathern Jews.

"So it would seem that this Barabbas is the very . . . what . . . pattern of a sinner?"

"You got it," George agreed. "Barabbas, he's the goddamn sacrificial goat. Keep this up, son, and you'll be a regular Bible scholar."

"Might make a preacher," Sammy said.

"Hot damn," I said.

CHAPTER NINE

I installed Sam in the barn across the road from the house, the same barn that we'd kept Ed Arrowood's body in while waiting for his sister. I figured to keep him mostly out of Mrs. Campbell's way and less of a bother in general. George helped him settle in, with his quilt and his goods, while I walked on to the house. There was a large, clean-shaven man sitting on the front steps. He had no visible disability, but I assumed he was one of the applicants. He touched his hat brim when I spoke, and when I went into the front parlor, I found May June waiting for me.

I explained about Sam and the barn, and she nodded, almost smiling. I figured she was expert at staying out of Mrs. Campbell's way herself and would appreciate my plan. When I asked about the man on the front porch, she just shrugged her shoulders and pointed to me and back to him—meaning that I had best find out for myself. Then she pointed to James Mitchell Randall of the Twentieth Kentucky Infantry on the printed list and pointed toward the back of the house.

"Kitchen?" I asked, surprised she would let anybody in her kitchen. She shook her head

"Privy?"

She nodded.

I lowered my voice. "Where's Campbell?"

She pulled me by the arm over to the table and pointed down at my own map, the map I had sketched from Jimmy Patton's master copy. She picked up her pencil and pointed to Marshall on the map, the county seat.

"Gone to Marshall? Court day?"

She nodded.

"Mrs. Campbell?"

She tucked her hand inside my elbow and made as though she were walking along beside me, even as we were standing still at the table.

"Gone with him?"

She nodded.

"Well, then, I imagine you're in charge."

She shook her head no, even as it was plain to see that I had pleased her.

I know what many of my former associates in Washington City would have said straight up—that I was a fool to let a Negro woman touch me, only they would have called her *nigger gal* or worse. But the plain fact was that I didn't just need May June. I liked her grit and her humor, the way that her eyes talked even when her lips didn't. And soon now, I had to know what she knew.

That morning, she and I set up shop and announced that we were open for business by throwing up the front windows and inviting the man on the steps in to be interviewed. I began by asking him his unit, and he only admitted to the Twenty-Fourth North Carolina.

"Well, then I reckon you're not Ezekial Goforth?"

"No," he said. "No, but I know Zeke. I'm told we're cousins."

"Are you claiming a disability?" I asked, studying his face. "I only administer the federal troops." Which caused him a good deal of mirth.

"No disability," he was finally able to say. "Though some of the voters in Madison might tell you I need one. Disabled in the head, they would say."

Our visitor was as young as me and carefully shaven, but there was no sense of weakness or hesitation in his manner. He had a concave face, like a shovel, and deceptive brown eyes—eyes that looked sleepy but roved constantly from my face to May June's and back. It was clear he was studying us rather than the other way around. Plus he was big, over six feet and thick through the arms and shoulders. He had removed a pistol belt when he came into the room and laid gun, holster, and belt on the table by the door.

"I believe you might be the sheriff of this fair county," I said.

"You might be right." He nodded agreeably. "Stephen Brigman at your service. Yours and Miss Washington's." He nodded at May June.

"I thought all Southern sheriffs looked like . . ."

"Hogs?" he asked helpfully. "Hogs that chew tobacco and take down any innocent stranger that happens to wander over the county line?"

He had me. "Just so."

"Well, now. I believe you're thinking of my opponent in the last election." He nodded at the memory. "I'm sorry you missed him."

"I'm not," I admitted. "Are you here because of Ed Arrowood?"

"He the dead man who turned up on your front porch?"

"Well, in the road in front of the house, but it looked like it was intentional. Looked like the killer meant us to find him there."

"I'm sure he did," Brigman said. He glanced at May June. "You see the body too?" he asked.

She nodded.

"What do you make of it?"

She looked helplessly back at him and then pointed to me.

"She's mute," I told him.

"Can you hear me?" he asked and smiled reassuringly.

She nodded, smiled, and again pointed.

"She believes you can parlay for her," he said.

"Yes, but trust me . . . if I misspeak, she'll let us both know it."

He laughed. "That's just how women do, I believe. You're right until you're wrong. Then God help."

Now, it was May June nodding and smiling.

"How did you know it was Arrowood?" he said, changing directions effortlessly.

"Because we'd just interviewed him a few days before and he was missing seven toes."

Brigman gave me a funny look.

"Seven total . . . off both feet."

The sheriff smiled. "Fair enough. That would do it. Don't see many three-toed corpses around here, and God knows we've got our share. I appreciate you taking care of the body like that and sending for Arrowood's sister." He nodded and smiled at May June again. "But that's not why you're here, is it, Mr. Ballard? Interviewing and grave digging—not why you're here?"

Again, he had changed directions with barely a hitch in his voice. But I had recalled that Vance had said I could trust this man, and I was ready for him. "I'm here to find out who's killing off the Union veterans."

He didn't smile at this. "Who sent you? The War Department?" May June's eyes were darting back and forth between us.

"No, the War Department couldn't care less who gets shot in Madison County. As far as they're concerned, North Carolina is still an occupied state under military rule. Governor Vance sent me."

Then he smiled. "You're a truth-telling son of a bitch, ain't you?"

"Depends on who I'm talking to."

"Well, since you're talking to me, you got any candidates for our killer?"

"Not really, but I would love to know a lot more about James Keith. Every time I dig down the least bit, his name rises up."

"I'd like to know a little more about him myself," he said. "I don't think he's in the county, truth be told, but the man is the original damn snake in the grass, and sometimes he seems to come and go like smoke on the evening breeze."

"Why don't you arrest him next time he materializes?"

Brigman smiled, though his eyes didn't shift or change. "You know I've tried. I've had capias and papers against him since the war, ever since he burned Thom Denver's mill down. I had him cornered in a church once last summer, and we traded shots till neither of us had a charge left and he climbed out a window. That's when he left out for South Carolina, and we had him picked up down there."

"But then he broke jail."

"Then he broke jail in Buncombe, and there's been a rumor or two of him, but his wife and family are gone to Arkansas, and he's rarely been seen since. If he was here, I think we'd know. Too many people up here would shoot him on sight."

I shrugged. "He's the best suspect I can offer up for the moment."

"I know how you feel," Brigman said sympathetically. "How I feel most days . . . all to seek. But here's the thing . . ."

I looked at him expectantly.

"This place is like a bear trap set with a hairspring. Has been since last summer when the soldiers started showing up to home, straggling in one at a time or in small groups. I fought for Bob Vance in the Twenty-Fourth North Carolina, Confederate troops, but I don't care one way or another. I just want to keep what peace there is and let the dead bury the dead."

"So you think the violence could catch fire again? Armed bands roaming the countryside?"

For the first time, he looked down at the floor, breaking eye contact with May June and me both. "The war starved this part of the country down to the bone and then sucked out the marrow," he whispered before looking up again. "There are desperate people everywhere. So if you do find out where Keith is laying out or some other bunch doing the killing, how about you send for me before you take off hell-for-leather up some lonely trail. You're a soldier. You know what reinforcements are for. Plus, I'd rather put this to rest without starting a whole new round of feuding."

I nodded. "If I have time, I'll come knock on your door myself before mounting an attack."

"Fair enough," he said and rose to go. "Fair enough for our kind of work." He paused as he was strapping on his belt and holster containing what appeared to be a long-barreled cavalry pistol. "You should know, just in case, last I heard Keith has shaved off his beard. Still sports a hell of a mustache from the war years, but his cheeks are bare." He grasped my hand, his own large and hard. "Miss Washington . . ." He tipped his hat to May June and then spoke further to her. "See if you can keep Mr. Ballard here alive for a week or two, you hear."

She nodded solemnly, taking him at his word.

*   *   *

UNCLE GEORGE HAD held Sam captive while May June and I were interviewed by the sheriff, but when Brigman walked out through the front door, Sam escaped long enough to ambush him by the front steps. Through the window, we watched as he convinced Brigman to show him his pistol, which looked like it would drop a mule in its tracks—and which made Sam jump up and down in illicit glee.

When I turned back from the window, smiling at Sam's antics, I found May June staring at me speculatively. She raised her eyebrows, forming a question with her face, as if to ask whether *she* could trust *me*. Asking why I hadn't told her the reason I was there, why I'd kept her in the dark as to my true intentions. "I never mentioned it because you didn't ask," I said. And at that, she had to smile.

*   *   *

TURNS OUT THAT Mitch Randall had fallen asleep under the sycamore, lulled by the midday heat while waiting his turn, so next we interviewed Mr. George Washington Freeman, Company C of the Second North Carolina Mounted Infantry.

Since I had already witnessed more than sufficient evidence of George's disability, I didn't have him raise up his mustache in the parlor, as much for May June's sake as his own. I was not about to send in a claim requesting federal script for a man with a split lip, so between us, May June and I described him as slowly starving to death from his broken mouth. This required some creativity, for he was partridge plump in a country where the men and women both were generally as lean as fence rails.

*   *   *

JAMES MITCHELL RANDALL had lost his left arm at the Battle of Chattanooga in November of '63. The interesting thing about Mitch Randall is that he hadn't intended to apply for a disability at all because he claimed that he could still shear a sheep, even a big ram, almost as fast as he could before the war. His father had convinced him, however, that he was owed something for the loss of his arm, especially as the old man himself had suffered mightily during the conflict. The Randalls were persecuted because of their Tory sympathies, and the Home Guard had visited the old man on more than one occasion, stealing his livestock and burning his barn.

Mitch himself was more disturbed about the loss of the barn than the loss of his arm, so he was pleased with the offer of five federal dollars a month. "Riches enough," he called it, "to settle Papa's score."

When he left Campbell's that day, intending to walk the turnpike down to Warm Springs, he shook my hand with an iron grip. "Listen here, Mr. Ballard," he said. "You ain't from around here, so you can see a little farther and a little deeper. Who you reckon is slaughtering us Yanks come home from the war? My papa is scared to death that I'm next, which I can't tell him no different."

I glanced at his face. He had the wary brown eyes of an old man, almost buried in his lively, young features. "I wish I knew," I said.

"I keep thinkin' the answer's right in front of us," Mitch said. "Somebody close by. Somebody related. I look at ever-body I meet on the road, ever-body I work for. Wonderin' if they got it in 'em to do these killin's."

"And . . ." I encouraged him.

"We all got some war in us," he said, sadly. "Some killin' instinct. Man or woman, don't matter . . . But whoever this is has got more war in his gut than you or me. More than . . . is natural." But then his face brightened. "Listen here. I'm workin' up at Freeman's at the head of the cove on Saturday. If you want to see what a one-armed sheep shearer looks like doin' his business, you ought to come up and see the show. Have a drink with Ben and George. They're good Union men."

I smiled back at his wink and grin, but then one more question occurred to me, a question I thought he could answer. We were standing in the road, almost exactly where I'd seen the murderer's prints days before. "Is it common," I said, "for mountain folks to go about with their mounts unshod?"

He shook his head. "Not if they can bribe the blacksmith. Ground's too rocky, work's too hard. In this country, a man will shoe his horse before he shoes his children."

"What if he can't show his face? What if he's hiding out?"

Mitch Randall's own face clouded over. "That would explain it," he admitted.

CHAPTER TEN

The Campbells weren't expected back till the next day, so I let Sam come into the house after Randall headed out for the river bridge. May June took charge, as one might expect, given that she was free for a while from the yoke of Mrs. Campbell's sharp eye and sharper words. She took Sam down to the river that late afternoon armed with fishing poles, and they came back with a catfish big enough to feed us all.

While they were gone off fishing, I sat at May June's parlor table and worked to compose a report to Vance. By the time they came back and were skinning their fish on the back porch, I had written out a half-dozen pages of notes, and I realized that I was still writing more to myself than to Vance. The story was getting longer and longer, as one stray fact attached itself to another. There was something that I was missing, something blood deep and important, but as yet, I didn't have the eyes to see it. As I worked to fill in my questions along with the notes, I realized I was going to have to start over to make anything like a sensible report.

I could hear May June and Sammy in the kitchen, the boy chattering away as he fired up the cookstove. And again, I was struck how much like a conversation it sounded, him talking as if she was talking back.

Before I started what I intended to be my actual report, rendered from pages fat with my impressions, I strode down the hallway to the kitchen and pushed open the door.

"All right, Sam, I got one for you," I said.

He straightened up from the stove, a chunk of firewood in his hand. "A riddle? You got a riddle?"

I nodded.

He stood up straighter. "All right. Go on ahead."

"*Spinning round, spinning round,*
Never makes nary sound.
Spinning round, spinning down,
Gets stuck out of town."

May June immediately fingered her sleeve and glanced out the back door where her answer sat on the porch.

"Not a spinning wheel," I said.

Sam slid the chunk of firewood into the open maw of the hot stove and closed the firebox door with a rag.

"Naw. Not a spinning wheel," Sam muttered to himself. "*Gets stuck out of town?* . . . Wagon wheel, wagon wheel." He was yelling and jumping up and down. "You know it's a wagon wheel."

*   *   *

THIS TIME, I wrote out my report to Vance in the plainest terms possible. Four men had been killed since I had arrived just a week before, bringing the total that I was aware of to thirteen. I went on to say that somehow my investigation into federal disability payments had seemed to speed up the killings if anything, making it more dangerous than ever to be a Union veteran. I was out in the countryside, finding my way, searching for answers, and getting shot at. The fact that I'd been shot at must mean I was making progress, but I wasn't sure just how. I thought of Mitch Randall and his speculations. *I believe the answer is right in front of me,* I concluded the letter. *As yet, I haven't sunk deeply enough into this place to take its pulse, to grasp the sinews of life here.* I thought of Sarah and Sam Freeman and the life they led. *But I intend to. And when I do find my way in, I think the killer will appear.*

*   *   *

MAY JUNE'S SUPPER was a grand affair, the three of us making a little family around the dining room table. There were slabs of fried catfish, cabbage fried in the same skillet, and big, doughy cathead biscuits. I sat in Campbell's place, May June defiantly in Mrs. Campbell's chair, and Sam in what we called the apostle chair, where I sat the first night I was there. We ignored the chairs of the two dead men leaning perfectly against the edge of the table with their ceremonious napkins draped over the chairbacks. It was darkening down outside as if to rain, but inside we laughed and ate. And slowly, ever so slowly, I fell into the rhythm that the two of them had created together when they were alone. The rhythm of conversation in which May June took her part, talking with her face and her hands, and of course with her full, brown eyes. Earlier in the day, she had seemed nervous for the first time since I'd known her, and several times I had caught her staring intently, almost as if trying to read my mind. At the supper table, though, she relaxed, caught up in the boy's foolishness.

When there was aught but fish bones on our plates and biscuit crumbs scattered on the tablecloth, Sam spoke up suddenly.

"Alright then, Jake, I got one for you."

"Did you already try it on May June?"

"Nope," he said cagily. "Nope, she don't know it. Neither one of you has a chance with it, I say."

"Go on."

He said it with an odd, incantatory tone, not unlike the rhythm his mother had used that morning with *whirly-go-whackum.*

"Threw a rock, threw a reel,
Threw an old spinning wheel.
Threw a sheep shank bone,
Such a riddle never known."

I noticed how Sam's face was thin and freckled like Sarah's. He was holding it perfectly still, his lips pressed tightly together. I thought about the day, searching for something that might have set the riddle in motion inside his head. Fish bones were piled on our plates.

"The river," I said. "The river throws up everything it swallows.

"Hell no," Sam said, "though that ain't such a bad guess." May June rolled her eyes—apparently she thought it was a god-awful guess.

"The wind," I said. "The wind throws everything around when it blows hard enough. Once, in the spring of 1863, just when—"

"Not the wind," Sam said, a hint of glee creeping into his voice. "Not even close."

May June stood up in her place, rising in frustration it seemed to me. Her lips were moving, as they often did, but no words came, of course. With her strong right hand, she sliced a jagged line down through the air from her shoulder to the tabletop.

Unnerved, I turned back to Sam. "I don't know," I admitted. "I don't . . ."

Sam turned to May June, giving her a fair chance.

"Lightning," she whispered.

Time stopped. Though the clock in the hallway kept ticking, not having heard. Sam was turned fully to her, mouth hung open. But she would not even look at him, for she was staring into my face in angry frustration.

"Is . . . *lightning,* you . . . cretin," she said in a rusty whisper.

CHAPTER ELEVEN

After Sam was safely asleep in the hay barn, I pulled May June by her bare arm into the dining room, where I forced her to sit with me at the table.

"When in God's name did you decide you could talk?"

She shrugged.

"I don't care. You understand that I don't care when or why or even how?"

Her whole body took on the same intensity as when she'd said the word *lightning* out of pure frustration.

"Who's doing it?"

Her wide eyes asked the question—doing what?

"You know why I'm here, and you keep adding your mysterious notations to the list. Who's killing off the Yank veterans? Who in hell is murdering these men?"

Her face took on a veil of what could only be sadness, and I got the odd sense that she was trying to decide whether to reveal what she knew out of concern . . . genuine concern for *me*. And as angry with her as I was, I resisted the urge to raise my voice or strike her. I was glad I did because she suddenly got up and walked around the end of the table and, with a startling dramatic flourish, picked up one of the two missing sons' chairs and slammed it down on all four legs and then picked up the carefully folded napkin and tossed it on the table as if it were waiting there for someone to take it up.

"Yes," I said. "I know both boys are dead and buried on the ridge behind us. That's not what I said. I asked who is—"

She kicked the other chair violently away from the table so that the napkin fluttered into the still air. The chair bounced off the wall and skittered on its back across the floor. She made a motion with her hand and arm as if she was hanging herself, as if to say *dead man*, and then pointed at the chair she'd kicked against the wall.

I stepped toward the downed chair and pointed. "That one's dead?"

She nodded so violently that sprockets of her braided hair shook loose from the bundle on the back of her head.

"Well, then what about that one?" I pointed at the chair that sat square to the table, its napkin lying before it.

She rolled her eyes in exasperation.

"Speak, damn it, May June. I know you can. If you can say *lightning, cretin*, you can say what is sitting in that chair!"

She walked out of the room and returned a moment later with our list of veterans and the penknife from her table. Laid the list on the table in front of the chair, as if setting a place for a meal. Folded the napkin and laid it carefully beside the list. Then she unlocked the blade of the knife from its handle and stabbed it down through the list with a solid *thunk* of steel into wood, pinning the list to the oak tabletop. She pointed at the chair and then at the list, looking at me with all the intensity of that knife striking.

"Lord . . . God," I muttered slowly. "That's the prison-camp son, isn't it? He's not dead, is he?"

She didn't have to nod, it seemed so suddenly, painfully obvious.

"He survived the camp somehow and he's laying out, killing as he goes?"

Her mouth formed a word, even though it made no sound. *Yes* was the word.

"How do you know this?"

She pulled me into the kitchen, where she looked around before taking a peck basket off the shelf. She put the basket on the table and mimicked putting food into it. Then she put the empty basket over her arm and became an eerie rendition of Mrs. Campbell. With the basket pulling down her left arm and her right crooked as if carrying the crazy woman's Bible, she marched to the back door and out onto the porch as if to head up the side of the mountain.

"I know," I said. "I followed her once. She only went as far as the cemetery. Where there are two gravestones, by the way."

May June shook her head furiously. She went back into the kitchen and tossed the basket aside and then knelt down beside the stove, where she acted out praying, her hands clasped in front of her face and her mouth moving, only this wasn't peaceful prayer—this was tortured, sweaty prayer. Then, quick as lightning flash herself, she stood up and pointing at the space in empty air where a second before she'd been Mrs. Campbell praying, she became simple May June again but with her hand cupped behind her ear and her head turned, listening . . . listening. *Jesus, Mary, and Joseph,* I thought, *she's even heard the crazy woman praying about him.*

"How long have you known this?" I demanded. "How the hell long have you let me wander around in the dark like an idiot?"

She raised her eyebrows at me in an ironic repetition of the look she'd given me that morning, the look that said I hadn't been honest with her till the sheriff showed up. And now it seemed, she was reminding me of that. "Fair enough," I said. "But how long have you suspected?"

There was a calendar hanging on the wall with a picture of praying Jesus for the illustration. She pointed to that very day and then skipped back in time with her finger—one, two days. She pointed at her ear and then at the imaginary figure of Mrs.

Campbell praying by the stove. She had heard the old woman praying while I was at the Freeman farm.

"Those marks on the disability list," I demanded. "You began those days ago. You could see the pattern even before you knew the killer?"

She shrugged and nodded.

"What does he look like?" I asked hoarsely. "The missing boy, what does he look like? How tall? How broad? How fair?"

Eyes wide, she considered. For the first time, I'd asked her a question she didn't know the answer to.

Suddenly, she raised her hand with a forefinger pointing up, as if sensing a new thought. She grabbed me by the arm and dragged me across the hall to the room where the Campbells slept, since Mrs. Campbell wasn't steady enough to navigate the stairs. There, faced with the closed door, she paused. I guessed that this was a room forbidden to her, and I could feel the muscles in her arms and shoulders tighten, as if she were gathering herself. Then she turned the knob, pushed the door open, and we crept in.

Nothing. Even with the moonlight through the window, it was too dark to see. The shape of a bed in the middle of the room, and dark objects against the walls, more furniture perhaps, but beyond that we couldn't see. She left me alone for a moment and then returned from the kitchen with a lighted candle, her bare feet brushing the floorboards.

The candle cast only the thinnest, flickering glow through the room, as if the darkness there was thicker than night, thick enough to snuff the tiny flame. But shielded by May June's hand, it gave us just enough illumination to find what she was looking for—a flat object like a small book bound in velvet, lying on the bedside table.

I carried it into the kitchen, where I popped the tiny catch holding it closed and opened up the two-hinged boards that held the image of the dead Campbell boys. On the left-hand board was the Twenty-Third Psalm pasted carefully in and framed by the edges of the faded velvet that bound the little book. On the right, was a tintype of two painfully thin young men standing on either side of a drum, ramrod stiff and tall, one with his hand thrust into his Confederate gray blouse like Napoleon and the other with his hand on the grips of an impossibly large pistol thrust into his belt. They each had the thin, sharp face they'd inherited from Obediah, thin shoulders, and long, lanky arms. I shivered in the dark, dense air. I didn't have to ask which was the prison-camp son, for I knew that version of the Campbell face already. It had appeared to me ghostlike in the middle of one long night, staring at the house in painful loneliness.

When May June first brought the lit candle into the bedroom, I had noticed a bulky Bible on the opposite bedside table. Now I led her back to the bedroom and moved her candle hand down close to the holy book. I opened the heavy pages to the middle, where the family records would be. At the very end of a long list of names, birth and death dates carefully recorded, were written *Thomas James Campbell* and *Matthew Mark Campbell*, recorded in a spidery script that swam in the yellow light. Beside Thomas's name were his birth and death, righteously recorded. The same beside Matthew's name—except that the second date, the date that should have noted his death, was struck through with one victorious slash of ink. May June's hand was shaking, and I heard her gasp. "And the angel of death shall rise again," I said, taking her arm to steady her. "Rise and walk the earth."

CHAPTER TWELVE

The next day, Friday, I intended to head back up the creek to Freeman's as soon as possible. If she was right and one of the Campbell boys was abroad in the country, then it made sense to at least warn the Yanks who were still alive, still looking over their shoulders everywhere they went. And the only ones I knew how to find quickly in all that tumbled country were Ben and George Freeman.

It was barely light when Sam and I shared a pan of eggs and a pone of corn bread with May June. I was already thinking of heading out. But even as we sat eating on the back porch, there came the faintest tapping from the front of the house. "Woodpecker," Sam guessed.

But it wasn't a woodpecker. It was a large, timid man named Alfred Dockery, who had fought in Company C of the Second North Carolina Mounted Infantry with the Freeman brothers and a number of others on our list. He was a farmer, like most of the others. Alf was tall, broad, and strong, but of all those we interviewed there in the mountains, he was the most shy and, therefore, the most maddening. I thought that I was going to have to threaten him with a broken head just to get him to sit down and tell his tale.

But sit he did, eventually, and I figured that a brief interview wouldn't delay for long the search for Matthew Campbell. I was glad, then, that I waited, because Alf Dockery had something long hidden to say.

With some embarrassment, he showed me his right hand, which till then he had kept hidden behind the bib of his overalls. His hand was perfectly whole, perfectly complete except that he had no thumb.

Dockery's thumb had been crushed while on bridge building duty on some lonely stream in Kentucky. He was a timid man, and he had fainted away when his hand was caught between two beams. When he came to, he found his hand wrapped in the town doctor's bandages, and he was reduced to standing one-armed guard duty while the rest of Company C played at reassembling a railroad bridge burned to the water by Reb raiders.

He signed his docket with his left hand, and when May June saw his handwriting, she nodded and pointed it out to me. It was ornate and yet perfectly readable. With Sam's prodding, he admitted that he had won fourth prize in a left-handed writing contest spon-sored by the *Soldier's Friend*, a journal for Yank veterans published in New York. To win, you had to establish that you'd lost your right hand or arm in the war and learned to write with your left. He was embarrassed to admit it because he'd only lost a thumb and he was competing against men who'd given up far more.

"You still had to learn to write with your left hand," I offered.

"I do console myself with that fact," he admitted. "But even so, I wonder if I should have accepted the fifty-dollar prize."

*   *   *

AS HE WAS leaving, I walked out to the road with him, this large, gentle man who seemed too quiet to have ever fought in a war.

"Did you know the Campbell boys?" I asked. "Before or during the war?"

"I knew them before," he said. "Once it all started, we seldom saw each other, as they were Confederate stalwarts and my father was a Union patriot. And then, as soon as the Sixty-Fourth was mustered, both the Campbell boys volunteered."

"One of the Campbells was killed in Tennessee, is that correct, and was brought home for burial?"

"Thomas. He was the eldest son, and his father's favorite."

"And the other?"

"Matthew. His name was Matthew. He was the happy-go-lucky one, his mother's boy, was meant to be a minister, believe it or not...Why do you ask, Mr. Ballard? He died of dysentery in a Yankee prison camp."

"Call me Jake. I ask because I'm trying to find out who is killing off the Union veterans."

He paused to consider. "George Freeman is a friend of mine, Jake. And he tells me that I can trust you. That's why I was willing to come here today, even with the killer lurking along the roads. So I will tell you that Matt Campbell and I were boyhood friends, but he refused to speak to me once I made it known that I wouldn't join the Confederate army. He and his brother could be . . . very high-minded."

"I think he's alive," I said. "And I think he may be involved in the killing. Do you have any idea where he might be if he were hiding out?"

Dockery shook his head sadly. "No. No, our friendship ended long ago. He's only a whispering spirit to me now." He turned to walk away so suddenly that I wondered if I had made a mistake in opening my mind to him. But after a few determined strides up the road he began to slow, and then he turned back to face me again. "The Matthew Campbell I knew was no killer. Just the opposite. I was insulted to hear you speak his name in such a fashion. But I will say this. Whatever Matt believed, he believed with all his heart. And nothing you could say or do would sway him. Do you hear me, Jake Ballard? Nothing." His voice was breaking.

I was nodding slowly, praying that he would keep talking.

"Foolishly, Matt believed in the war. He believed God was on the side of the South and because of that, the South could not lose."

"Would he keep fighting even if most of the known world had given it up?"

He paused again, longer this time than before. "When I heard that he had died at Douglas and was brought home in a box, I wept for the loss of it all. He was such a . . . beautiful young man. But now that I hear what you say . . . well, I hope he did die."

I was still nodding.

"He was too good for this world, and I hope that his soul has fled. I hope that he revels with the angels while we grovel here below."

*   *   *

BEFORE SAM AND I left for the Freeman farm, I confronted May June while the boy was packing his things. "I want you to leave," I told her. "Before Campbell and that witchy wife of his get back from Marshall, I want you to go on home and stay there."

Her eyes looked a question at me.

"I don't trust Campbell to keep his hands off you. That's why."

She shook her head impatiently and held up both hands, her fingers curled like claws, and I suddenly realized where the scratches I'd seen on Campbell's face had come from.

"Maybe you can fight him off," I admitted, "when she's in the house. But there's more to this now. If angel boy Matthew is behind the killings, then she at least knows it, and we just went pilfering through their bedroom. Go on home where you'll be safe."

She stood up straighter then and squared her shoulders. Tapped her chest and made a hard fist out of her hand. She meant to say that by God, she could take care of herself, and unfortunately, I believed her.

CHAPTER THIRTEEN

Sam and I reached Anderson Branch and Sarah's cabin by noon. We found her at home, weaving. She was in the middle of a difficult section and shouted down that she couldn't stop, so I climbed the ladder to the upper floor and watched her work. The pedals and beam of her loom continued their steady flow up and down, to-and-fro; she worked so fast that the whole affair seemed to hum like a beehive as she threw the shuttle.

"What's wrong?" she asked after a moment, glancing up for an instant from her work.

"What do you mean?"

"I can tell by your face that something's happened. You know something."

I told her about Matthew Campbell. That I thought he was alive, that he was laying out, that he might still be fighting the war.

"He lived through Camp Douglas? That's what you're saying?"

I remembered that Young had died in Douglas. "That's the way it seems," I said quietly. "I think I had better warn Ben and George."

A stray strand of copper hair kept falling free into her face from where she had it pulled back, and she would twist her mouth to blow it to the side, out of her way, her hands busy at the loom.

After a moment, she spoke. "George will likely be in the orchard. Sammy can show you. Ben'll be up at his still. Sammy can take you there too . . . Here, come hold this thread till I can tie it off."

I held with my right hand where she showed me and watched how quickly and deftly her hands moved inside the workings of the loom, just at the edge where a complex web of brown thread met the solid weave of the cloth. "You can let go now," she said. "It's tight." She let her feet slip down to the floor from where they'd worked the four pedals, and somehow the sight of her bare feet moved me. They were small but strong, capable in a way I couldn't name. She straightened up from the sloped bench she'd been sitting on.

Without thinking, I reached out and tucked the stray hair behind her ear. She looked at me closely, her green eyes searching into mine in that single, quiet moment. "I'm sorry about Young," I whispered. "I don't mean to keep reminding you of him."

The corners of her eyes drew up ever so slightly, *almost smiling*, I thought. "Thank you," she whispered. "Here lately, I don't remember him so well as I used to . . ."

*   *   *

GEORGE WAS WORKING his own and several of Ben's boys in the orchard directly above his slapdash house. They were gathering apples for brandy making and pruning dead branches out of the trees. When I told him about Matt Campbell, he spit onto the ground beside a bushel basket half full of small, speckled green apples. "Could be," he said. "Could be the Campbell boy. He was awful bad to believe in things. If 'tis, we'll have to factor where he's layin' out and visit with him."

"Sammy's going to take me up to warn Ben."

George grinned. "Think you've earned the right to see into the family business, do you?"

"Well, I . . ."

"Don't signify, Jake. Once you've been there, you just take care to forget where it is. That's all that matters." He started laughing while he scrubbed at his mustache with a clotted handkerchief fished out of his overalls.

* * *

FROM THE ORCHARD, Sam and I walked up the path to Ben's cabin and beyond, past the springhouse, past the barn, and into the woods. When we entered the trees, the path became much less obvious, and I was glad then that I had Sam to show me the way. Freeman's Den was buried in an almost impenetrable laurel thicket where a shelf of rock was undercut to make a shallow cave, perhaps ten feet deep and thirty feet long. Where the rock face broke the dense web of mountain laurel, a stand of hemlocks had grown up, mostly hiding the cliff itself and creating something very close to a wall in front of the cave, so that the den was completely hidden from view. Ben Freeman himself was fond of saying that if it weren't for the smoke that seeped out when they were cooking the mash, not even a crow could tell where the operation was located.

The other advantage to Freeman's Den was fully illustrated when Sam led me up to it. You had to crawl on your hands and knees forty or fifty feet through the laurel hell to get to the cave, and as Sam explained, gasping, while we struggled through, Ben or George or whoever else would always hear you coming and could shoot you a half-dozen times before you could find a spot to stand up in. When we were about halfway through, a cold, clear voice from farther in clearly pronounced one word. "Abraham."

"Lincoln," Sam called back.

I could hear Ben Freeman chuckling from the green depths. "Come on, then," he said. "Mind your pecker."

When we finally reached the rock face and were able to stand, I saw that Freeman himself was seated on a cane-bottomed stool, smoking a pipe. He was situated at the mouth of what looked like a stone oven built against the rock, up under the roof of the cave. The double-barreled shotgun leaned against the face of the cliff not far away.

After we sat and caught up with our breathing, I told Ben about Matthew Campbell. How May June had named him, so to say, and Alf Dockery explained him.

"Matt Campbell *was* an awful pretty boy," Ben said after a moment between puffs on his pipe. "Seem to you that maybe Alf had some unholy yearnings after young Matthew when they were boys together?"

I nodded. "The thought crossed my mind."

"Funny he would tell you what he did then, isn't it?"

I glanced at Sam, who was crouched beside his uncle, studying the fire inside the oven.

"Maybe Dockery tried to do something about those yearnings, and Campbell didn't like it. Maybe Dockery got his feelings hurt."

Ben Freeman grinned through the smoke writhing around his beard from the pipe, and for a moment he reminded me of his brother George. They both saw the humor in the human condition. "Hell has no fury like a woman scorned," he offered.

"I've heard that said," I admitted. "'Course Dockery's still alive, so Campbell must retain some friendship for him."

Ben shrugged. "What do you think pushed Campbell over the edge? Prison camp?"

"I believe he was part of the firing squad that shot those men in Shelton Laurel."

Freemen glanced up from the fire. "Why do you say that?"

"Johnny Norton told me that both the brothers were there the morning of the execution. And being part of a firing squad has a way of eating the soul out of a man, especially a young, sensitive thing hardly more than a boy."

"I take your meaning," Freeman said quietly.

Sammy began to poke at the flames with a long pole that seemed shaped especially for the purpose, and I saw that the oven was deep, the coals themselves perhaps three or four feet back under a huge kettle that was built in on top of the firebox. Whatever was cooking had a strong, thick, sour smell, and I noticed bees circling the top of the kettle, looking for a way in.

"How in the world did you ever find this place?" I asked Ben. "Not hunting rabbits, that's for damn sure."

He grinned through the smoke again. "No. Back during the war, after a number of us decided we'd had enough of the Sixty-Fourth and came home to live, we discovered that the Home Guard wasn't having any of that. They intended to hunt us down and send us back under guard. Or hang us, shoot us outright. They hung three boys they caught over near Tennessee without benefit of judge nor jury. One was named Simmons, I recall."

"Seems like it would be easy to hide out. I couldn't even find myself back in here, let alone somebody else."

Sammy began to feed the fire, chunks of split wood from a stack farther under the lip of the cave.

"Oh, there's caves and shelters all up through the high mountains. But here's the thing about the Home Guard, when it's your cousin or your uncle who's huntin' you, he knows the territory just as good as you. And maybe he wants your land or your wife or your horse, so he's got what the lawyers like to call a motivation."

"A motive?"

Ben nodded. "He's got a motive to track you down and kill you, plus he knows from the start where you'll most likely run to earth. Not too hot, Sam. You'll scorch the mash."

"Ain't I been doing it?" Sam muttered.

"Don't say *ain't*," I said. "So who found this place?"

"I did. When I ran off from the Sixty-Fourth to get away from Keith and Allen, I thought I could live back home in peace, laying in the lap of my sweet bride. But damn if she wasn't worse than the Home Guard. So it wasn't long before I had double reason to hide out, and I needed a place where even she couldn't find me."

"I like it," I said, standing up to stretch. "Is there a back door?"

Sammy started to answer, but Ben cut him off. "A back door to hell? Of course there is, but you don't need to know where. Not just yet anyway."

*   *   *

BEFORE SAM AND I started down the mountain, Ben let Sam explain how they made a run of whiskey. The kettle, as they called it, was a twenty-gallon copper pot that was fitted carefully over the firebox and chinked in tight with rocks and clay. The mash, fermented corn was all Freeman used unless he was making brandy, was poured into the kettle when it was ready and cooked slowly until the alcohol began to evaporate off the makings. He called it "vapor-ate." The alcohol spirit or gas could only escape the kettle through a long copper tube that was coiled down through a barrel of cold water. "That's why they call it *spirits*," Sam said solemnly, obviously echoing his uncle. The gas turned to liquid again inside the tube because of the temperature of the water in the barrel, which ran constantly down from above by virtue of the wooden trough Ben had built to funnel it from a small spring in the rock. The spirit of the alcohol "densed" inside the tube, according to Sam, and when I glanced at Ben, he mouthed the word "condensed" around his pipe stem. And what dripped out the end of the copper tube where it emerged from the cooling barrel was pure alcohol.

Sam started into what happened next, what they did with the pure oil that came from the "first run," but Ben stopped him. "School is out for today," he said. "It'll be black dark before you've talked it into the jug ready to sip."

After a moment, the boy began to nod, lulled by the heat. When his chin was all the way down to his chest and he was slumped against the rock face, I asked Ben about the man he and George had supposedly killed.

He didn't hesitate for a moment in his reply. "He was a Ray

from over on Spring Creek. Had hair so red, you would call it orange, and an ugly scar that ran from one ear all the way under his chin and round to the back of his neck on the other side."

"Somebody tried to cut his throat," I said.

"Or tried to cut his damn head off. He was one of those who joined the Home Guard just to steal stock and roust out women and girls. He met his match with Harriet Freeman, though. He's lucky she didn't kill and eat him, especially when the detachment found our only horse and rode away with it."

"You figure that justified killing him after you got back home?"

"We didn't set out to kill him. We set out to get the horse back. It was midsummer of '65, but we figured we could still get a crop in, and at that point, getting a crop in meant survival. That horse is the prettiest strawberry roan mare you ever saw, and when we heard tell of her over the mountain in Spring Creek, we went looking, and we found Ray plowing with the very horse. So there was the orangey hair, the scar, and there was the damn horse."

"Seems fair enough," I admitted. "Judge and jury."

"We walked up, each holding a locust fence rail we found handy, and actually offered to parlay a bit, but then he pulled a knife and called George a harelipped son of a bitch. In case you haven't noticed, your fence rail is longer than your clasp knife, and we laid him low. George went into a fit and started stomping on him once he was down. Seems my brother didn't care for being called a harelip. After a bit, we collected the horse and came on back home. All I know beyond that is that he was still breathing when we left him lying in that field."

"So you didn't kill him outright?"

"Of course not. He didn't die till three days after. Could have died from most anything in that time. Probably caught a cold." Ben was grinning. "Besides which, there was a horse involved, which meant living or dying for a lot of us, so most mountain people would call what we did fair."

"Not like the man I'm after."

"The man *we're* after is killing indiscriminate, killing because he enjoys it. Hell, he can't even claim it's personal. The man we're after clomb up the ladder out of hell, and it's time we sent him on back."

CHAPTER FOURTEEN

Sam asked that I be allowed to sleep up in the loft that night. After a nod from me, Sarah agreed, only shaking her head and hoping out loud that the boy didn't rattle me like teeth in a gourd.

I fell asleep while he was still talking, telling another adventure of the mysterious Jack who could get himself into and out of any trade or trouble. Something about Jack and a magic bucket. At least I think it was a bucket. And later, if he tossed and turned, I was too tired to know it.

What I found out in the morning is that I woke Sam up instead. In the late, middle watch, a few hours before dawn, I kicked him awake by thrashing around, fighting some invisible forms, crying to be let go. I scared him so badly that he leaped down the ladder to get his mother, who came back up with him, bare armed in her shift. Together they held me down and she talked me partially awake. When she realized just how lost I was in some dark place, she wrapped herself in her shawl and sent Sam downstairs to sleep in her bed. Only later did she tell me that he was so scared that for once he went without complaint. At the time, I didn't know it because I was on . . . *that hard, cold wooden tabletop. My uniform blouse is wadded under my head, and a bloody sheet thrown over me. Two Negro men are tying my arm to a plank, and a man I had never seen before is standing behind . . .*

Somewhere a voice is whispering. "Say it. Say it all." I think it is a female voice.

"Chloroform?" he asks the empty air. "Done gone, boss . . . Been gone, boss." And I beg and beg for my arm. Try to raise it, but it is already lashed down. Chop off the fingers, I say. Please chop off my fingers.

"Chop off my fingers," her voice whispers. "Please not my arm."

Leave me a hand. Please, God, you can manage. God says if I leave the hand the fever will destroy you. Please, God, please. And almighty God lays down his bloody saw, wipes his own hands on the edge of the sheet, and picks up a heavy, double-edged catlin. I began to rise up, rise above the bloody tabletop.

"No, no," her voice says. "Tell it all. You must tell all of it."

And God says let his hand be held down on the plank. Say the Negro men, "What hand, boss?" What's left of it, God says. Wipes the catlin on his sleeve and bends to his task. With the pain I began to slip deeper into that hole, and what light there was above seemed as distant as a star.

Suddenly I felt my left hand rise up from the splintered plank and float in the black air. Then, most strange, the palm of that battered hand came to rest against a woman's living breast. I could feel the weight of her breast against my hand and the pulse of blood within. I could feel the faintest stirring of her nipple, like a ripening berry. I gasped in wonder.

My head lay not on a bloody Union blouse but in Sarah's lap. There was a single flickering candle that seemed to flame in her hair. It came to me that I might be in her barn rather than that hell hole outside Fredericksburg. Or no, not her barn . . . but could it be the loft of her cabin? "Please don't cut off my arm," I whispered to her. I wanted to feel her breast forever and ever. "I don't want to die," I tried to say. "I don't want to die."

"No, no," she said gently. "I will never take your arm, just your fingers. You are not going to die here. Not now." She shifted in the wavering candle light, moved her legs out from under my head, and pulled Sam's feather pillow there. Her face was even closer now, but her breast seemed to float away from me. I could see her eyes so close; they were forest green even in the pale-yellow light. "But I am going to take your dream. I'm going to take it from you now, Jacob Ballard, and you will never have it again." She leaned closer still, and I could feel her warm breath on my face. "*Fly three angels from the North, ride three angels from the South. Winter, spring, summer, fall.* Open your mouth, Jake . . . Open your mouth and blow out all the air that is in you. All of it. *Father, Son, and the Holy Ghost.* Slowly . . . slowly . . . blow. *Fly three angels from the North, ride three angels from the South. Winter, spring . . . Ahhh!*"

She closed her eyes tightly. There was no color in the loft then, only shades of gray-black. She sucked into her lungs, into her soul or so I thought. All my dark breath, with a long, shuddering gasp, she took it all in. And then, ceasing to breathe at all, collapsed beside me on the narrow cot.

And so I became *her* nurse for the first time. As the candle guttered out, I wrapped her in Sam's quilt and held her while she shuddered and shook and cried out in a deep voice. Cried out from some place far deeper than sleep, fallen into what I could only assume was a barn full of demons with knives and saws. I held her more closely than I had ever held anyone before in my life as she suffered through the horrors of a dream that even then was fading from my memory. Held her because it was all I knew to do until she stopped shaking.

In the early, misty light of dawn, her breath came easy once again. And as she slept, I gently wiped a froth of blood from her lips with the tail of my shirt and gazed into her face. Even the scattering of freckles over her nose and cheeks were pale now. I was dumb with wonder. Bending over, as gently as I could, I kissed each trembling eyelid.

CHAPTER FIFTEEN

Sarah was nervous and still all that cool morning, even sitting quietly by the fire while I fried the three of us some eggs in a skillet over the coals. I had never known her quiet before, and it was upsetting to me. Even with Sam chattering happily away, eating up my lesson in camp cooking, there was a stillness inside the cabin that felt damp and cold. Almost a stillness of the battlefield or the prison camp.

Once, when Sammy was gone to milk the cow, I offered to find or fix anything she might want.

"I'm so cold," she said. "Midwinter cold. Would you stir up the fire and bring me the quilt from the bed?"

I did so and asked her about her mind, whether it was haunted by saws and knives.

"No, no. Nothing like that. But I want to tell you something that came to me in the night. Something true, I think."

I knew enough to sit quiet and listen.

"I feel like I know you now, know you from the inside. And I want to be fair with you. I know you are a good man, but it broke my heart and most of my mind when Young died, and I can't walk through that valley again. I cannot lose another and live. I cannot. So when I push you away, you need to understand. It's not that I sleep with a ghost. It's that I can survive with sleeping by myself. I'll never be widowed again, and I can live out my time till Sammy is on his own."

"That's no life," I said, although with real horror, I saw that what she described was exactly what I'd been doing myself. Sleepwalking through the days, more dead than alive.

"No. No, it isn't. But it's safe. It's sure. And if I think of myself as Mrs. Young Freeman, waiting patiently to be reunited in heaven, then nothing can ever cause me that kind of pain again."

"I'm little better than a dead man myself," I whispered. "I admit that. But you are more deserving than I am. You have earned better than a corpse for a husband. There's too much life left in you for that." I thought of her living breast, the nipple stiffening against my palm. "Your heart is beating even now."

*   *   *

AT MIDDAY OUR salvation arrived in the form of Mitch Randall, who came striding into the yard leading a pack mule and singing a sprightly version of "The Battle Hymn of the Republic."

He set up shop inside a lean-to shed at the top of the pasture, where once Sam and I shepherded an ewe through the front of the shed, Sarah could slide a rail into the door framing and trap the sheep in with Mitch. He would then grab the ewe by her wooly head and slam her into the wall of the shed or throw her on the ground, and then pull her up against his body so that she sat on her tail with her legs stuck straight out in front of her, pinning her against his stomach with his half-an-arm and shearing with his right hand. Once the ewe was off her feet and pinned against Mitch, it relaxed completely, and he could begin to work. The first time I saw him do it, manhandling the hundred-plus pound ewe with what was left of one arm and shearing away long swaths of wool with his only hand, I realized with a shock how incredibly strong he was—strong like a smith is strong, but a smith working with kicking, bleeding life.

The day was hot, and the smell of raw lanolin, sweat, and manure mixed with the faint iron tang of blood from where Mitch nicked first one and another with his shears. Fate was not allowed in the pasture during shearing and howled from where she was tied at the cabin.

But I have to report that it wasn't so much the shearing that brought Sarah back to life; it was watching Sam and me herding sheep. Yes, I slipped and fell again and again, once into the edge of the manure pile. Yes, the boy and I ran into each other, both of us cursing. And yes, it took us longer to corral one of the ewes than it took Mitch to shear it. At one point, when I looked up while helping Sam to his feet, I saw his mother sitting on the ground laughing, laughing so hard she couldn't stand up.

After the ewes came the two rams, and Sarah took pity on us. She shook shelled corn in a gourd, and they came lumbering up to the shed. Even so, Mitch waved me into the shed with him to handle those two brutes, one by one. The rams each swung a ball sac between his back legs that would have done justice to a much larger beast, and the rams themselves were hell on the hoof once they were trapped in close quarters. We would each grab a horn, which would earn one of us, usually me, a bone-crunching throw into the shed wall. The language inside the shed grew heated, and at one point Mitch kicked one of the rams so hard it began to choke. But shear them he did, and when we emerged victorious, our arms draped over each other's shoulders, Sarah threw her own arms up in the air and danced a jig.

While Mitch and I washed off in the creek below the pasture, I told him about Matthew Campbell, and because he couldn't recall his features, I described the boy in detail. He thanked me and said he'd spread the warning as he worked his way from farm to farm.

He and I climbed back up through the pasture, and we all drank fresh cider under the shade of the ancient oak tree that guarded the side of the cabin. Drank deep and reenacted our epic battles with the sheep.

*   *   *

WHEN MITCH LEFT, taking a quarter of the wool as payment, Sam accompanied him down as far as the road, leaving Sarah and me suddenly and unexpectedly alone. "Let's sit in the sun," she said after a minute. And we helped each other up, awkwardly, and eased out into the light, sitting down again on the edge of her front porch.

I didn't know what to say after our morning despair but spoke anyway. "Are you sure that you're all right? . . . I mean after last . . . ?"

"After eating your dream?" she asked without opening her eyes. She was leaning back against a porch post, letting the sunlight wash over her face.

"Yes. The nightmare you took from me, does it . . . ?"

"It goes *through* me, Jake. I'm like an open window. It blows through me and away."

"Are you certain sure? It never . . ." And only then did I realize that the dream no longer had any purchase within me.

"It's gone, isn't it?" she asked. "I can tell by your voice."

"Yes, but . . ."

"Don't worry. That place and time have left this world." Without opening her eyes, she grinned, and the sunlight in her hair flashed red and gold. "Elseways, it would haunt us both now, wouldn't it?"

What I didn't know how to say to her—not then—was that even though the dream was washed out of me, the deep stain of it might remain.

CHAPTER SIXTEEN

That afternoon, Sam was dispatched to take Uncle George across the mountain path to Big Pine and up to the barn at Worley's, where the dance was to be. Not so much to get him there but to get him back again at midnight, Sarah explained, when George would be spinning in his boots, drunk on whiskey and music.

Sarah and I took a more leisurely route, walking over the ridge farther down by a well-traveled trail, so that she could show me a thing or two about what she kept referring to as "your country."

We crossed Big Pine Creek on a broad chestnut footlog. After a few minutes walking up the Big Pine Road, we came to a silent crossroads beside a log church so small that it couldn't have held more than two dozen saints packed in shoulder to shoulder. Sarah pointed on up ahead and said, "That way's the way to the dance. And that"—she pointed up the smaller dirt track to the right—"that's the way up to Bearwallow Gap."

We were halted at the crossroads, standing in the sun. She slipped her hand under my left elbow and rested it there, almost as if she was supporting me. "We have time for a visit up there before the dance if you want to see where you grew up."

"I don't believe there is a place called Bearwallow Gap," I said. "It sounds like something out of a dime-store novel."

"I guess there was a bear in a wallow," she said and shrugged. "Some years, there are more bears than people around here. They eat calves and stray children, you know?"

"Do they eat Yankees?"

"Like you?"

I nodded.

She shook her head slowly. "Meat's too stringy."

"How do you know where I grew up anyway?" I asked suddenly. It sounded mean up against her playfulness, even though I tried not to say it that way.

"I asked around," she admitted. "After Sammy and I found you naked in the ditch, I was curious about where such a creature as yourself might have come from."

"Even after you saw what I looked like?" For some reason, I was smiling.

"You didn't look like much that day, I grant. Are you afraid to go up there?" She nodded toward the gap.

I didn't say anything.

"What are you afraid of?"

"I don't know. Maybe that I'll recognize it. Maybe that it will look like home."

"See, just like when we first met. Me asking you ten dozen questions, and you not even remembering your own name."

"It might be Jacob," I said. "God knows."

She cocked her head to one side in her friendly way, her eyes alight with humor. "Well hell, Jacob," she said. "If coming home scares you that bad . . . then you need to get it over with."

*   *   *

WE CLIMBED UP and up the trail, for that's about all it was, winding back and forth across the face of the ridge. We walked slowly, in part because I wasn't used to the country, and the cool air under the trees burned in my lungs. Sarah herself seemed dreamy, almost as if strolling along rather than climbing a steep place. I was sure she was walking easy, letting me keep up.

"Hold," I called out after a bit. "I'm not used to this."

"Don't they have any hills in Washington, the District of Columbia?" she asked innocently.

"Flat as a plate," I gasped, "plus, there are streetcars . . . You can ride . . . most anywhere."

"A streetcar?" she asked. "Describe it to me."

*   *   *

AFTER WE TOPPED the ridge and worked our way down on the far side, she became something I had never seen in her before that day. *Solemn*, I suppose I should call it. Quiet, like she had been that morning, but this was different. She was quiet now out of respect for where we were, the place we'd come to.

She led me first off the trail up a narrow animal path through an old, overgrown field. I noticed some scrubby apple trees lost in a sea of tall summer weeds. We made our way through the brush toward a single tall stand of trees on a rise in the middle of the field.

"It's a grove of those trees you called . . . hemlocks."

"Look deeper, under the trees."

I took a step forward, farther in, and saw a stone chimney rising up. Another step, and I could see that there was a stone foundation built out from the chimney, a rectangle of carefully laid fieldstone, perhaps ten feet by twenty. There was a large, flat rock just before the open mouth of the fireplace, a hearthstone, I realized.

I walked forward into the dense, green shade of the trees, into the depths of green light and shadow. My legs took me forward of their own volition, and I stepped over the lip of the foundation and into what had been the floor of a log cabin. Opposite the chimney, there remained a notched corner of dark-gray chestnut logs, still woven tightly together, ends blackened by fire—the fire that had taken the rest of the place. I found myself on the hearthstone and knelt there, and then I reached out with both hands to the rocks of the chimney. Locked my elbows and leaned forward with my hands—good hand and bad—pressed hard against the cold stone of the fireplace. My eyes were closed, and I was listening. Listening for what, I wasn't sure. Voices, perhaps.

"What do you remember?" she whispered.

"I used to crouch right here in the mornings," I began. "Right here by the fire to try to get warm after crawling down the ladder out of the loft. I would pretend I was a mouse and that I was so small no one could see me."

"Was your mother here? Was she cooking?"

"She was. Corn mush. Porridge, she would call it, if there was even a scrap of meat in it. And when it was done, she would call me to come to the table, looking all around as if she couldn't see me by the fire."

I turned slowly and let myself sit. Sit with my back to the side of the fireplace and my legs drawn up against my chest.

"Where was your father?"

"He was outside already, doing his chores. We couldn't eat till he came back in. We could hear him coming along. In the winter time especially, hocking and spitting as he came along the yard boards."

"Did you have milk . . . with your porridge?"

I nodded, the back of my head scratching against the cold rock. "He would bring it in the bucket when he came in. He had already milked. My sisters . . . my sisters and I would have milk and porridge. Sometimes an egg."

"Did he love you, your father?"

"Well, you know he did." I could feel the hot tears burning down my cheeks. "When he came in, he would call for me, and my mother would pretend like she couldn't see me anywhere. He would hand her the bucket of milk to strain so we could drink it, and then he'd pick me up from the fireplace." I patted the hearthstone. "He'd pick me up and toss me in the air. His hands and his clothes were cold. In the winter, they were hard and rough with the cold. And he would carry me to the table where . . ."

"What? What is it?"

"Where there were five of us. Mama and Daddy and sisters. Mean old beanpole sisters."

"What's wrong, Jacob?"

"I don't know. I feel like I've been missing him my entire life. Wondering and dreaming about him. Stuck off in Pennsylvania with a pack of damn women and missing him."

My tears had stopped but even so she came and sat beside me on the hearth and held my ringing head against her chest. In the stillness under the trees, I could hear my own heart beating, and just there, I could hear hers as well.

"They wanted you," she said. "He loved you, and they wanted you."

I nodded that it was true. My ear and the side of my face rubbing against the soft cloth of her dress, I nodded. "They did want me," I whispered. "It was so long ago, and there's not been much wanting since, but when my father was alive, they wanted me."

CHAPTER SEVENTEEN

At the cemetery, we found them. Across the gap and up the face of the little round hill beyond, we found a cluster of Ballards, my father and his kin. Most of the graves were marked with simple, rough fieldstones stood on end, but here and there was a chiseled name—Buckner and Robbins and Anderson as well as Ballard. There they were, and there he was. The stone, though flat and simple, was granite, meaning someone had loved him, according to Sarah, loved him past caring about the cost.

NATHANIEL JAMES BALLARD. 1821–1852.
The Lord is my Shepherd.

We sat together, she and I, resting against the low stone wall that surrounded the Ballard plot. The simple wall around the graves reminded me in an eerie way of what was left of the foundation of the cabin up on the hill. She showed me a relic she'd found at the home place. It was made of wood, intricate and worn from use.

"What is it?" I asked quietly.

"A shuttle," she said. "Your mother must have kept a loom, for there's no other reason for it to be there."

"Is it like the one you use?" It was pleasant in the sun, and our voices were quiet.

"Exactly like. Made of dogwood, I expect."

"Dogwood . . . tree?"

She nodded. "It's one of the hardest woods there is. Harder than maple or walnut. Not so pretty, but much harder. It's almost impossible to fashion but it lasts forever."

She let me hold it, and it was heavier than I expected.

"I don't remember a loom," I said. "The cabin was so small."

"On the porch maybe," she shrugged. "Most folks dismantle a loom and store it in the barn in summer when they're too busy to weave." She nodded at the grave that was only a few feet away. "What else do you recall," she asked, "about your family?"

"About him, not so much. Overalls hanging on a peg. Coughing while he slept. The pine box laid out when he died, and my sisters whispering in a corner. But more and more, since I've been back, I remember things. Smells, sounds—little, small details rinsed in light."

She turned slightly such that she could see my face more easily. "Like what?"

"I recall that we had a little book, a primer, that my mother would teach me out of. There was a picture of a bull beside the letter B, a picture of a lady's fan beside the letter F. I asked what was a *fan*, and she was puzzled to tell me, as she had no fan . . . I remember the smell of the horse in the barn when I had to stand on the bucket to brush him. His name was Bill, that horse, and I would make up songs to sing to him while I brushed him . . . And I recall that no matter the day or the hour, my father always told me to put up my tools. 'Son, put up your tools, and they'll be there tomorrow when you reach forth your hand.' And I remember that when my father died, my mother said over and over 'I hate this place, I hate this place,' while she wept."

"She blamed the mountains for killing him?"

"She thought life here was too harsh and the work killed him . . . I expect she blamed her father too. Probably the whole Vance family."

"What do you think?"

"I think he must have died of consumption. My earliest memory is of him coughing in the night, keeping me awake. After two years in the hospitals, listening to men die of every possible disease imaginable, I think back and I believe it must have been his lungs that killed him."

"Do *you* hate this place?" She was frowning in concentration.

"I meant to, I confess it. I came down here ready to hate this place. Hit and miss, here and gone again. Back to Washington City."

"What do you intend now?"

"I don't know. I don't know where I belong. I never imagined there was anything here." I nodded at the headstone just in front of us. "Anything like him. Or anything like you."

"What do you mean?"

"I intend to find out for certain who's killing off the Yanks. I do intend that. And if it's this damn Matthew Campbell, I intend to deal with him."

"What do you mean, *anything like me?*"

"Isn't there any real law in this place? The sheriff seems like a good man, but Lord, there's a dozen men dead—"

"What do you mean, Jake?"

"By what?"

"By *anything like me?* You didn't know there was anything like me in . . ." she waved her arm as if to indicate all the towering mountains around us and said, "this place?"

"I never saw anybody with such a funny damn way of doing as you. I never . . ."

"Well, the hell with . . ." There was a hot flush rising from her neck up into her cheeks, and she struggled to push up and away.

"When the sun hits your hair, it gleams. And so many freckles! I never knew there could be so many freckles on one woman's skin. I never knew."

She eased back down beside me on the grass, having finally realized I was teasing. "You haven't seen the half of them," she said ruefully.

"No, I never imagined that I would care about this place. Or about you."

"What are you saying, Jake?"

"I have no idea." It was true. The words were coming out before the thoughts themselves had time to form. "I have no idea what I'm saying. But I would like to count them. God knows."

"What in the world? Count what!"

"Those freckles. All of them. One by one."

She was grinning, there in the sun. "Just how do you propose to do that? Some of them are hard to find."

"Why, I'd count 'em with the tip of my little finger," I said with all the seriousness I could muster. "Or the tip of my tongue for the harder ones."

"Oh, my Lord God!"

She jumped up then, sure enough. But she was laughing, laughing so hard that she almost tripped over a gravestone as she ran away down the hill toward the path. Leaving me to follow her as best I could.

CHAPTER EIGHTEEN

The music in Henry Worley's barn came and went in great tides of sound and liquor and dancing. People also came and went, children as well as grandmothers and grandfathers. There was dancing, so I suppose you could call it a barn dance, like we had in Pennsylvania, but the dancing was sometimes inside and sometimes outside by the bonfire that burned high out in the open space before the barn. Sometimes there was a banjo brought back from the war and several fiddles outside by the fire and a lonely fiddle inside, playing the most plaintive melody while an aged grandmother sang ever so softly a ballad tune that could only have come by ship from the old country. And once I recognized George's version of "Soldier's Dream," played fast as a dance tune. As jar and jug made their rounds, there were at least three fights that boiled up, two between hard-fisted men and one between equally hard-fisted women over the prostrate body of a man both claimed an interest in.

I sat or stood, sometimes with Ben Freeman, as early in the evening we made a point of warning the Yanks in attendance about Matthew Campbell. Sometimes I went about with Sam as he introduced me to children, dogs, and grandfathers so old and toothless their noses scratched their chins. And yes, he introduced me to the Anderson girl, who was too shy to speak even a word where I might hear it.

I mostly went about with Sarah, I confess it, under the devilish influence of the music. And listened to the banjo and fiddle while she sang under her breath the words that accompanied, letting me hear what story followed the ringing, swinging notes. Dancing? Why, even an old soldier like me, wounded in heart and mind, can dance like a heathen when he's chased a swallow of liquor with a dose of brandy. And Sarah was happy, happier than I had seen her. That was the thing. If you care about someone, her happiness opens up a wellspring inside you, and that night she was happy. She taught me many a square and many a round outside by the fire, and we stole a warm kiss or two inside the barn where it was cooler. The first kiss, I recall, seemed to occur by accident, as if neither of us would take credit for it, were surprised by it. But the second, longer kiss, seized back behind a stall door, was of our choice, a talking in tongues. It felt like she was tasting me, or more likely, tasting herself to see if she felt anything.

Once as we danced, a lightning bug got caught up in the flying mass of her hair and with each spark, cast a golden glow over her shining face. I stopped her in midreel, both of us gasping, and pulled her to the side, under the trees, to remove the lightning bug and cup it in my hands, just for a moment keeping the light. It was like holding a throb of lamplight from Sarah's hair as its tiny flash echoed the swirl of the music.

By the time the moon was high in the star-strewn sky and the fire had burned down to glowing coals in the barnyard, I could not have told you my own name, but not because I'd been struck in the head. Rather I had been struck in the heart. By the place and by the moonlight, by the music and by the chestnut-haired soul of it all.

I saw—or think I saw—Sam being sent off with his Uncle George, down the Big Pine Road toward home. I seem to recall Ben still talking in the shadows with men I knew to be in danger, asking I assume about Matthew Campbell and where he might be laying out. I saw various men and women grinning at either Sarah or me as if enjoying that we were somehow together.

As we started on the long walk home, alone in the dark with no one to follow, we came in time to the small log church at the foot of the trail up to Bearwallow Gap. Tired from the day, from the drink, from the dancing, we paused there to wash our faces in the creek and lift up a cold, fresh sup of water. Me feeding her a drink out of my cupped hands and she feeding me the same, with tongues lapping against fingers.

As if in a dream we fell together, there below the church on the creek bank, using our clothes as a sort of pallet against the dew-chilled grass. One or the other of us above, below, beside the other. One of us inside the other, striving for completion, for release, for salvation. It was as if we pulsed with sudden, piercing flashes that lit and blinded us, dancing as we were to a high, ringing fiddle tune. And there, below the church, with the water rushing, surging baptism past, we ceased to be separate. We did not cease to be, though for a moment, we neither one could breathe nor think. But rather came into each other like lightning in the velvet night.

PART THREE

CHAPTER ONE

I felt a stranger that next morning, I admit. As if there was not only someone else inside my skin but also as if my skin itself was newly stretched.

"Sam?" I asked quietly, while watching her put a pot of coffee to boil on the hearth.

She pointed up, toward the loft, and smiled shyly. "He was asleep by the time we got here," she whispered. "I checked on him."

I think we were both a little in shock. But walking outside helped ease us, me following her through her chores, carrying eggs and wood into the cabin while she milked. The coffee helped, black and strong. That and the fact that Young Freeman's likeness was nowhere to be seen.

*   *   *

"ARE WE GOING to the revival meeting at the Springs?" she asked while we ate cold cornbread with fresh, warm milk for our breakfast, along with coffee boiled over the fire.

"I expect that I should," I said after a minute. "Somehow I keep thinking the Bible thumping and hollering have to do with . . ."

"With the Campbell boy and the killing?"

I nodded. "If for no other reason than the whole family is obsessed with this preacher. Plus, I need to track down the sheriff and tell him what I know."

"Where did you learn to call it hollering?" she asked after another bite, the lilt slowly returning to her voice, the willingness to laugh.

"Jimmy Patton said you mountain folks call it that." I was teasing and she knew it.

"Well, we mountain folks like our preaching loud, it's true." And then, after another bite, "And if we're to catch the morning stage, we need to start out soon, as soon as I change."

"You don't have to—"

"Change? I only own one dress that I intend to be seen in down at the Springs. And you, Mister Jake Ballard, will have to step outside while I—"

"No, I meant *go*. You don't have to . . ."

"You're going to chase after a killer," she said. "And you're going to do it down at a resort hotel overrun with every kind of humanity, including women I don't care to think about. All that and you still have trouble remembering your own name. What makes you think I would let you go off by yourself in such a state, never to be seen again?"

"My name is Jacob Israel Ballard," I replied. "Are you saying you care, one way or another?" I was trying not to smile, but I couldn't help myself.

"Maybe." She paused to consider. "Maybe not. I suppose you could say that I like you reasonable well. And now that I've found you, I'm not anxious to lose track of you again while I make up my mind."

I stood and carried my cup and bowl to the washbasin on the back porch. "I'll wait outside," I said and bowed as I said it, causing her to grin.

"Why don't you wash up a bit your own self," she said. "And if you'll heat a kettle of water, I'll shave you."

I did bring another bucket of water from her well while she changed and set some to boil on the hearth. I rinsed out one of the rags from the back porch railing, took off my shirt from the day before, and washed off. Threw some of the cold well water on my face, and when I did, felt the thick bristles there. My razor had lain on the shelf at Campbell's for the past several days, but I hadn't had the time to consider the result.

I sat on a low stool on the front porch, shirtless in the cool morning breeze. I could hear her indoors, mixing something, and when she emerged, it was with a bowl of lather she'd stirred up out of lye soap and almost boiling water. She sat the bowl on the railing and then returned a moment later with the oldest straight razor I've ever seen, the wooden handle cracked and the blade worn thin.

"Good Lord," I said involuntarily. "Will it . . . ?" I had started to say "cut my throat," but stopped myself in time.

"It was my father's," she said. "Still sharp, for I keep it wrapped in an oiled rag up where Sammy can't find it."

She laid the razor on the railing and began to massage the lather into my skin with her fingertips. Her hands and the lather smelled strongly of smoke and flowers.

"Lay your head back," she said after a moment. "So I can reach your neck."

"What . . . smell?"

"Be quiet or you'll get soap in your mouth." She slapped me lightly for emphasis and kept kneading at my jaw, my cheeks, my lips. "It's dried lavender that I threw in." Just the tips of her warm fingers rubbing in circles.

Her hands were gone for a moment, for more lather, and then she was standing behind me, her stomach pressed against the back of my head, her fingers reaching around to work the hot soap into my throat. Everything in me began to breathe—my face, my neck, my shoulders—began to relax. I could feel myself slipping into a trance.

Her stomach tensed slightly as she reached to the rail for a rag to wipe her hands on and then again for the razor. She bent over me from behind and, while pulling my chin up with one hand, began to shave my neck from the bottom up with long, smooth strokes.

"Be still," she warned. "I haven't done this in years."

"But your . . ." I said. Her breasts were pushing against the top of my head and moving as she moved.

"None of your concern." She stifled a laugh. "Be still or I'll slice you." Another long swipe of the razor.

I rubbed my head back against her softness, still in the dreamy place of fingertips and hot lather. "Die happy," I muttered.

She leaned back to fling the lather off her razor into the yard. When she did, she rapped the top of my head sharply with her knuckles. "Stop it. You're getting soap on my good dress." She walked around in front of me and began on my face, at the top of my jaw. "Quiet or I'll cut your ear off." Trying to be stern but giggling as she said it.

Which made it hard for me, for I was chuckling back at the look of her—her eyes squinting in the early light, her lips trying not to smile. And so it was my fault, she claimed, when she nicked me several times about the face. With a razor blade that was forged before either of us was born.

*   *   *

SARAH NAPPED ON the stage down to the hotel. Her only dress she thought fit for the Springs was blue linen, a light blue that matched her eyelids as she slept. Sometimes resting comfortably against my shoulder, and other times with her head nestled in my folded coat against the side of the coach. And each time we came to a rough stretch in the turnpike, she would be jolted briefly awake. At one point where the roadway slid into the river, the driver stopped to let the horses blow and dip their dusty heads to drink. And for a moment, as we seemed suspended above the river itself, we both stuck our faces gratefully out through the stagecoach windows into the sun. She showed me a kingfisher sitting close by on a branch overhanging the river. Female, she explained, pointing out the bird's rusty brown belt. It was chattering, calling out, and then suddenly it rose from its perch, hovered impossibly for a long second and then flashed down into the water. It struggled up a moment later with a small silvery fish in its beak and beat up again to the same branch, where it paused to swallow its catch.

*   *   *

SHE NAPPED AGAIN, and the wonderment rose inside me. Wonder at this strange man I seemed to have become in only a few weeks' time. Attached to a woman for God's sake, when I had so long distrusted women, even disliked them. What she and I had done on that creek bank . . . it had seemed easy, like drinking cold, sweet water or resting beside a midwinter fire. Not forced, not purchased, not angry. And even more surprising, here I was almost comfortable, almost at home—not just with her—but *here* in a place that I had dreaded, a screeching wilderness where every snake was meant to bite you and every rock to break you. Could a man like me become younger in a place like this? This North damn Carolina of a place?

CHAPTER TWO

We arrived at the hotel in late morning. As we climbed down from the stage, we could see several hand-painted signs, first on the bridge and then on the hotel porch, announcing the afternoon's *Grand Revival Meeting by the River. The Great Profit Abednego Rogers . . . Gods Man of the Mountains . . . Come to Fite Sin and Defeat Death . . .* and so on. Three o'clock that afternoon, in the field beside the hotel, the Holy Spirit would be *A Flame Among the People.*

We went into the cool lobby and walked together to the long bar of the registration desk, where Johnny Norton was working alone, business being slow on a Sunday morning. Sarah spoke to Johnny in a friendly way, though she didn't seem to know him by name, and he replied in an equally easy, local sort of way. He almost smiled, covered his mouth self-consciously, and then stuttered a bit when he spoke to me; apparently I was still the outsider, whatever I might think.

"Johnny Norton," I said, "meet Sarah Freeman. Sarah . . . Johnny. Johnny, I'd like to get the key to my rooms, if I still have rooms. Miss Freeman and I would like to rest before the revival meeting his afternoon."

Johnny smiled shyly at Sarah, who smiled easily back. "It's the Laurel Suite still," Johnny said as he handed me the key. "And Mr. Patton wants to see you first thing."

"Is he in his office?"

Johnny nodded, and we started to turn away. "Don't you want your mes . . . ?"

"Messages?" Sarah said quietly.

"Yes, ma'am."

I nodded, smiling, pleased at how just the tone of her voice had gentled him. He handed me three envelopes, which I stuck in my pocket. When we reached the rooms, Sarah poured out glasses of water from the pitcher on the chest and we sat across from each other. Priscilla Cushman and I had sat in almost exactly the same places on the night she had turned herself into Lady Macbeth. *Was she still here in the hotel?* I wondered.

Sarah interrupted my thoughts. "I'm sorry. I have to do this." And in the first blush, I wondered, *What? Do what?* But then she bent and pulled off her shoes. "I'll never get used to it," she said. "Wearing shoes inside during the summer . . ." She got up and began to examine the rooms, her bare feet whispering against the wooden floor—feeling the curtains, pushing the windows up to let in a breeze, sitting experimentally in the desk chair—and then she was gone, into the bedroom. As curious as a cat, I realized, to see something she'd never seen before. I exhaled.

I pulled the pistol out of my coat pocket and laid it on the low table. And then the three envelopes. One from Vance, telling me to hang on, he'd likely see me soon. And at the bottom of the page, as she was like to do, Harriet had filled in the details: *Zeb wasn't allowed to take office, still a traitor in the eyes of some, coming back home to practice law.* The second envelope was from Jimmy Patton, asking me to see him as soon as . . . But the third, the third was perfumed, and the brown ink was applied with a flourish. It was, of course, from Priscilla Cushman.

Kind Sir,

You will be pleased to know that my fortunes have righted them-selves. Your good friend and associate, as he styles himself, Mister Joseph B. Lyman, has offered to assist me in returning to New York City, as a paid associate in the effort to colonize the Warm Springs area with worthy individuals. According to Mr. Lyman, someone of my character and reputation is needed to endorse their plans, and we are leaving on the 23rd*. This will serve to get me back to New York at least, where horizons will open.*

I also received a small grant-in-aid from young Mister Norton, funds which I believe were originally intended for your use. But as you have been absent from the scene for some time, I explained to young John that you had meant all along to assist me in my travels, and he came to see it in that light as well. So, thanking you for your understanding and support, I am . . .

Fondly Yours,
Priscilla C.

After a moment's reflection, I followed Sarah into the bedroom. She had thrown back the drapes and opened the bedroom windows as wide as they would go. You could hear the sound of voices from outside and the distant rush of the river. She was standing in the door to the bathing room, hands on her hips, staring at the bathtub in astonishment.

"Where does the water come from?" she asked. "And how do they ever heat up enough to fill that thing up?"

"It's mineral water come straight out of the ground. Already hot. But before I order you up a tub full, I want you to do some-thing for me."

She must have caught the tone of my voice, because she turned and looked closely at my face.

"I want you to come out on the porch with me, sit a rocker for a few minutes, and read these." I handed her all three envelopes.

"What are they?"

"Just about everything you might want to know about me, all in a neat, little bundle."

We sat and rocked in the shadow of the porch roof. She opened first the note from Jimmy Patton. "Hadn't you better go to him? It says as soon as you arrive."

"In a minute," I said.

Then the note from Washington. After reading it through twice, she looked up at me. "Is this *the* Zeb Vance, the governor?" I nodded. "He seems to think he's your uncle." I was still nodding. "You didn't tell me that part."

"I'm telling you now."

She blushed a little as she read the third note. Her neck flushed and then, ever so slightly, her ears. She raised it to her nose, snorted in disgust, and then read it again.

"She stole that money, didn't she?"

"Yes."

"Your money. Took it from that boy at the front desk."

I nodded.

"Did she . . . him for it?"

"I imagine she did."

"What day is it?"

"I believe it's the twenty-third."

She glanced down at the page again. "Today . . . Well, I believe there's a woman in the hotel I need to see."

"Why?"

"Don't you want your money back from the harlot, after I've scratched her damn eyes out." She wadded up the note with its envelope, stood up, and threw it into the trash bin on the porch.

"No. I'd say let her keep the money. Sounds like she earned it."

"Do you still have feelings for this woman, Jake? This . . . *Priscilla*, for God's sake?"

"Not now."

"How do you mean, not now?"

"I might have. Once upon a time. But it was before I got to know you. Here of late, I haven't thought of her at all."

"So you don't mind if I tear the hair off her head?"

"Why would you go attacking an actress from New York City if you don't care about me?"

She almost smiled. "I might care. Might not. But damned if some . . . hussy is going to . . . Are you glad I'm here, Jacob? Here in your room in the flesh?"

"Yes, damn it. How do you want me to say it? I'm glad so long as you're willing to live in the here and now. Let Priscilla Cushman and . . . Young Freeman . . . let them both go. Let the dead bury the dead."

She stood before, over me really, her hands on her hips. After a long moment, the smile that had only flickered before crept fully onto her face. "I'm willing to lay Young to rest, but I'm not promising anything as concerns this New York woman. I won't track her to her lair, but if we should happen to meet up accident, I might have to take counsel with her. Give her to understand that the situation has changed."

CHAPTER THREE

Jimmy Patton was in his office, seated by an open window, reading. Another one of his leather-bound volumes, I noticed. Reading and enjoying a cigar, the smoke from which he casually blew out the window.

"You can't sell to that son of a bitch," was the first thing I said to him when I tapped on the open door and walked in. "He's trying to finagle you out of your property."

"Which son of a bitch?" he said without looking up. "Been several around here lately."

"The New York one," I said.

He grinned even though he was still looking at his book. Then, after a moment, he folded down the corner of his page and looked up. "You mean the one who left out of here this morning claiming his mysterious syndicate has all but bought the place? The honorable Joseph B. Lyman? *That* son of a bitch?"

"That's the one. You can't do it."

"I'm curious, son. If their money's good, why not?"

"Because they have no respect for the people who live and work here. They have no appreciation for the beauty of the place. They plan to *colonize*, for Christ's sake."

Jimmy Patton started laughing, which led to the wheezing I remembered from the first time I met him. Wheezing to coughing. I picked up his half-smoked cigar and threw it out the window.

"You got to stop smoking those damn things."

"You got . . . to stop making me . . . laugh like that. When did you of all people start carrying the flag for the people who live here? I don't . . . recall you mentioning the beauty of the place before either."

"I've had my eyes opened some," I said defensively.

"Well, good for you. You want to own a local hotel? This one here's for sale."

"What the hell? I thought you said you sold it to Lyman's crowd?"

"I didn't say I'd sold it. I said he left here *saying* they'd bought it. Big difference. When I pushed him right to the limit, he suddenly began to equivocate. You know what *equivocate*—"

"I know what it means. Why do you think he . . . backed off?"

"'Cause they're a bunch of confidence men. They aim to collect shares from every poor fool in New York who yearns for the land of Eden and then claim the deal fell through. Keep the money for expenses."

I pulled up a chair. "So he really is a crook?"

"You mean Lyman? It's possible he's just a fool and the men behind him are crooks. If they needed somebody to go to jail at some point, don't you think Lyman'd be the perfect choice?"

I felt a grin spread across my face. "I think he'd make a fine choice."

He leaned forward and peered over his spectacles. "You threw my cigar out in the yard."

"Enough of that coughing. You can't get sick—you got a hotel to run."

He shook his head slowly, still smiling about Lyman. "I'm near to eighty years old, Jake. I can smoke a tree stump if I want to. And I was serious about the hotel."

"I haven't got enough money to buy one room out of this place, let alone the whole thing."

"Zeb'll back you. I finance it, he buys it, you run it."

"You're not serious."

"Now, listen son. I expect you've seen some things since you got here. But you can't go stomping around raising hell about Yankee businessmen who have neither heart nor soul—and then not step up to your duty when the bugle blows. You think about it. Once we get this other mess straightened out, you think about it."

"What I think is that I know who the killer is," I said to change the subject.

"Do tell . . . Fetch us both a cigar from that box on the desk. Bring the matches. Tell me what you think and why you think it."

Soon we both had our cigars drawing there by the window, and the smoke was strong and sweet going down. I told him what I believed, that two local people, May June and Alfred Dockery, had together identified Matthew Campbell. I admitted that I had probably seen the killer myself standing in front of his own home in the middle of the night before I knew what I was witnessing.

"There's only one thing I can't understand," Patton said after a moment. "If you're right, why would he keep fighting? After all he went through, the killings at Shelton Laurel, nearly dying at Douglas, you'd think he'd crave peace, not more of the same."

"From what I hear tell," I offered, "the prison camps were the worst of it all, North and South. Probably be enough to drive a man crazy."

"So, it's revenge. You think he's still taking revenge for the camp?"

I shrugged. "Maybe. But my guess is just hatred, pure and simple hatred . . . Sometimes the things we do are worse than the things that are done to us. I think he was at Shelton Laurel on the day of the executions, and he made one of the firing squad. What must that have done to him?"

*　　*　　*

IN THE MIDDLE of that afternoon, all the church bells in the hamlet of Warm Springs began to ring out, signaling folks to gather on the hotel lawn. The churches that had organized the revival had pulled a large, old-fashioned farm wagon up into the open field beside the hotel for a pulpit and spread hay on the ground in front of the wagon. Sarah explained that when Rogers got warmed up and began saving souls, the ground just before the wagon would be covered over with kneeling and fainting men and women, with the local preachers and deacons moving among them, praising and singing out. "A big meeting like this one tears up soft ground like you wouldn't believe."

I was more interested in watching the crowd before the wagon than I was the preacher himself, even if he was the Apostle of the Mountains. It had occurred to me that that Mrs. Campbell might well be in attendance, along with her shadowy family members. We found a place to stand back among some large rocks in a small copse of trees. Thirty or forty feet from the wagon and to one side. I explained again about the Campbells, adding James Keith to the mix, and asked her about Matthew. She thought she remembered Keith with a thick black beard before the war but had never seen the boy.

A chorus of shape-note singers warmed up the crowd. They were standing in the straw spread before the wagon, with their songbooks in hand. A man and a woman were standing in the wagon bed, each marking time with one hand while holding a songbook between them. I couldn't make out what they were singing. The notes were clear and high and stirred your blood, but the words were indistinguishable to me. I glanced at Sarah and she leaned toward me. "*I'll Fly Away*," she first whispered and then almost shouted, so I could hear her over the shriek of the music. "*I'm tired of this dark world. Some bright morning, I'll fly away . . .*"

The singing served to gather the people. From the main street behind the hotel, from the hotel itself, over the bridge from across the river—they came. One humpbacked grandmother stopped to talk to Sarah for a moment. When Sarah introduced me I didn't catch her name in the din, but I did hear her say that this was "better than a hangin' for bringin' God's people together."

After the third song, something about being *born to die* and *laying this body down*, the choir directors came down off the wagon and the choir dispersed, leaving the space just in front of the wagon clear. Then I saw the great man himself emerge from an army field tent pitched just behind the wagon and walk slowly forward, flanked on one side by my old friend Mrs. Loudermilk and on the other by a tall, lanky boy I didn't recognize. The boy assisted Rogers up onto the wagon, using an upturned bucket that had been placed beside the wheel as a step. Then he climbed up behind the apostle and stood beside him, holding the largest Bible I have ever seen. The apostle bowed his head and began to pray silently, and the crowd fell silent as well. When it was so quiet that I could hear a wren fussing in the tree branches above us, the boy began to read from the Bible in a high, reedy voice that strangely penetrated the silence. "Book of Genesis, the thirty-second chapter." You could see the mass of people before the wagon lean forward ever so slightly, following the boy's words. "Verse twenty-four. *And Jacob was left alone . . .*" The hair on the back of my neck stood up at the sound of my name. I could feel Sarah glance at me and smile.

> *. . . wrestled a man with him until the breaking of the day.*
>
> *And when he saw that he prevailed not against him, he touched the hollow of his thigh; and the hollow of Jacob's thigh was out of joint, as he wrestled with him.*
>
> *And he said, Let me go, for the day breaketh. And Jacob said, I will not let thee go, except thou bless me.*

"Who?" I whispered to Sarah. "Who is he wrestling with?"

"Just listen," she whispered back. "Pay attention."

. . . is thy name? And he said, Jacob.

And he said, Thy name shall be called no more Jacob, but Israel: for as a prince hast thou power with God and with men, and hast prevailed.

And Jacob asked him, and said, Tell me, I pray thee, thy name. And he said, Wherefore is it that thou dost ask after my name? And he blessed him there.

And Jacob called the name of the place Peniel: for I have seen God face to face, and my life is preserved.

In the silence that followed this eerie reading, the boy laid the open Bible on the wagon seat where Abednego Rogers would have it close to hand and then climbed down, leaving the old man alone there.

It was almost cold under the shade of the trees, among the rocks. I couldn't tell if the air had chilled me or the boy's high, shrill words, but it must have affected Sarah too, for she took my arm and pulled me close.

"In each of our frail and fallen lives, there is a time when we come to the ford of the river." The man's voice struck deep bass notes, almost like a drum, but melodious still, despite its depths. "When we must cross over into a new country or stay behind in the desert. When we may go on to something rich and fine or stay behind mired up in sickness and death. There is a choice to be made, and a hard choice it is."

The old man waved his arm to indicate the crowd before him. "Some of the preachers out there that don't know any better will tell you it is an easy thing to cross over." And then lower again, as if he was just speaking normally. "That giving yourself to the Lord is just a step away, plain and simple. But I tell you here today that is a lie! Oh, my brothers don't mean to lie to you. They make it sound easy because they want you to come over and add to the host." Suddenly he shouted out again, "They yearn for your souls to come home to God." And then more quietly, "But they stoop too low, I say. They stoop too low. God is not easy. He loves you, but He is not easy. And the way home is not so soft as that. You have to give up who you were before and cross over.

"God will meet you halfway, in the ford of the river, with the water swirling around him and his arms out to lift you up. But if you come to him in sin . . . if you come to him unsure . . . if you come to him still full of the liquor from your past life . . . he will grip you in those terrible arms and you will feel what Jacob felt. You will feel your old life torn from you. Your sins ripped out of your soul!

"When Jacob came to the Jabbok River, he was not a holy man. Oh, he was a successful man of this world. He had many wives and he had many possessions, but he was afraid. He was to meet his brother Esau, and he was afraid. Before he would cross the river, he sent his possessions on ahead as gifts to Esau so that Esau would not kill him." Rogers pointed to the open book on the wagon seat. "The Bible records that he sent over two hundred female goats and twenty male goats, two hundred ewes and twenty rams, thirty female camels with their young, forty cows and ten bulls, and twenty female donkeys and ten male donkeys. He was a rich man, was Jacob, but when he had sent all on ahead, given it all up, he was left alone, as poor and frightened as you or me.

"Just as each of us is alone. Alone and in the night when we come face-to-face with the almighty God and nothing of this world to protect us from his questions. *Who are you?* he will ask. *What is your true name?* And you will have no choice but to answer. *Are you ready to live eternal . . . ?*"

The voice of Abednego Rogers so mesmerized me that I didn't notice Sarah had slipped away. For a long moment, I looked among the shaded rocks, and then I saw her striding purposefully toward a man and a woman who were standing off to the side—like us, apparently not wanting to be seen. I realized with a shock that the woman was Mrs. Campbell, Obediah's wife, dressed in her dusty black, and the man beside her was . . . not Obediah . . . and too old to be her ghostly son.

Sarah stopped in front of him, hands on her hips, in that familiar attitude. The man had not removed his hat, as most had out of respect for the preacher. From what I could see of his face, he had sharp cheekbones and a long white mustache that hung down over his mouth, obscuring the bottom half of his face. Suddenly, with a chill, I recalled the man I had seen at Goforth's Store weeks before, on the night I'd been knocked senseless. Sarah had confronted him about something, and I could almost hear her voice questioning him as I hurried forward.

Mrs. Campbell saw me coming and jerked at the man's arm, pointing toward me and saying something. In the same rushing moment, Sarah reached out and grabbed at the man, at something on his vest, and without a pause he struck her down to the ground with his fist. Hit her so hard that she was driven to her knees, and then he turned to run. His knuckles to her face stung me from twenty yards away.

Since the day I charged toward Marye's Heights in that dissolving wave of blue, I had not felt such a surge of hot blood. I could hear shouting all around, and I was running as fast as I could past Sarah, who from the ground was pointing at his fleeing back and yelling something, Mrs. Campbell screaming his name—*James . . . James!* This surge of hatred was personal, for he had knocked Sarah down as casually as a man swatting a fly, and I meant to have him.

I grabbed into my coat pocket for my pistol and remembered with a wash of shame that I had left it behind because we were going to a religious gathering. The man ahead was not such a fool; he reached his fist back toward me as we ran and fired a shot. Once and again, and the second time his pistol misfired.

We were that quickly on a dirt street at the back of town, over the Spring Creek Bridge and slowing. I was gasping, and he was slowing but running still. He cut up a lane to the left, past the last house in the village, and I was closing the gap. He spun and drew down again. When his pistol misfired this time he threw it at me and in dodging sideways, I fell.

I was quickly back up again and behind him as he started across the creek on a footlog, meaning to lose me while I was down. And it was there that I caught him, halfway across, by diving at his legs and bringing us both down into the rocks and water below.

He was my height, or a little taller, and he was heavier, stronger, and now that his hat was gone, I could see that his hair was dark even though his mustache was stark white. He had two good hands to grasp and throw me down. His knee was on my chest and his hands pushed my face under the water. I had him by the shirtfront with my one good hand and set to gouge his eye out with my left finger and thumb. He was drowning me but my thumb digging into his eye socket threw him back. ". . . me go, you son of a bitch." He was growling as he kicked at me and rose to run. And again I tackled him around the waist, intending to hold.

We threw each other into the rocky creek bank, and I gasped out as we lay there, ". . . arrest you, James Keith . . . for the murders of . . ."

He laughed. Actually laughed. "God . . . almighty," he gasped. "You're that same . . . shitheel Yankee Pinkerton . . . ain't you? I thought you'd a . . . run back North by now. Save your . . . worthless life!" Somehow he struggled to his feet, still laughing. Still gasping and laughing, he lifted one heavy boot and kicked me in the privates so hard my eyes went dark. "I ain't . . . killed nobody dead since the spring of '65 . . . you . . . you . . . whatever the hell your name is." And he climbed up the bank, still laughing to himself, and was gone.

CHAPTER FOUR

It was Sarah and Jimmy Patton who found me trying to climb up the creek bank. When I chased Keith across the Spring Creek Bridge and in among the buildings, she had gone immediately to find Jimmy, sure he would help.

I was staggering as we walked back, I confess, aching all the way up into the pit of my stomach. As we backtracked toward the hotel, we found first Keith's hat and then his pistol. Sarah, it turns out, had his watch, or rather my father's watch, which is what she had been reaching for when he struck her down. I carried the pistol and Jimmy the hat as we eased through the back hallways of the hotel.

We found Sheriff S. G. Brigman waiting in the office. Jimmy poured us out each a tot of brandy, Sarah included, and we laid our evidence on the desk. When Jimmy offered Brigman a crockery cup full of brandy as well, he turned it down politely.

He could tell that I was having trouble with my chair, Keith's boot heel having made it all but impossible for me to sit down.

"Little bit of the tale I hear says you found our man Keith," he said pleasantly. "From the looks of it, you caught up with him."

"After he tried to drown me, he kicked me in the privates."

"Sounds like him," Brigman agreed. "Surprised he didn't shoot you for good measure."

"He tried," Sarah said. "I heard the shot."

Brigman picked up the revolver off the desk. Carrying it back, I had noticed how heavy it was, much heavier than my pocket pistol. "Starr revolver," Brigman offered. "Made in New York state before the war." He sniffed the barrel and rotated the cylinder. "Looks like one chamber fired and two went cold . . . Rest of the chambers are empty." He glanced at me in a friendly way. "How the hell did he miss you? You're a big enough target."

"How did he miss you in that church you told me about? You're bigger than I am."

He grinned. "I had a pew to hide behind," he said. "I had the advantage of you."

"Yeah, well, we were both running hell-for-leather, and he was shooting back at me."

"And he thought he had two more loads," Brigman added thoughtfully. He laid the pistol on the floor beside his chair. "What else y'all got to show?"

Sarah held up the watch by its broken chain.

"You stole Keith's watch?" Brigman asked her.

"No," she said. "I retrieved it from him. Belongs to Jake. Ish Goforth said a man with a long white mustache bought it off him for some silver dollars, and when I saw that mustache in the crowd, I went up to speak with him."

Brigman grinned. "You asked nicely, and he gave it to you?"

I could tell it hurt Sarah's bruised face to smile. "No, sir. I grabbed it, and he knocked me flat on my ass."

"How do I know it's yours?" Brigman asked me.

"Initials *NB* scratched inside the back cover. It's all I have of my father's."

Brigman's sharp brown eyes darted back and forth from Sarah to me, and he laughed. "Fair enough. I'll let you secure it from Miss Freeman. I'm afraid of her . . . That Keith's hat?"

Jimmy tossed it to him. As Brigman turned it over in his hands, I noticed for the first time how sweat-stained and dusty the hat was. Brigman turned the inside band out and found several pieces of paper. He tossed me the first one, a copy of the wanted poster that Jimmy Patton had shown me weeks before: $300 *Reward. Broke jail in Buncombe County on the night of* . . .

The second piece of paper made him whistle. "Look at that," he said. "Let's just hope they issue him a replacement."

"What is it?" Sarah asked.

"Railway ticket to someplace called Jonesboro, Arkansas. A long damn way from here. As I believe I told Mr. Ballard before, I thought he was already gone. Till he and I conferred the other day, I thought Keith'd already followed his wife and children down to Arkansas."

"You think he's mixed up in the killings?" Jimmy Patton asked.

I started to interrupt, but I could see Brigman was already shaking his head. "No. No, I don't think so. Oh, I'm sure he knows of it, but he's been mostly down in South Carolina since he broke jail in Buncombe. Besides," Brigman glanced at me and said, "the man you want shot George Lockaby from bushwhack this afternoon in Marshall and wouldn't have had time to attend revival services after."

I remembered Lockaby's name from May June's list. "Did he kill him?"

"No, but he shot him through both cheeks."

Sarah's hand went involuntarily to her face. "My Lord . . ."

He grinned. "Not his face, ma'am. Shot him where he sits. Howsomever, the doctor in Marshall says old George will live to ride again."

It was then that I told Brigman about Matthew Campbell, the possibility that he was alive, that he might be hiding out and taking his revenge. I could tell he didn't like it that the county clerk was involved, but he was more concerned about something else. "Don't know if you've thought this through, but not only do you know who the killer is, he knows you now. And if he was only interested in warning you before, now he has to shut you up. Assuming he's in his right mind . . ."

"Are you saying Jake's his next target?" Sarah interrupted him.

"Maybe," Brigman replied, "or somebody close to Jake. Maybe it's you or one of the other Freemans, but however it plays . . ." He shifted his sleepy gaze from Sarah to me. "You're in the middle of it now, Jake. Good news is you won't have to hunt for him. He'll come to you now."

"I've already seen his grave," I said. "If he does come for me, I'll put him in it."

"Don't mind if you do," Brigman said. "I might just help you shovel in the dirt. But along the way, let's make sure there's only one of him. Let's make sure he hasn't gathered up a company, aiming to raise the countryside. I'd rather you not catch a killer and start a brush war. You follow me?"

CHAPTER FIVE

Once Brigman was up and gone, Sarah and I rose as well. It was early evening, dark enough for a lamp inside the office. Jimmy offered Sarah a room for the night, noting in an offhand way that the last stage south was already gone. She didn't hesitate but said that since I'd been allotted three rooms at least, she could share my quarters without shame. And it was obvious I needed nursing.

She was right. I was about to topple over. My clothes were still clinging wet from the creek, and I was shivering from the chill despite the brandy. The inside of my left thigh was so stiff from Keith's boot heel and sitting on the hard chair that I nearly fell back when I tried to stand. My eyes went dizzy from the pain.

Jimmy considered us both for a moment, kindness in the wavering eyes behind his spectacles. "I'll order a tub of hot spring water brought in," he said to me. "I suggest you sit in it till you feel whole again . . . And a bowl of cold cloths for your eye, daughter," he added, smiling at Sarah.

Once we were outside the door of Patton's office, Sarah offered to take my arm.

"I'm all right," I complained as I shuffled along.

"Are you?" The dark-blue bruise around her eye stood out in stark contrast against the pale, freckled skin of her cheek. "When you told the sheriff that Keith kicked you, did you mean where I think you mean?"

I nodded, suddenly embarrassed.

"Are you permanently disabled?"

When I glanced at the side of her face, I could tell the corner of her mouth was twitching. "I expect to apply for a pension," I said. "Injured in the goddamn war."

"The proper sort of doctoring might save you," she offered, still with a perfectly straight face.

"What sort is that?"

"Biblical sort. In the Old Testament, when the King would grow old and staggering around like you, they would bring in a young virgin to cherish him, and he would get some heat."

I stopped still in the hallway, trying not to laugh. I knew just how much it would hurt to laugh. "You aware of any virgins?" I asked.

"Close enough," she said and finally smiled outright. "Setting aside the other night at Big Pine Creek, it's been so long that I could qualify myself."

*   *   *

SHORTLY AFTER WE hobbled back to the Laurel Suite, Johnny and several other boys employed by the hotel arrived, each carrying two covered buckets of steaming hot spring water.

I went first to the water closet off the bedroom, from where I heard Sarah talking gently to Johnny, who had returned with a covered bowl. "For your eye," he said without a stutter.

Sarah ordered me into the inner room off the parlor, the small bathing room, to undress and climb into the water. There was no lamp lit, so it was restful dark. I could hear her moving about in the other two rooms, opening windows again and this time pulling the curtains closed. Then suddenly, I heard her gasp.

"What?" I called out. "What is it?"

"It's ice."

As if in a dream, I limped out into the parlor, wearing only my smalls and those half unbuttoned. With the windows open and the curtains pulled, the evening shadows had invaded the room. Sarah had set the bowl down on the low table and was staring at it. I touched the cloths and shivered.

"But how in the middle of summer?" she asked.

"They cut blocks of ice in winter," I explained. "And pack it in sawdust in the basement of the hotel. Welcome to civilization."

She laughed, almost as if to herself. "Into the pool with you," she said, "before you freeze. I'll lie out here on this . . . with a cloth on my eye." She was pointing at the couch.

"Go on to sleep." I managed to say as I eased back into the bathing room.

It had only been a few minutes since they'd carried the last of the steaming water in, and it was still gloriously hot. It all but scalded me as I eased first one leg and then the other over the lip of the tub and let them sink in. Chicken flesh raced up my back and arms from my legs being bath-hot and the rest of me creek-cold. I let myself slip slowly, carefully down until the shrunken, bruised part of my body was immersed. And it hurt, hurt deliciously from knee to waist, such that tears squeezed out of my eyes clenched shut.

"Are you all right?" Sarah called.

"What?"

"You groaned. I couldn't tell if you were alright."

"Right," I gasped. I let myself slip slowly down until I was up to my chest, only my head resting back against the cool metal rim of the tub.

I must have dozed. Or just fainted, more like. Drifted in and out of reality without knowing, some dream, some real. I could hear

Sarah moving about after a bit, and she must have thought I was asleep, for she was humming, singing quietly. Perhaps it was a dream, or perhaps real, or something folded out of both . . . inside and out.

> *The battle being ended,*
> *She rode the circle round,*
>
> > *. . .*
>
> *Her darling dear she found.*
> > *Sing ree and sing low,*
> > *So fare you well, my dear.*

Was she saying good-bye, I thought, deep in my mind. Fare you well, my dear. Would she be gone when I . . . I felt a deep stirring of panic, I think, for she seemed to keep saying *fare you well, fare you well*, and I thought to climb out of the deep tub and bring her back . . .

> *This couple they got married,*
> *So well they did agree;*
> *This couple they got married,*
> *And why not you and me?*
> > *They got married,*
> > *Why not you and me?*

The last were slow and hoarse, as deep I had ever heard her voice. Repeated slowly as if by the mourning dove. What did they mean, those words? Were they a spell?

The water surged around me as she slipped naked into the tub . . . bringing me up as she sank down, the peccable part of me rising to meet her and both of us gasping at the heat.

*   *   *

LATER, IN THE unremarked middle of the night, a summer thunderstorm blew through the French Broad valley. A moaning wind tossed the curtains of the Laurel Suite, and the lightning flashed into the room where we slept together in my bed.

Waking to the sound of thunder on the mountain, we rolled together without thought, our two skins cool and touching from toes curling tight to hands tangled loosely in her hair. She rising to float over my hips as if in a dream, her naked breasts beautiful above me in the gray light, nipples hard as ripe, brown berries. Her body was rocking over me like a loom, I thought in my addled senses, weaving something tight and wet out of threads of fire. A dream of us weaving and woven, making one fabric out of hot, spattering light.

Thunder woke us and lightning lit us, and the air gusting in after was as sweet and clean as it is possible for air to be.

CHAPTER SIX

We weren't alone that morning. When we climbed on the stage to travel up river to Barnard, there was already an aged matron in charge of a young woman on board, they seated directly across from each other. From their elegant dress, and the amount of luggage loaded on top, they must have been long-term guests of the hotel. The girl was sleepy still and trying to mind her chaperone's admonishment "to sit up straight and cross your ankles" while also composing herself against the side of the coach to nap.

Sarah sat down beside the girl, leaving me no choice but the matron, who had taken up most of the opposite bench with her bulk and her bustle. I automatically slid my bad hand into my coat pocket as I wedged myself into my corner.

As the coach began to move, the matron directed her eyes resolutely out the window, and by her unmistakable gestures, directed her young lady to do likewise. The lady however, promptly yawned, closed her eyes, and fell asleep. And, surprisingly enough, she was followed by the matron, who snored like a sergeant.

By the time we were across the bridge and well onto the turnpike, it was obvious we were all but alone. Sarah handed me an advertisement she had picked up in the hotel that morning.

HOTEL TO LET.

The <u>Right</u> <u>Man</u>, with a capital of from $5,000 to $7,000,
can have a lease for a term of years, on very favorable terms,
of the Warm Springs Hotel, Madison Co, North Carolina.
Apply on the premises, to Mr. James Patton.

"What do you think it means?" she asked.

"Means the old man is tired of playing nursemaid to folks"—I nodded at our fellow passengers—"like these here."

"Hush, you'll wake them up. What do you really think it means?"

"I think he's old and he's sick, and the world keeps interrupting him while he's trying to read. With one thing and another, wars and such, I think he's tired of trying to make the place pay. Where did you get the flier?"

"He gave it to me. And if I'm not mistaken, winked at me when he did."

"Jimmy Patton gave this to you?"

She nodded, smiling that ironic smile of hers. "Ask yourself," she said in a deep, mocking whisper. "Are you the *Right Man?* Do you *have a capital of from $5,000 to $7,000?* Are you—"

"Hell no," I muttered. "I don't have a capital of $5 to $7, let alone thousands."

"What are you going to do, Jake Ballard, when all of this is over?"

"I don't know."

She looked at me in earnest then with those frighteningly clear green eyes. Searching . . .

"Ask me when the time comes," I said. "Nobody's ever cared whether I came or went. Left or stayed. I'm not sure I know what to make of it."

"I care," she mouthed the words, as the young woman was stirring beside her.

"I thought with you it was always maybe."

"*Maybe* I care."

"What about your attorney? What about Mr. Egyptian Breese? I've never heard you give him up entirely, and I'll never amount to anything near a lawyer."

Her eyes continued to search. And it struck me forcefully that she was the best looking woman with a bruised face I had ever known. With or without a black eye, she was striking just as she was.

"What if I'm the sin eater?" I said.

"What?"

"What if I was sent here to eat the sin out of this place? It sure seems like what Vance and Jimmy Patton want me to do, suck the war out of Madison County. And what if I'm not like you?"

"What do you mean, not like me?"

I could tell that my words frightened her, but I couldn't stop. "You said that the nightmare you took out of my mind went through you, flew through you like you were an open window. But what if I find Matthew Campbell and put him down? This place might be healed, but the death could stick in me like a poison. What if it doesn't pass through me, and I'm ruined with it, worthless to you or anyone else? What then?"

She didn't answer but only looked down into her lap. And when I glanced to the side, I could see the girl beside Sarah staring, wide-eyed, directly at me—frightened nearly out of her wits.

*   *   *

IT WAS WHEN Sam met us at Barnard with Fate that Sarah and I got into our first real skirmish. Not our last, although for a time, I thought it might be. She was determined that I was to come up to Anderson Branch and commence my search for Matthew Campbell from there. Or, failing that, she would accompany me to Campbell's. Either way, she would go with me.

"Hell no," I snapped as we stood in front of Goforth's Store. She was shocked, for the first time in my memory, I realized.

"We've reached the place where you and I must part," I said. "I know that when you say *help me*, you really mean *protect me*, but this is real, damn it. You didn't see Ed Arrowood's body lying in the road with a leather strap cut so deep into his neck that it had to be dug out with a knife. You need to take Sam home and let me do what I came here to do."

"I've been hearing that all my life, Jake Ballard. Sit at home, little sister, while the men go off to fight. That's all fine and good, but in my experience, you don't come back and we're left to starve."

"What?"

"Young never came back, and we've been grubbing two potatoes out of the ground ever since. Do you have any idea?"

"You're not making one damn bit of sense. I'm not Young, and I mean to come back."

"No, you don't. You already said so."

There was a long, breathless pause, while we each tried to grasp what we'd just said. I realized that Sam had been following the course of the argument, his face pivoting back and forth from one to the other.

"I didn't say I wasn't coming back or staying here, or whatever the hell I'm trying to say. I never said that."

"You didn't say you were. I wish to hell you would make up your mind. You said you weren't Young, and you're right. Young never even grew up enough to shave. And I'm done with lawyer Breese. I haven't said it before, but I'm saying it now. It seems to me that we're into the middle rows here, you and me, and . . . and we have a chance at something. But not if you get yourself killed or . . . your parts stomped off in a creek bottom."

Both my hands were out to her now in supplication or frustration . . . or both. "I don't plan to get myself killed. For the first time in years, I've got a reason *not* to get killed, damn it. I'm not going anywhere."

Ish Goforth and several of his loafering customers had come out onto the porch of his store and were listening with undisguised interest.

She seemed to hesitate. To change her mind about what she'd been about to say. "Look," she finally said, "I know you think you're one tough Yankee son of a bitch, with your mangled hand and all." She reached out and took my butchered left hand in both of hers. "But you just don't have any idea what these people are like. You don't have any idea what this Matt Campbell will do. He'd as soon shoot you as spit on you."

"These people?"

"My people. You don't have any idea . . ."

"They're my people too."

"Well, then you don't yet know what *our* people are capable of."

"Maybe," I said. "But I've seen just about the worst humankind has to offer, and that's exactly why I can't let you go with me. I can't let anything happen to you . . . or Sam. What kind of man would I be?"

Another long pause. Again, she was considering. "Maybe . . ." Her voice broke ever so slightly. "Maybe you're right."

"I know I'm right."

"Come on, Sammy," she said finally and squeezed my left hand before dropping it. "Let him go get himself killed—just to show out he's a man. Let him get himself shot dead in the dirt just for us to have to dig the hole and roll him in it . . . Damn you anyway, Jake Ballard."

Dragging Sam along behind her, she started resolutely over the bridge toward the trail home. After staring at me thoughtfully for a moment with her head cocked to one side, Fate turned and trotted after them.

"That's the way to tell 'em, Jake! Don't let her boss you, boy, or you'll never lay on top agin! That'll sure enough shut up her mouth!" These proverbs of wisdom from Ish Goforth's companions on the porch, all while they cackled and slapped each other on the back.

CHAPTER SEVEN

I arrived at the Campbell house just as it was coming on midday. My new watch, or at least my old watch returned, claimed through its cracked crystal that it was close on eleven o'clock when I walked up the front steps. The front door was standing open, as it almost never was, so I stepped in after knocking on the frame. I had no idea what to expect after chasing down Campbell's brother-in-law the day before. I hadn't taken two steps down the hall before I heard Obediah's voice, slow and stern, summoning me into the parlor.

Even though I'd been gone only a few days, it struck me that the house felt smaller somehow. The parlor itself even felt smaller, as once again I had a fleeting sense that I was the applicant and Obediah Campbell the judge.

"Jacob, come in and sit down." He was sitting in the chair where I sat to interview pensioners, and he didn't get up to greet me. The room was dark, and before I sat I pulled open the curtains to allow in a little sunlight. Campbell was immaculately dressed, with his tie tight to his neck and his vest buttoned down to his waist.

"Obediah," I said evenly, "I've missed you these past days."

He nodded, and his nod was more of a jerk or a twitch, mindful of his scarecrow nature. "You have been a busy man, Jacob; although, I must say that it appears your activities have gone far beyond your official capacity."

"How so?"

"Your only charge was to interview those poor unfortunates who think they should be paid for having fought against the glorious South. I conjure you to forget these murders you keep speaking of."

"The glorious South is no more, mister. We're all one country now . . . under God."

There was the sound like leather creaking, and I remembered his laugh. "Almighty God knows full well the difference between the North and the South, Jacob. It is written that he shall divide the sheep from the goats."

"You remind me, Obediah. I went to church only yesterday. I met your brother-in-law, and he tried to shoot me."

"I'm certain that he was provoked beyond the limits of his patience."

"I'm sure he was. I also saw Mrs. Campbell at the preaching. I didn't have a chance to speak to her except in passing. Is she here?"

"I don't know where she is," he said absently and glanced about the room, as if he were referring to a lost cat. But something in his calmness screamed at me, even as he continued to rock slowly back and forth. And there was a faint smell of decay in the room that reminded me of Matthew Campbell. I got up and opened the window.

Other than the sound of his chair rocking, I realized the house was extraordinarily quiet, so quiet I could hear the river.

"Where is May June, Obediah?"

"She is no longer with us."

"Then where the hell is she?"

"She broke one of our strictest rules, and she had to go away."

I could feel my left hand and arm begin to tremble. "What did she do?"

"Why, she went into the bedroom that I share with my wife, and she disturbed our most precious belongings. She knew that she was never to invade that private . . . nay, sacred place. The bedroom of a man and his wife is sacred, an altar unto God."

"Did she look at the tintype of your sons?"

He nodded, again jerking as if his head and neck were being pulled by a string. "Our sweet, dead boys," he murmured.

"One of them's not dead, Obediah."

He stopped rocking, suddenly, as if I'd surprised him. "That's what Zilpah said," he whispered, "but I don't believe her."

"Who's . . . Zilpah?"

"Why, my wife, Mrs. Campbell. Have you met her?" Despite the open window, the rotting smell in the room was growing stronger. I couldn't tell if I was imagining it or if it was real.

"Yes, Obediah, I saw her only yesterday." I felt like I was talking to a child rather than a very confused old man. "I think your son Matthew is alive," I said quietly. "I think . . . Zilpah is right."

"Have you seen him? Have you seen Matthew?" I suddenly realized that Obediah Campbell was crying. He didn't seem to notice, but there were tears on his cheeks. "I looked for him in Illinois, you know, and I found where they had buried him with his legions, but I could not bring him home."

"I was given to believe that you had brought home his body."

"Oh, I hired some local niggers who worked there, and we dug up a box full of bones after dark, enough to pass for a body. I brought them back so Zilpah would have something to bury. I never told her the truth for fear it would kill her. She believed both her sons had come home to her, and she could rest at night."

"I believe he's come home on his own, Obediah, and in the flesh." I paused. "I would like to meet him."

"He did not fight for the Union army, Jacob. You cannot offer him a disability."

"I know, but I think he may be a great hero, and I would like to shake his hand. Do you know where he is?"

His head jerked from side to side. "No, Jacob. But I will ask Zilpah if you'd like . . . Mrs. Campbell! Mrs. Campbell, will you come here please!" He called out this last in a loud voice, choking a bit as he did so.

There was no sound in response. Except the river and some sort of bird chattering near the front porch. There was daylight outside, though it seemed to be growing darker and steadily colder inside the room.

"Where could she be?" Obediah complained. "She was here last night and demanded that we send May June away, but now she's gone again." He leaned forward to confide in me, and I confess, I rocked back without thinking, repulsed by his odor. "I had to sleep alone last night, Jacob, and as one man to another, I will tell you that I don't enjoy that."

"Mrs. Campbell . . . Zilpah . . . is gone again? Gone back to Matthew?"

"Why, I believe she has." He brightened at the thought and began to rock again. "Thank you for telling me."

I stared at him for a moment, holding my left arm still with my right and shaking my head in dismay. He seemed to be slipping further and further away even as I was talking to him, slipping into some deep hole inside his mind. I made myself lean forward and touch him. I grabbed his knee and squeezed it hard. "Think, Obediah, where is May June? When was the last time you saw her?" I could feel my own voice growing hoarse.

He grimaced, whether at the pain in his leg or at some sharp splinter of a thought, I couldn't tell. "Why, she was visited by an angel, don't you know," he said with wonder. "An angel came to take her away."

I stood up and struck him hard on his cheekbone with my open hand, and he grunted. "Where did the angel take her, Obediah?"

"I believe he spoke to her in the springhouse. A lowly place I know, but remember that our Lord was born in a manger."

The springhouse was a small rock building of perhaps ten feet square dug into the side of the hill behind the house. I had only glanced into it once before, enough to see that a stone trough took up all of one side, and that a stream of fresh water ran constantly into the trough before draining out through a siphon in the lower end. The trough was where crocks of cheese or buckets of milk were set to keep them fresh in the summer. I ran out of the house, jumped down the set of shallow rock steps, and ducked inside the springhouse through the low door.

May June's body was floating face down in the spring water. Her shoulders were so wide that he had been forced to shove her down into the trough by brute strength, and one of her arms was still bent back at a horrible angle where she had fought for purchase on the near side of the trough. I knelt there in the wet earth to lift her hand from the stones, and the flesh on her fingertips was torn away down to the bone where she'd clawed at the rock. I lifted her arm slowly, gently and rolled her over in the frigid water. Her dress was soaked and clung to her, submerging her legs though her shoulders and her head still floated, her hair loose like a sodden black pillow around her face.

The horrible thing was that her face was utterly natural, perfectly formed and perfectly kept by the icy water, though her mahogany skin had taken on a gray tinge. Her lips were slightly parted as if she might actually speak, the gray tip of her tongue barely visible between her teeth. The rivulets of spring water that drained from her cheeks and lips might have been tears. Her eyes were wide open, and though as empty of life as glass marbles, they screamed at me.

CHAPTER EIGHT

It was just then that I heard a man's voice calling me from the road outside, yelling my name.

Ben Freeman and Tom Boon were standing in the road in front of the house. Boon carried his Gillespie rifle and Freeman the shotgun that I'd first seen him with. Freeman was waving me down to the road.

"Come on quick," he said. "We know where the Campbell boy is. Tom's seen him."

"He was here last night," I said. "He murdered May June."

"That deaf-and-dumb nigger gal . . ." Freeman began.

"Don't call her that, damn you!"

They glanced at each other to consider, but only for a moment. "Well then, we got some work to do for her too," Boon said. "She in that springhouse?"

I nodded, trembling.

"She'll keep then. Get that little pistol you carry," Freeman said, "and whatever other armament you can scratch together. Gird up your damn loins, and let's go."

*   *   *

IN THE NEXT two hours, we nearly walked our legs off. We passed the gap where my father was buried. Ben Freeman was limping on his bad right leg by the time we left the trail down along someplace they called Doe Branch and crept through a thicket up to the lip of a low hill. From a stand of laurel, they pointed out an old, run-down farmhouse in what once had been a prosperous field with a creek. The fences were mostly down, and the field itself was grown up in weeds, but the house itself was built out of sawn lumber and had a covered front porch. There was a smudge of smoke at the chimney.

"Keith's old place," Freeman whispered. "Where he left out of to go to war."

"Where did you see Campbell?" I asked Boon, having finally caught my breath enough to whisper.

"Seed him first time on the path where we just come along." Boon jerked his thumb over his shoulder. "Then I seed him out to the privy and back early yesterday mornin'." Nodding toward the farmhouse itself.

"Did you have a clear shot at him?" Freeman asked.

"Clear enough," Boon said. "But I wasn't fond to take it."

"How does it go from here then?" Freeman asked Boon.

In response, Boon actually rose up on his knees and sniffed the air. I glanced at Freeman.

"He's smelling for sign. He's hunting."

I glanced up at Boon—his own odor was something fierce.

When I looked back, Freeman had a thin smile on his yellow face. "He's like a damn bear," he whispered. "He don't smell himself."

Boon lay back down. "Woodsmoke, mostly red oak, some bacon grease," he whispered. "And coffee. Son of a bitch has real coffee . . ." Boon looked wistful. "Here's how it plays. See that persimmon tree there in the front yard?"

I saw a lone tree twenty feet from the front porch, so I nodded.

Boon continued. "Jake, that's your spot. I'll back you from that downed poplar beside the creek. We'll give ol' Ben here ten minutes to creep around to the back door. He'll give a whistle when he's set. Then you step up an' hail the house. Don't call him by name, for that'll stir him up and he'll likely shoot you from the window. Just call out, *hello, the house, can I have some rations* or such as that. He'll either come to the door or more likely he'll break out the back and Ben will take him. One or t'other."

Boon started to rise. "Wait," Freeman whispered. "Jake, check that Colt you got . . ." I eased the pistol from my pocket, broke it open, and tapped each load in turn. Replaced one of the caps that had dislodged when I spun the cylinder. "Here's the thing I'm telling you, and you better listen," Freeman said. "If there's a gun in Campbell's hand, rifle or pistol don't matter, you shoot him. You understand? Don't wait, don't talk to him, and for God's sake, don't stop to consider."

From where he knelt above us, Boon nodded. "Thing to remember, Jake, is he's likely seen you. Watched you from cover. After a minute or two, he may decide he knows you. And he don't like you worth a damn . . . I'll be there as well, drawed down on 'im with my good eye, but don't you let that son of a bitch point anything at you."

Quarter of an hour later, I walked out of the woods and waded through the weeds up to the tree we'd agreed on. We'd heard Freeman's bird whistle from behind the house, and I had pulled my hat low over my face. The strangeness of it all was nigh over-whelming. My throat still ached at the thought of May June, and my heart beat a tattoo in my ears. I handled the pistol so hard in my coat pocket that my sweaty right hand was slippery on the grip.

"Hello, in the house," I yelled. "You got anything to eat for a lonely man?"

Nothing . . . Not a sound.

"Hello, the house," I cried.

The door swung slowly open and a rifle barrel appeared. My heart nearly stopped. "Walk on, stranger. There's nothing for you here!" It was a woman's voice. A harsh voice I knew—Mrs. Campbell's voice.

"I been a long time on the road, and I'm hungry," I said. "Out of Christian charity, could you spare me a bite?"

"Pull that hand out of your pocket and step up here on the porch where I can see you." Still that harsh, grating voice.

There was nothing else to do, so I put my hands up and stepped out toward the porch. "Don't block the door," I heard Boon hiss behind me.

"What?" she screeched.

"I said I'm coming to the door."

I stepped up onto the first step, then the second, and onto the porch itself. She peeped around the edge of the door frame, and I could see that what I'd thought was a rifle barrel was only a broom handle. "Damn your Yank soul," she cried and charged through the door.

*   *   *

IT TOOK BOON and me both to subdue Zilpah Campbell and take her broom away. While the battle raged, we could hear Ben Freeman working his way through the house from back to front.

"He ain't here," he said when he finally came out through the front door. "Lord God, what happened to you boys?"

"I whipped them sons a bitches," she growled from where we'd tied her to a porch post with a piece of plowline we'd found. "Limbs of Satan that they be."

Freeman grinned. "Well, I'm glad you didn't kill 'em outright," he said.

"That's my Matthew's job," she replied. "Had he been home, you'd be dead men."

"Somebody would be," Freeman said. And his voice was suddenly cold, so cold that for the first time I knew why so many were afraid of him. "Come inside a minute," he said to me. "I want to show you something."

When we stepped through the door, we were immediately inside a large, open room with a stone fireplace at one end. There was enough flame in the grate to throw a subdued, flickering light into the center of the room.

"Look," Freeman said and pointed. Over the fireplace was a large, square flag prominently displayed. It was the full stars and bars, a Confederate regimental battle flag, stained and torn from years in the field. Stitched in faded white cloth along the bottom edge were the words *Allen's Sixty-Fourth No. Carolina.*

"I thought all of those damn things were surrendered at the end," I said.

"Oh, it gets even better," Freeman said. "Look inside that cupboard in the corner." I turned and pulled back the double doors on a large wooden cabinet. Someone had carefully stacked a dozen Enfield muskets inside—clean, oiled, and apparently ready to fire.

"I will be damned. So Vance was right about arming the countryside."

"What in hell do we do with 'em?" Freeman asked.

"We can't carry them and we haven't got time to bury them. Did you see a well?"

*   *   *

AFTER WE DUMPED the Enfields down the well behind the house, we came back around front to Mrs. Campbell, who was glaring at Boon. "Where's your boy Matthew gone?" I asked her. "I'd like to meet him."

She shook her head fiercely, side to side. She would not talk.

I thought of May June. "Mrs. Campbell, I will tie you to this post and whip you till the blood runs down your legs. I'm done with you and your whole goddamned family."

She looked down at her feet and cleared her throat before looking up again. "His head and his hairs were white like wool, as white as snow; and his eyes were as a flame of fire."

"What the hell?" Freeman said.

"And his feet like unto fine brass, as if they burned in a furnace; and his voice as the sound of many waters."

"Book of Revelation," Boon whispered. "Best let her finish."

"And he had in his right hand seven stars: and out of his mouth went a sharp twoedged sword: and his countenance was as the sun shineth in his strength." Still she stared straight at me, a fierce hatred in her eyes. "And when I saw him, I fell at his feet as dead . . . That's my boy Matthew. Beware you find him out."

I held up my hand before Freeman could curse at her again. "He's looking for me," I said to her. "For I am captain of the Yankees. I have come here from Camp Douglas to take him back. If you tell me where he is, I will go to him now."

She smiled a savage, feral smile and nodded at Ben. "Then why don't you go along home with Mr. Freeman?" she said with a chilling courtesy. "And you'll find that sweet Matthew has been there before you."

CHAPTER NINE

I had thought the walk out to Doe Branch was hard, but coming back was a forced march at the quickstep. For we were all of us afraid. Ben Freeman feared for his children, and he growled as he dragged his increasingly lame right leg over the roots and through the leaves on the trail. Tom Boon was angry because he'd brought us on what he kept calling a wild goose chase, led away from the nest where true danger lay. And I . . . I was terrified for Sarah and Sam. I had already let May June get killed, and I was riven by guilt for leaving them alone after she'd all but begged me not to go.

We took a faint trace high over the Divide Mountain, and they took no pity on me, even though as Ben grew stiffer, I was better able to keep pace with him. Boon ranged out in front of both of us, picking his trail and listening for gunshots. During the one time we slowed for rest at the very top of the Divide, Boon wondered aloud whether we should have left Mrs. Campbell tied to that post.

"She'll chew her way loose . . . by nightfall," I gasped.

"Yeah," Freeman muttered, "or if we miss the Campbell boy, he'll circle back around to her. We probably should have cut her throat and been done. Come on!" He pulled himself up with his shotgun and began to half limp, half jog on the downhill trail, his overalls flapping in the chill mountain wind. Boon and I followed.

*   *   *

WE CAME OUT of the woods in a cornfield at the head of Anderson Branch, from where we could hear an unearthly screaming. We all, each in his own way, broke into a dead run, and I was the quickest on my feet. We came straight down the branch and so to the back of George Freeman's ramshackle, run-down house. The screaming was coming from directly in front, and I broke around the edge of the house. I had the pistol out, but it was too late for that.

George was lying in a pool of black blood on his front porch. His shattered fiddle lay beside him. His wife was kneeling in the blood screeching. I pulled her back and knelt in her place just long enough to roll him on his side. The ball had passed through him, and he was moaning and singing to himself. After taking a deep breath to steady myself, I reached into his mouth and pried the chaw of tobacco out and threw it in the weeds. I didn't want him to choke to death if he had any chance at all. His wife was still screaming that he was shot, shot, shot from the trees.

Boon came around the side of the porch next, followed just behind by Ben. I grabbed them both by the arm. "George is shot through the lung," I hissed. "Clean through. I can't stay. I'm gone to Sarah's."

"I'll doctor him," Ben said. "After I slap that woman quiet."

Boon nodded. "I'll check on your chirren, see if he went for you next."

At least I think that's what he said, for I was already running around the head of the creek and starting up the path through the corn. And then, like to a dream, time slowed. I was laboring up the hill when I heard Fate give a howl that sent shivers down my back.

There was more howling and the flat clap of a shot fired, but no matter how hard I tried, my legs wouldn't lift any faster. A second shot—different sound, the crack of an old muzzle loader—and I was over the edge of the rise and out of the corn.

Fate was running to meet me. I could see that she'd gnawed through her rope and was dragging it behind her leather collar. Beyond, dear God, I could see Sarah pulling herself upright. She was up now and hopping toward the corner of the porch, using her musket as a crutch, one of her legs limp. I ran straight to her without pausing even to look around me, ran straight to shield her with my body if I had to. I drew up beside her. "Are you—"

"No, no," she screamed. "He shot me through the meat of the leg."

"I've got you," I wheezed. "I'll protect—"

"No! God no, Jake. He took Sammy. Dragged him into the woods beyond the field. Go get my boy, Jake . . . please!"

"Can you get into the cabin?" I asked, already turning away. "Get inside."

I spun on my heel and Fate was there, nervous and growling. I grabbed Sam's shirt where it lay on the porch bench and rubbed Fate's nose with it roughly. "Take me," I whispered into her long ear. "Take me." And we were gone.

Everything till then had been playacting. The long climb up to Doe Branch in midday heat, the hard trail back as fast as Ben Freeman's paralyzed side and my city legs would allow, even the sprint behind George Freeman's house with his wife's screams in our ears—all that was a picnic with a covered basket compared to the dance that Fate led me then.

We tore around the side of the cabin and scrambled over a low place in the pasture fence, where someone had thrown down the top rail. Then we flew down through the hard tufts of pasture grass, Fate howling like thunder as she ran, her tail ramrod straight in the air. I fell once and just let myself tumble and roll as that had to be faster than seeking my feet. Even the dog went down hard onto her chest and muzzle, but still she howled to the sky.

A section of the lower fence by the branch had been knocked down and we ran straight through, splashed through the creek, and rushed into the trees beyond. As we started up the flank of the hill, Fate slowed to a walk, and with her muzzle down in the leaves casting for scent, she began to growl. First almost as if she were breathing deep in her belly, but then louder and more harshly. The sorrel hair on her shoulders hackled up. I reached out and grasped the end of her leash line and wrapped it around my strong right hand, for I didn't want her to leave me behind.

We were into a pine thicket, the ground open but dark and slick with needles among the roots. There was a voice then under the dark trees. I knew it wasn't mine, for I was still breathing too hard to speak.

"Far enough." The voice was curiously slight and high-pitched. "You've come far enough, pilgrim."

I straightened to look up through the trees. Less than a dozen feet away stood a figure bathed in light. He was standing in a small clearing where the sunlight reached down to the ground. He had a thin, sharp face like an ax, his father's face, and he was holding Sam Freeman tight with one arm choked around his neck. There was an Enfield strapped over his shoulder and a strange-looking pistol in his hand. Sam was trembling, and there were tear tracks down his cheeks; tears of pain and fury, for he had seen his mother shot.

I held Fate's leash wrapped tight around my right hand, the line embedded in my flesh. The single finger and thumb on my left contracted spasmodically, but the pistol was in my right hand coat pocket where I couldn't reach it.

"Matthew Campbell," I said with all the ease I could muster. "I am glad . . . to finally . . . make your acquaintance." I slowly unwound Fate's rope from around my stiff fingers and shuffled my feet to gain traction in the pine needles.

Campbell was clean-shaven and had a young face for a veteran, a beautiful, pink-cheeked face that I recognized from the tintype. He was so pretty that had you met him in the street, you would have smiled at him without thinking. He tipped his head to one side. "I do not believe you," he said. "For you are a Godless man, of that I make no doubt, or you would not interfere in my work. And as you are a Yankee, you do not want to know me." His voice was quiet, cultured even, and I had to strain to hear him.

"What is your work, Matthew? Besides killing?"

"Oh, my work is to purify the land and its people. I mean to finish up what we started here in the winter of '63, God willing." He paused to consider, and I could hear Sammy gasping as he struggled. "God gave us this last, great war as a blessed opportunity. With the war came the chance to cleanse this land of the human trash that live back in these coves. To rid ourselves of the Scotch-Irish drunks and whore-mongers who breed like rats. If I had my way, I'd castrate every man from these mountains who fought for the North. But you wouldn't understand what I'm talking about as you are not from these parts."

"Oh, but I am, Matthew. Born and bred. And I mean to cleanse the landscape of you and your crusade . . . here, now, this very afternoon." I finally had breath enough to speak a whole sentence. "But this is between you and me. All this long trail. The boy is nothing to the argument."

Sam was trying to speak but as the breath was near choked out of him, it came out as little more than a grunt. Fate was crouched low and pulling hard against the lead, growling deep in her chest.

"Perhaps," he said. "He was too young to have been there, in the war." He shook Sam like a shock of fodder. "But I have business beyond, Godly business, and if you do not retreat back across that creek and leave me be, I will kill this boy where he stands." He pointed the pistol at Sam's head. "He's a Freeman, and that's enough for me. A Yankee sow breeds a Yankee shoat."

Fury almost blinding me, I let Fate's rope go, and she sprang forward, straight at Campbell's legs. As he brought his pistol down to shoot her, Sam shoved hard against him, nearly knocking him off his feet. He reacted by flinging Sam down to the ground and aiming his pistol back toward the boy. But he was too late, too slow.

As he shifted his aim from one target to another, I brought out Patton's pistol, ran up close, and shot him through the neck. He staggered back but then lifted his arm toward me as if finally he had made up his mind, but again he was too slow. There were too many thoughts in his mind that day, too many enemies to choose from. I knocked his arm aside roughly with my bad hand even as his revolver finally went off, shoved my pistol hard against his chest, and shot him again.

He was down then, and Fate was on him, tearing at the wound in his neck. When I helped Sam to his feet, he kicked the body as well, and had I not stopped him, would have spit in Matthew Campbell's bloody face.

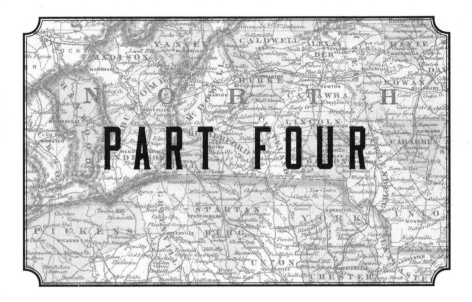

PART FOUR

CHAPTER ONE

We established Sarah's hospital room at the Warm Springs Hotel, in the Laurel Suite. I didn't ask Jimmy Patton's permission, but only that he move another small bed, a daybed, into the parlor. I slept on the daybed and Sam slept on the couch when he was there. Sam went back and forth in the days just following the shootings, taking care of Sarah's stock, moving the cow down to George's barn where she would be milked, and checking on the sheep. On the day he brought Fate back with him, he walked all the way to the Springs because the driver wouldn't let him bring a dog onto the stage. "Not a gol-damned huntin' dog," Sam mimicked the driver. "Now, iffen it was a hotel lapdog . . ." Fate took up residence on the hotel porch and soon befriended Miss Fay and Miss June in the hotel kitchen.

It made Sarah absolutely furious that we would not let her travel upriver for George Freeman's funeral, but the hotel doctor and I stood firm. He had dug the ball from Matthew Campbell's Enfield out of her leg and sewn the ugly wound closed. The ball had torn a gash on the inside of her thigh, halfway between her knee and hip, but had missed the bone, thank God, so the wound was more spectacular than crippling. But George was to be buried only two days after she'd been shot, and neither the doctor nor I would hear of Sarah going, despite her fussing.

So she sent me instead, along with Sam. At the funeral, the entire Freeman clan treated me casually as almost one of the family. George was buried with the remains of his fiddle, which he'd been playing when he was shot and had been shattered by the same ball that killed him. After he was safely beneath the ground in the cemetery on the ridge, we ate the abundance of food spread out on planks laid across the backs of the church benches. As the meal and the storytelling filled the afternoon, I walked up to Sarah's cabin alone and collected most of her clothes and several of her coverlets from the trunk in the attic and rolled them up in the quilt off her bed. She had asked for clothes and the herbs that hung along the beam nearest the fireplace. In particular, I was to bring back her powdered poke root, which was in a small paper envelope in the chest in the loft. She needed poke root in case of lung trouble, she'd said, which often came from lying too long abed.

During the hot summer day while we were gone, Jimmy Patton himself sat and read to her from Dickens. He began *Great Expectations*, a title she had not seen before, and I was then required to finish the book in the days that followed, as she was determined to know what happened to Pip. Even Sam, once he sat through an entire chapter, demanded that we only read in the evenings, when he was there. So often I would read a chapter during the long afternoon just for Sarah, and then she and I would take turns rereading the chapter to Sam in the evening.

The first time that Patton and I sat alone together, we talked about Matthew Campbell and the final chase. He poured us both out a tot of brandy. "To the end of the war," he intoned, and I had to drink to that. After we paused to swallow, he asked me if it bothered me to shoot Campbell.

I hesitated. "Not much," I finally admitted. And then after another sip. "After I saw May June's body floating in that spring-house, I'd have cut his throat at the church altar."

"I expect you'll hear from May June's family before this tale is told."

"What do you mean? If they blame me for getting her involved and getting her killed, then it's no worse than what I think myself."

"No, no. I doubt they blame you. My guess is they will thank you putting an end to Matt Campbell."

"I wish you may be right."

"As for Campbell, he wanted killing," Jimmy said simply.

"I believe he did. But I hope I'm done with that business now . . . for good."

"To the end of the war," he repeated and sipped. And I with him.

*   *   *

I WAS GLAD to be Sarah's nurse and rarely left her for more than an hour or so. She doctored herself with a poultice of ground yarrow root, which she applied to the wound, and a tonic that I made for her from a very small amount of the ground-up poke root stirred into a small glass of Ben's white liquor—taken twice a day. The yarrow root would help the wound heal without infection, she explained, and the polk tonic would prevent the pneumonia, which made sense to me, as I had seen dozens of men cough their lungs out in Washington hospitals even as their wounds were healing. She made me take a glass of tonic with her twice a day as well, minus the poke root, because she didn't like to drink it alone. This sort of doctoring, I told her, should go into the same Biblical almanac with the application of a virgin, for Ben's liquor definitely brought some heat and perhaps a little light.

We had company there in our makeshift hospital. Jimmy came each day to sit with Sarah, and as time passed, Sam became his particular companion. The two of them would walk along the river, and Jimmy would tell Sam all the old-time tales of the Springs, characters and events, including the skirmish that had been fought on the hotel lawn when some fool major named Woodfin from Asheville had been shot down on the bridge and left behind when his own troops ran away with their tails between their legs.

Sheriff S. G. Brigman showed up the day we brought Sarah downriver to the Springs. After speaking kindly to the patient, who was still in some pain, he invited me out to the porch rockers to talk. I told him the story straight through from when we last had met. How Obediah Campbell had buried a collection of bones in his son Matthew's grave, how he'd finally lost his senses, how I'd found May June's body, our hunting down Mrs. Campbell at James Keith's place, the hurried chase back to Anderson Branch, and the events that followed.

"What happened to the body?" Brigman asked.

"George Freeman or May June?"

He shook his head. "No, the Freemans will take care of George, and May June's family has already collected her. What happened to the Campbell boy?"

I gazed at him in consternation. "Why, I guess he lays there still, in that pine thicket. I never even thought . . ."

He grinned. "If it makes you feel any better, I've lost track of a few bodies myself these last years, especially during a busy season. But don't you fret, I've got an old, one-eyed mule that don't mind the smell. I'll deliver the boy to his father and see if Mrs. Campbell ever made it back down from Doe Branch. It may help them both to finally bury him."

I told him about the Enfields thrown down the well and the Confederate battle flag. "Shouldn't Mrs. Campbell at least be charged with harboring a fugitive?" I asked.

"What do you think?" he asked evenly. "Everybody in these mountains has harbored a fugitive one time or another. Besides, the community will mete out the proper punishment to her and Obediah."

"Then leave them be," I said, albeit reluctantly. "What about James Keith? Any word on that devil?"

"Pickens County sheriff sent word that he was seen in South Carolina day before yesterday in the train station. Bought himself another ticket for Arkansas."

"I hope to never see that man again," I confessed. "In this world *or* the next."

"I've had the same thought myself." He nodded pleasantly. "What are you going to do now?"

I discovered that I liked this sheriff, with his sleepy eyes, and I didn't mind him asking. "Well, I . . ."

"For a living, I mean."

"I'm going to finish up the pensioner interviews. And then I frankly don't know. I might go back to Washington City."

"I misdoubt that. You're not a farmer, though, are you?"

"I grew up on a farm, and I liked it so much that I ran off to war the first chance I got."

"How would you feel about being a deputy sheriff?"

"Why no," I said in surprise. "I don't have the talent for any such as that."

He laughed out loud. "Oh Lord," he cried, "that's the best I've heard in a long time. Hunting down malefactors might just be your God-given talent, Jake."

"I hope not," I said.

"You think on it," he said. "Even if you just come along for the ride when I have a special occasion on. Damn crazed killer running loose in the woods, which seems to be your specialty."

CHAPTER TWO

He was followed, a few days later, by a thin, very properly dressed Negro man who had with him a boy, perhaps ten or twelve years old. The boy was wearing a white shirt and overalls so clean that they looked stiff to walk in. When the man said softly that he was looking for Mr. Jacob Ballard, I invited him to sit with me out on the porch. The boy sat down on the step below us, and when the man lowered himself slowly into the porch rocker, I realized that he was older than I had thought.

"My name is Isiah Washington," he said when he had caught his breath. "And this young man is named August."

"Did you know my friend May June Washington?" I asked.

"You are kind to call her your friend," Mr. Washington said. "She was my daughter."

"I had no idea. I'm terribly sorry that she's gone."

He nodded and looked down at the work-worn hands folded in his lap.

"I blame myself, sir, for not having caught her killer sooner and for involving her in the first place."

He looked up to search closely in my face, a gesture almost unheard of in a Negro man in those days and yet so mindful of his daughter that for a moment I sensed her face staring out at me from his. "You must give that up, that notion," he said. "Her husband was a Union soldier like you, and she was equally fierce in her own way."

"I admired her greatly. She was much smarter than she allowed anyone to know."

He smiled. "That is the way with our people." And after a moment, "I have a feeling you understand what I'm saying."

"I wish there was something I could do for her now . . . or for you."

"That is why I'm here," he said. "I wanted to meet the man that she called her friend, and I wanted you to meet her son." He nodded at the boy sitting on the steps.

"My Lord," I muttered, staring at the boy, who met my gaze with mute curiosity. "She never said . . ."

Mr. Washington chuckled, and when I looked back at him, I grinned as well, struck by the irony. "She spoke at the end, you know," I admitted. "Called me a cretin."

"Well, she had strong ways. And she had begun to speak at home as well. She wanted to speak for August's sake."

"I don't wonder."

"And now this young man needs a position."

"August needs a job?" I glanced at the boy again and saw more clearly his mother's strength in his neck and shoulders. "I'll speak to Mr. Patton. I'm sure he would consider it."

"Mr. Patton has instructed me to speak with you. He also suggested that you might offer August his found and one federal dollar per week."

"I don't have any say here. I'm just another guest until Mrs. Freeman can walk and fend for herself. There are a few more petitioners for me to interview, but then . . ."

"Mr. Patton says it is you who must decide about August." He was determined.

I looked back at the boy. "If you're going to work here, August, you have to speak for yourself. What can you do?"

"I can learn to do anything you got goin'," he said brazenly, and I realized I was hearing his mother's natural voice for the second time.

*　　*　　*

AS EACH DAY passed, Sarah got a little stronger. Even though I was her only nurse, she had refused from the beginning to use the chamber pot but instead insisted that I help her to the water closet. As for washing, while she let me bathe her feet and hands, she was modest otherwise, and during those first days gave herself a bath with a soft rag, soap, and water—first in bed and then standing precariously at the washstand.

Just five days after she'd been shot, she asked me to help her out to the porch, where we sat together in the rockers and soaked in the healing sun. She rocked gently with her eyes closed, humming to herself a melody I didn't recognize. Only the shadow of her black eye remained, and the freckles on her nose and cheeks stood out like tiny pricks of rust. She had managed somehow to wash her hair that morning, and it gleamed again like new copper in the dusty sunlight.

"Sarah Freeman, how are you truly?" I asked her.

"Right this very moment, I feel like I'm being hatched," she whispered, her voice somehow staying in rhythm with the tune she'd been humming. "Lord, how I've missed the sun."

"Have you sufficient presence of mind to answer a question?"

She didn't open her eyes, but her lips twitched the way they did when she was flirting with a smile. "I have barely any presence of mind at all, Mr. Ballard."

"Everyone here seems to think I am going to lease this hotel," I said, smiling at her closed eyes. "Patton brought me a contract this morning as he and Sam were heading out to make their rounds of the garden, the barns, and such. Said for me just to drop it by his office after I'd signed it."

"What's your question?"

"What am I to do?" I asked.

"Do you even want to manage a hotel, Jacob?" Her voice still had a musical quality, and she continued to rock easily back and forth. "Do you want to see Sammy grow up? Do you want to learn to sing the old songs? Do you want to see what the fall of the year looks like up here—in the high mountains?"

"I think I'd like to get married in the fall," I said. "Up here—in the high mountains. After the leaves change."

That stopped her. She frowned and her eyes popped open, emerald in the sunlight. "And just who are you planning to marry, Jacob Ballard?"

"Don't know," I said. I let a long pause grow longer. "But I have a test worked out for any woman who might be so inclined."

"What kind of test?"

"A riddle. I figure any woman who can answer this riddle, then it's a sure sign she might be worthy."

She pursed her lips. Her eyes were blazing hot, but she wasn't smiling. "*Worthy* is it? Line it out, then, Jacob. Let me hear it."

"You can call me Jake."

"Say the riddle, Jacob. Don't make me get out of this chair."

"*Lightning soft, lightning bold,*" I whispered.

"*Strikes me down, into the earth.*

Lightning bug, lightning bold.

Knocks me down, gives me birth."

It was a small miracle all its own—to watch her face relax after a moment from such a fierce frown into that grin of hers, almost a laugh, the tip of her tongue glistening between her teeth. She closed her eyes again and relaxed back into the rhythm of the rocking chair. "The answer to your riddle is me," she said.

"Yes," I said back to her. "I believe it is."

CHAPTER THREE

August Washington and I finished the pensioner interviews by late September, when summer had all but exhausted itself and you could feel old fall slipping down the mountain. In the night, autumn would advance down from the ridges but then retreat during the days, under the radiant pressure of the sun. Everything was cooler than I had known before, however— the days as well as the nights. By the middle of the month, Sarah had Sam clean out the fireplace in the parlor room—where he and I still slept—as well as the fireplace in the bedroom. Each evening he would build fires in both rooms and nurse them for as long as we sat up to read.

By the first of October, the mountains themselves had taken on an aged and tarnished look, as if they truly were millions of years old, which Jimmy Patton claimed. But I have to say that they were beautiful in their autumn colors, with a depth and grace that I could not have imagined, and the river reflected back the beauty of the mountains as it swept gently past. As Sarah and I took longer and longer walks during the warm afternoons, her pain and stiffness began to fade, and she taught me the names of the trees according to their fall dress. I learned the red oaks, yellow chestnuts, golden maples, and the rusty blood brown of the dogwoods. All this a tapestry set against the still, deep greens of the hemlocks, which kept their stately color even as they dropped dozens of tiny cones among the fallen leaves.

During the mornings, I toured the hotel from cellar to attic with Jimmy Patton or sat beside him and Matthew Reevis as we went over the great ledgers in detail. I found that I was delighted with the order and symmetry of the place, with the faint possibility of profit. After a time, it also occurred to me that in all that great edifice, no one was wounded or dying. There were no wards or nurses, no long cabinets of drugs or medical instruments, and the hotel doctor spent most of his afternoons napping on the porch. But as taken as I was with the inner workings of the hotel, I found that I longed to be outside. For the first time in my life, I wanted the world outdoors more than I wanted the world within. It seemed to me that there was wisdom in the mountain weather that I couldn't discover anywhere else.

The days shortened, one by one, and the sun traced a cooler course closer and closer to the corner of the bronze sky. Sarah began to have Sam build up the fires in the morning as well as the evening.

And so we set a wedding date according to the seasons. We chose the last Sunday of October, when there would still be some color on the hills and before the iron cold of November could settle in for good. Without saying a word, Sarah let me know that her wound would be sufficiently healed for what we shyly called the wedding night, and sometimes, jokingly, the *honeymoon*. And for the first time in my life, I realized the word might refer to a time of year, not an excursion, a celestial alignment that was especially sweet like the harvest or hunter's moon. She also let me know that we had better not wait too long to sanctify our union, for it seemed I was to be a father in blood as well as marriage.

I began to wander out at night as well, and quietly watched how that October moon of 1866 first drew down to darkness and then began to seek its maturity again, almost as if light itself was being reborn. For the first time in my life I saw that, in the dark of the moon, the stars were simply magnificent.

We each wrote our wedding letters or sent messages by word of mouth. Ben Freeman himself came calling to assure us that the distillery up in the laurel hell was running hot and that there would be no shortage of liquor and brandy for the wedding. While Sarah and I sat laughing with Ben on the porch, she asked if we could spend a few nights after the wedding at her cabin. Just the two of us, with Sam left behind at the hotel. We would, when we returned, borrow Ben's wagon to bring back her chairs, her loom, and her spinning wheel. When I asked about her livestock, or her other furniture, she wondered aloud if we might rent out the farm with the stock included excepting the cow. She would be much more comfortable living in town, she said, if she had a cow to milk. It was her decision, I said, but I thought we might do all of that—including the cow.

I wrote to the man who I now felt truly as uncle, to Zeb Vance and his wife, Harriet, the only people beyond the mountains I could think of to invite. Sarah asked after my sisters, but they seemed far, far away from the autumn mountains and the shifting moon. I would write later with the news and, perhaps, with an invitation to visit. After several failed attempts at a full letter to Uncle Zeb, each longer than the last, I confined my final invitation to one close page—mystery solved, date set, family gathering. And the odd thing was, I meant it when I ended with "please come." And before I sealed the envelope, I underlined the words.

*   *   *

I COULDN'T THINK of anyone else to write to, for it seemed to me that most all my family that counted was there already. I had an older friend who was much like a father to me and who was determined to teach me the hotel trade. I had a friend who was a bootlegger who was fast becoming like a brother—a brother who claimed paralysis on his right side, complained of it with a grin and a wink. I had a young friend who stuttered, though less and less each day. I had an adopted nephew named August, who had taken up with Sammy such that when they weren't working, you rarely saw them apart. I had an uncle who was perhaps the most famous man in the state and who wasted no time in writing me to say that not only would he and Harriet be there, all the Vances and Ballards from up and down the river would be there. He had taken it upon himself to spread the word for my mother's sake.

I had the strange urge one night late as I was falling asleep on the parlor daybed to invite my father. I made a mental note as I slipped down toward sleep to write to him the next day, and then suddenly I jerked awake. I couldn't write to him, for he rested in the cemetery on Doe Branch. Without pause, I said the words, "Please come." I whispered, "You and mother, please come."

"What?" Sam muttered from the couch.

"Hush," I said quietly. "I'm praying."

*   *   *

OF COURSE I had no idea what it meant to have a son, though I was beginning to find out. When Sam wasn't walking the property with Jimmy or fishing with August, he would follow me anywhere and everywhere. I finally had to have a man-to-man talk with him, just to explain that I needed some time alone with his mother. He was incredulous. "You two? What the hell for?" My explanation made little sense to him, but we finally agreed on a secret signal. When I winked, he was to make himself scarce for at least one hour. He liked the secrecy of the plan and the secrecy of the signal. I had less success getting him to stop cursing—perhaps I was not much of a pattern after all—and the words "yes, sir" would not come out of his mouth.

Nor had I told him that if his mother was right, and the autumn gods were kind, he was to have a brother or sister. I assumed that news could be delivered in its own time, when Sarah was certain.

Since her mother could not be there except in spirit, Sarah wanted her mother's brother, who was a preacher, to marry us. Uncle Robert Hicks was over seventy, but he would come from Watauga, though it cost him slow days on horseback. He would come for Sarah.

*   *   *

SUNDAY, OCTOBER THE twenty-eighth was born unseasonably cold, with a chill breeze in the trees. It had rained and even sleeted during the night, and the ground was slick wet. Dark-gray clouds were scuttling across the early morning sky. Uncle Zeb and Aunt Harriet had arrived late the night before, and he and I met for breakfast. He promised by handshake—I'd forgotten how bone crushing were those hands—to fund my lease on the hotel, and he laughed long at my obvious nerves. The second time I spilled my coffee, he got me up from the table and took me for a walk outside.

We talked about the private war of Matthew Campbell and how it had finally come to an end. I don't now recall everything that was said, because at every turn there was a wagon or buggy, a clump of folks I'd never seen before on the porch or in the yard. I thought they'd come to see the famous politician, for he stopped to hob with everyone we met, calling most by name. But when I asked how they knew he was there, he only chuckled. "They're not here for me, boy. They're here for you and Sarah."

*   *   *

I ONLY RECALL a few things about the wedding itself, held that midafternoon in the great lobby of the Warm Springs Hotel. There were so many people in attendance that the children, except for Sam and August, were required to watch and listen through open windows from the porch, the room itself shoulder to shoulder with adults. The local men carried guns as they came in, and at first I was afraid that somehow hostilities had been rejoined, the families rising up in arms. Another murderer lurked in the trees, I thought, James Keith returned. But no one else seemed the least concerned, and I was, I confess, too preoccupied to ask. The Reverend Uncle Bob Hicks was an ancient man, from another age entirely, but he stood ramrod straight and said his piece true with a twinkle in his rheumy eyes. It was me, of course, who lost his voice. When I opened my mouth to promise, I croaked like a frog rather than spoke. Everyone who was close enough to hear—except Sam—laughed out loud, and on my second try, I managed to stammer the words.

After the ceremony, we walked outside to find the great bonfire in the side yard already lit and the food set out along the porches. It was then that the men, Yank and Rebel alike, raised pistol and rifle and shotgun and fired a stunning volley into the air, which set Fate and every other dog on the place to howling. It seemed to me then that they were one army, neither North nor South but mountain bred. It was then that the music and the dancing began, along with the feasting, drinking, and long storytelling.

*   *   *

SARAH AND I sneaked away early that evening, as dusk gathered around the still-burning fire, as the visiting went on unceasing. We climbed up to a suite that Jimmy had arranged on the third floor, high up under the eaves. And for the first time, bathed in a pool of yellow lamplight, we saw each other perfectly free of clothing, each sanctified by our scars. We danced for a bit to the fiddle and banjo music that drifted up from below, our tired feet on the thick, warm carpet and my face buried in her dark-red hair. But we didn't dance for long, because we had other business in hand. And so to bed we went like any country couple, and it was there, slow as sunset and moonrise, that we began to heal.

AUTHOR'S NOTE

A few of the events and a handful of the characters in this novel are based on a dark period in Western North Carolina history that is well-known locally and all but forgotten outside the region. Most prominent of these elements is the Shelton Laurel Massacre. On 18 January 1863, a contingent of the Sixty-Fourth North Carolina, Confederate Troops, under the command of Lieutenant Colonel James Keith, executed thirteen men and boys suspected of being Union sympathizers in an isolated valley of the Southern Appalachian Mountains. This event outraged North Carolina Governor Zebulon Vance, who was a native of the region, and it was widely publicized in Northern newspapers. The account of the massacre embedded in this narrative is based as closely as possible on primary sources, many of which are now obscure. This event and the other wartime experiences of the men and women in this book are in no way exaggerated but rather true to the time and place. The postwar murders that are part of this book, however, are entirely fictional and are not based on any historical events.

The ongoing process of interviewing Union veterans in order to determine disability payment for wounds received is historical. The only liberty I have taken is moving the disability investigations up in time to a period just after the war when, in fact, they took place fifteen to twenty years later. The Western North Carolina Cooperative Manufacturing and Agricultural Association, based in New York, did attempt to colonize the French Broad River Valley following the war, and the account given here is based on the historical record.

Among the many books of both fact and fiction that fed this narrative, two stand out. The first is a 2008 study of "Death and the American Civil War" titled *This Republic of Suffering* by Harvard historian Drew Gilpin Faust. This powerful book explores how the truly staggering death toll of the war changed almost everything about American culture, North and South. The second is Betty Smith's fine book titled *Jane Hicks Gentry: A Singer Among Singers*. Most of the riddles and songs in the novel, as well as Sammy's version of "The Heifer Hide," trace their lineage here. These two books helped breathe life into the story of Jacob Ballard and Sarah Freeman.

The character Benjamin Franklin Freeman is based on my great-great grandfather, and it was tales surrounding his life that set this whole story in motion.

MY OWN HERITAGE

So far as I can tell, I have at least four family members from Madison County, North Carolina, who fought for the Union Army during the Civil War and at least two who fought for the Confederate Army. William Anderson (b. 1843), the older brother of James Anderson (one of my great-grandfathers), George W. Roberts (b. 1844), the older brother of William Harrison Roberts (another of my great-grandfathers), and George W. Freeman (b. 1837), the younger brother of Benjamin F. Freeman (my great-great-grandfather) all joined the 2nd NC Mounted Infantry (Company C) on September 26, 1863, and apparently were all a part of that unit until it was disbanded in 1865. The 2nd NC Mounted Infantry was a unit in the Union army made up primarily of men from Western North Carolina and Eastern Tennessee.

According to his own testimony after the war, Benjamin Freeman spent three months in the 64th NC Infantry (Confederate Troops) in late 1863, apparently deserted, and then joined his younger brother and the others in the Union Army on October 1,

1864. There is also a George W. Roberts on the rolls of the 64th, so it is possible that George Roberts did much the same thing.

Benjamin Roberts, the younger brother of Evan Roberts (my great-great-grandfather), also joined the 64th NC Infantry relatively early in the war. He enlisted on October 16, 1862, was assigned to Company C, and was later promoted to Corporal. He was captured by the Union forces at Cumberland Gap on September 9, 1863, and was eventually sent to Camp Douglas, an infamous prison camp in Chicago, Illinois, where he died from chronic diarrhea on September 23, 1864. Benjamin was also the uncle of George Roberts, who joined the Union Army (perhaps after having deserted from the 64th North Carolina).

This brief snapshot of family history, lit by muzzle flash and campfire in the dark night of history, suggests just how tangled and ambiguous were the loyalties of that place and time. It also reminds us that these men, along with the women and children who missed and mourned them, were fully as complex as we are ourselves. They were not stick figures; they were fully human. *That Bright Land* is my attempt to honor them.

—Terry Roberts

Terry Roberts's direct ancestors have lived in the mountains of Western North Carolina since the time of the Revolutionary War. His family farmed in the Big Pine section of Madison County for generations and is also prominent in the Madison County town of Hot Springs, the setting for both *A Short Time to Stay Here* and *That Bright Land*. His debut novel, *A Short Time to Stay Here*, won the Willie Morris Award for Southern fiction. Born and raised near Weaverville, North Carolina, Roberts is the Director of the National Paideia Center and lives in Asheville, North Carolina.